SAGE COURAGE

❧ ❧

HEATHER McLOUD

For Kayo —
Enjoy the novel
and may your life
be full of zest !
— Heather McLoud

DEDICATION

To my husband.
You believed in me first.

Contents

CHAPTER ONE

Between building road weariness and constant glancing into the rear-view mirror, Leila forgot to look at the gas gauge. The analog needle sat low in the orange mark when it did catch her eye.

She looked around, more aware for a change of her surroundings than of the receding road in her mirrors. Fenceposts. Sage brush near and far, the near ones standing tough and prickly and proud, the far ones nothing but gray-green dots on the prairie. To her left, an outcropping of red rock. Rolling prairie under an impossibly big sky. No side roads. No sign of civilization as far out as she could see. And here in central Wyoming she could see a long way.

A new anxiety built itself on the bedrock of her constant nervous tension. Soon the car would start to choke, jerk, and stutter and then she would be stranded with not a person in sight and not a single place to hide the car. Stu would find her. She wondered if, when her husband came for her, she would run. The thought made her legs rubbery.

Three stressful miles later, a modest green sign announced "Elk Crossing" in white letters with an arrow to the left. She turned, hoping this place wasn't far and furthermore had its own gas station. So many towns out here merited signs and then consisted of nothing but a few weather-beaten, boarded up buildings.

Pressure behind her eyes, a dry mouth, the rear-view mirror, the gas gauge, the mirror. And then, like an oasis, a tall sign announcing a universal brand of gasoline came into view.

She pulled up to the nearest island and popped her door open. The wind almost pushed it closed again and her legs barely held her upright. The crumpled money which came out of her pocket amounted to $11.37. So Elk Crossing was it. No more play in her finances. Her stomach felt tight and small under her waistband.

Four dollars of cardboard hoagie and six dollars of gas later, Leila shifted from one size eight shoe to the other at the cash register. She could hear Stu mocking her as she struggled to ask a desperate question of the teenaged girl behind the counter.

She firmed her trembling chin. "Um. Is there any work around here?"

For the first time in their interaction, the cashier's blue eyes met Leila's brown ones and actually focused on her.

"I don't think we're hiring," the girl said, flattening her hands on the counter between them. Leila noticed her blunt, square fingernails, the calm way the hands rested, fingers pointing across the counter.

The stillness of the girl's hands somehow kept Leila from crying, although she wanted to.

"No. I mean..." she took a deep breath, "I mean I'm looking for a job—any kind." She glanced up, saw a fleeting wince of pity, looked at the hands.

"You'll want to talk to Randy at the hardware store. Straight west into town. It's the one with the flags on the right. You can't miss it."

"Thank you," Leila managed, and fled.

***

Leila's flight from her husband Stu started the day before in Sunnyvale, California. With a gasp of panic, she awakened beside Stu and lay there, heart thudding in the pre-dawn. She checked the clock and released her gasp of breath when she saw it was the appropriate time to wake up. All her weekday mornings started like this. Stu wouldn't allow her to have an alarm clock because it would disturb his sleep. But she was required to have coffee ready and breakfast on the way by the time his alarm went off.

She handed him his backpack and a hot travel mug and held the door for him, both hands gripping the frame. As he did every morning, he pinched her bruisingly on his way past her. She waited, shivering, until he got into his red Mustang and closed the door.

The morning diverged from normal at that point. Instead of going to the kitchen to cry and wash dishes, Leila stood facing the curtains over the door glass and shook. Her thoughts whirled fast and then faster until she couldn't identify an individual thought at all, simply the drive to get out.

She stumbled to the laundry room and dug down into the box of detergent. Soft grains of detergent lodged under her nails and with a revelatory bit of insight Leila realized it didn't matter if all the detergent ended on the floor. She wouldn't be there to pay for the mess and then clean it up.

The detergent spilled onto the floor, a wad of fragrant cash falling out last. She stuffed it in her pocket without counting. No matter the exact amount it would have to be enough. She was leaving.

***

Leila's misgivings about the cashier's simple directions proved unfounded. The town of Elk Crossing rose up out of the prairie over the next rise. The highway transitioned into Third Street. She passed a stop light, the first she had seen in hundreds of miles. Four blocks down, she saw another but before that was the hardware store, a squat building with American flags flanking the doors.

"I can do this," Leila said as she sat in the ancient Buick and stared though the plate glass. She shuddered. The bald statement had carried her through too many years of picking herself up from the floor and going on as though she hadn't been knocked down.

A bell rang when she pulled the door open. She stepped out of the sun and wind into the cool exterior of a store which smelled of wood and fasteners and fertilizer.

"May I help you?" asked a man.

Leila turned to see a diminutive older gentleman with a nose which seemed too sharp for the rest of his features. She breathed once, twice, and fought the tears of desperation.

"I—I'm looking for work?"

"Well now," the man said, "what sort of work?"

"I can do a lot of things. Cooking, cleaning, secretarial work—I was an English major in college."

The man stood silent beyond a point Leila thought she could bear. She lay her shaking hands flat against her thighs and lifted her chin to keep from crying, both techniques she had used with Stu many times.

The man nodded and came around the counter. He neglected to offer his hand, but he did offer his name.

"I'm Randy. Randy Ostermyer. There is a job—I just don't know if I should tell you about it. Maybe not for the faint of heart..."

She recognized the contrast between how she acted and what she knew of herself. After what she had just escaped she knew she could handle whatever she had to.

"Anything."

"The man's name is Bill Colvin. Owns a horse operation. He's looking for someone to watch his kids. I've got his cell number around here somewhere."

The man—Bill Colvin—answered her call on the first ring. Randy had dialed for her using a grimy, old rotary phone which sat on the equally grimy counter. Leila focused on the smudges in the dirt and said the first thing which came to mind.

"This...this is Leila?"

"Yes?" The snap in his baritone voice told her she should get on with it.

"I was wondering—I heard—do you need someone for your kids?"

"I'm in town. Where are you?" Bill demanded.

5

When she told him, he instructed her to wait at the hardware store. Randy said she should wait inside. She stood near the front door and looked out the plate glass window, her view framed by the handles of an upturned wheelbarrow.

A large, red truck pulled into a diagonal space in front of the hardware store, fenders hanging out over both flanking yellow lines. The man behind the wheel jumped down and strode into the store, catching the door behind him when the wind caught it. He spotted her immediately and, cowboy boots striking the floor a pounding blow with each step, closed the distance.

"Miss Leila?" He said.

She nodded and he offered to shake. She had to look up quite a bit to meet his eyes even at her five foot ten height.

"Bill Colvin." His large, rough hand felt as if it had square edges. His browned face was also rough, starting with a forehead truncated by a red cap and ending in a square jaw.

He looked around and made a face. "Let's talk somewhere more private," he said. "Get in the truck and I'll tell you about the job."

Leila walked out the door behind him despite the alarmed voice clawing for purchase in the back of her mind. She mocked herself for her alarm and her compliance, thinking of the experiment where the dogs slobbered every time a bell rang.

Colvin's hand on her elbow helped her negotiate the high step up to the truck's cab. Her expectations of the character of a ranch vehicle were quashed by the plush comfort of the interior and she relaxed. He let the wind slam his door shut, cutting the noise level.

6

"Miss Leila, I'm not going to beat around the bush here. I haven't had a vacation in longer'n I can remember. I need to get away for a while. But someone's gotta watch the kids. Are you interested?"

Leila quelled the urge to tell the man she had no experience with children.

"I'd be honored."

"All right." He hesitated a moment then turned to look at the dashboard. "How're you doing for gas? It's a drive."

"Only a couple of gallons," Leila said, also looking down.

"Meet me at the gas station on the way out. That'll be your down payment."

The alarmed voice in her head ratcheted up its volume. Despite her need for food and a place to stay and the ever-present, gnawing worry about Stu finding her, a question emerged.

"What? That's it?"

Bill turned to her. "What's it?"

"You—" she cut herself off, afraid of losing the job. "You're giving me the job?"

He chuckled and his gaze caught hers for a moment before she looked down and away.

"I flatter myself," he said, "on my instincts about people. You're the perfect person for the job. Trust me."

***

Bill's red truck turned off the highway onto an unpaved road and accelerated. Leila concentrated on pushing the old Buick fast enough to keep him in sight. Bald tires struggled to grip the road and the car slewed and fishtailed when she changed speed. The

7

truck disappeared over the top of a ridge. Leila held her breath until she topped the rise, too, and saw the truck speeding into a valley.

Yes, Leila thought, as they raced around corners and up and down ridges, Stu will never find me out here. Elation drew her lips into a smile made a bit tense around the corners by her struggle to keep the car on the road.

Half an hour later she began to wonder whether the drive would ever end. Hard on that thought came the fear that Bill had some nefarious purpose in mind, that he had lured her to the middle of nowhere to hurt or kill her.

She remembered his strong, calloused hand wrapping around hers. A chill crept down her back. The sensation obliterated her awareness of the dust and the stiff feeling in her hands from gripping the wheel too hard. Despite the sensation of doom, she urged the Buick up another rise and saw the red truck pull off the road and into a wide graveled space next to a house.

With perfect irrationality, she heaved a sigh and her hands loosened. The existence of a house, a destination, reassured her Bill's intentions were honorable. She continued at a more reasonable pace, watching as Bill jumped out of the truck before the dust settled behind him and strode into the house.

Safe in the drive, Leila sat for a moment and worked to consciously relax her shoulders. As she climbed from the car, Bill reemerged with a suitcase. He heaved it into the truck's bed before walking to her.

"Payment up front," he said, and handed her an envelope. She took it, wordless in the wind and sunlight. The last of the dust settled in her wake as the truck started and backed up. She stared in shock for a second or two. The truck came to a stop on the road. When she saw Bill shifting and turning the wheel she began running down the drive.

"Wait," she yelled. "Wait!"

Bill turned toward her. He smiled and waved as the truck tires spun rocks up and sped off.

Later, she would try to lie to herself about what happened next, ashamed of her mindless panic. She actually did, however, sprint after the truck for a short way, yelling and begging, and stand in the dust long after the tail lights disappeared over the rise.

***

Finally, because there was nothing else to do, Leila walked back toward the house. Accusatory questions occurred to her every couple of yards. How long did he say he would be gone? Why didn't I ask how many kids he has? How old are they? Gravel shifted under her when she stopped in the drive and stared at the house.

She thought back to the hope she had allowed herself this morning when Bill offered the job. The unfamiliar sensation had lifted her, carried her to this place, and dropped her just as happened with her marriage. The realization shook her with the understanding it is possible to feel really good about something and have it go horribly wrong.

The longer she stared at the house, the less interested she felt in going in. The windows lacked curtains, the gutter over the front door sagged, and the paint stood up in little peeling cups.

9

The texture of the paint on the eaves reminded her, inexplicably, of the smell of a decaying carcass. This impression of a putrid scent threw her back to the first time she experienced it.

"You never could do anything right," Stu had said.

She had spilled coffee grounds on the kitchen floor and he beat her right there, holding her face to the tile like rubbing a puppy's nose in its own shit. Then, she lacked the distance from the experience to consider why she smelled rotting meat. Now, she had too much time to stand and consider. No matter how she considered the question, however, she could not form even a theory about why she smelled rotting meat—then or now. She decided it must be an oddity of her brain.

The wind gusted with such force that a chunk of her curly, dishwater blonde hair ended in her mouth along with a teaspoonful of grit. She staggered back a step and wondered whether the wind itself was trying to tell her not to take the job. She gave herself a mental slap, a reminder it was too late for doubt. There were children inside waiting for her, needing her.

Leaning into the wind, dragging her feet forward, Leila eyed the house even as she moved toward it. The wrong angle of the eaves, the shadows crawling on the green front door, and the blank windows conspired with the wind buffeting her face to make her imagine fleeing.

The familiar safety of her battered Buick called to her. She clutched the envelope to her chest, acknowledged its power to buy her a lot of gas money, and kept slogging to the front door.

Touching the door knob required effort. She didn't know what she expected, something unpleasant, but the sun-warmed knob turned easily. Pushing the door open turned out to be another matter. It wouldn't budge. She tucked the envelope under one arm and pushed again. No luck. The door stuck fast in the frame.

She pressed her lips together and shook her head. She could feel the relentless wind bearing the house out of true, warping lines so the door wouldn't budge. Stashing the envelope under a gritty, red rock by the door, she turned the knob, set her shoulder against the door, and shoved so hard the shock of impact traveled to the balls of her feet. The door gave a little then snapped back.

Desperation took over. She needed to get inside. Had to. A brief prayer welled spontaneously from the depth of her need. Please let me get in. She mocked herself for the plea. Prayer ceased being an option years ago, when she noticed Stu beat her whether or not she beseeched God for mercy.

Acknowledging the certainty of a sore shoulder in the morning, Leila leaned back and threw herself at the door. With a splintering sound, it bashed open so hard the door knob jerked out of her hand and the door slammed against the inside wall. She put a foot inside, bent and freed the envelope from the rock, and walked in.

The stink didn't hit her until she closed the door. The house reeked of filth and dead things. The smell brought to mind an overflowing outhouse stuffed with dead mice. Outside, she longed to run away when she imagined the smell of rot. The reality cowed her into shoulder-slumping defeat. She saw the sunlight streaming through the kitchen window as dimness. The ruddy tile of the floor, the rough-hewn trestle table flanked by benches, even the white refrigerator, everything she saw was transformed into muddy unreality by the smell.

"Holy shit." She breathed the words into the dead, fetid air and it seemed to smother them before they lived. She recalled Bill's sun-lined face and simple, practical clothes and wondered who really lived inside those clothes, behind that face. Who on earth would live like this—especially who on earth would let his children live in such a place? Leila formed a plan. She would gather the children and get them out of the house.

"Hello," she said.

The word, her first attempt to carry through her plan, emerged feeble and meek but still elicited a response. A low, muttering growl filled the room. The hair on her neck prickled up and she turned toward the sound. The darkened doorway at the opposite end of the kitchen had obscured the dog's massive form. Now it lifted its head, German Shepherd ears stiffly pointed in her direction, and rumbled again.

Leila whimpered. The world went wobbly around her and she needed to sit. Slowly, inching her way down, never taking her eyes off the dog, she lowered herself onto the nearest bench. The angry dog's presence destroyed the last wisps of her hopeful mood and the words "not fair" were stuck on repeat in her brain.

Her vision swam as the tears started. Once she realized the inevitable breakdown she gave in, cushioned her head on her arms, and started sobbing. A well of self-pity opened before her and she jumped in and began listing every single damn thing which seemed specifically designed to make her life a living hell. With each remembered insult or obstacle, her sobbing ratcheted up another notch.

Something hard poked upward under her biceps. Dimly, she wondered what poked her. She cracked open an eye previously squeezed tight in denial and looked down. There sat the dog by her side, its eyes now soft and wide, its shaggy front paws planted primly side by side on the tile floor, less than a foot from her. The reversal of the dog's mood and the release of a good hysterical break-down served to calm her.

"Well, look at you," she said, and with great care reached out and touched the dog's head.

Underneath the thick, silky fur she felt hard ridges of skull. The dog allowed her to pet it, a gingerly process which produced no reaction in the animal. It was, Leila thought, tolerating the experience for her own good.

The dog's solicitous behavior released the last of the tension in her shoulders. She sighed. The dog sighed. The envelope sat fat and cockeyed on the table before her.

The abundance of the money inside shocked her.

She counted the thick wad of one hundred dollar bills and found fifteen of them.

Stu managed all their money during her marriage. She'd never seen so much before. Again she wondered how long Bill would be gone and heard Stu's voice repeating one of his maxims about her: You are so stupid.

A deepening of cold in the kitchen alerted Leila just before the dog's head turned toward the living room. The stink in the house once again pressed on her consciousness and she dreaded looking up. A conviction settled on her that something horrible stood in the doorway to what she presumed was the living room. A small scuffing sound magnified the silence instead of breaking it.

The dog's tail brushed the tile once back and forth. She looked up and saw a little girl framed by the door. Still as the dead, her pale, expressionless face reflected the white of her nightgown.

Leila startled and jumped up. Without a sound the girl whipped around and disappeared into the gloom.

"Wait!" Leila's voice sounded weak and hopeless, an echo of her life to date.

Either a ghostlike child or a childlike ghost inhabited the house. Leila decided for the ghostlike child. She didn't believe in ghosts and Bill had hired her to watch children.

***

She knew finding the children should be her first priority. But something within her refused to wander through the house, refused even to let her raise her voice to call out. Irrational fears haunted her. She thought again of calling for the children and could only imagine something evil crouching in the shadows, waiting for her invitation. Her imagination of touring the house terrified her even more. She searched for some reason for her profound foreboding and found nothing. She hunched her shoulders. The physical action recalled how she always held herself in Stu's presence. When she thought of her constant fear and anticipation of being hurt when she was with Stu the memory seemed clear and rational compared with her current experience.

The thought of Stu brought up a knee-jerk reaction to make dinner. It must be ready on time. It's getting late. She hadn't brought a watch with her when she left California so she looked around the kitchen and saw the microwave oven didn't have the time programmed, the gas stove lacked a time display, and no wall clock decorated the kitchen.

"Whatever," Leila told the dog. "It must be around dinner time."

She paused in front of a door which looked like it should lead to the pantry, her heart beating hard. She would open the door and behind it would be something horrible, something terrifying.

The dog contradicted her, dancing from foot to foot and poking its nose repeatedly at the door. The eager behavior encouraged Leila and, still prepared to scream or faint or something, she swung the door open to a completely normal, rather large pantry. In rushed the dog and shoved a bag of dog food with its nose. Leila looked at the shaggy animal and stroked its side, finding the thick fur hid a row of protruding ribs.

"Oh, you poor thing," she murmured, "I'm sorry, I'm so sorry." She filled its dish to overflowing, refreshed the water bowl, and watched with pleasure as it inhaled the chow.

She studied the boxes and cans stacked on the pantry shelves with a dull confusion. Which one of these is not like the other? The shelves bowed with the weight of their contents—everything she could imagine was stacked there, not just one but two, three, four of each item. The disparity of the smell in the house and the poor condition of the dog with the abundance in the pantry created a dissonance in her which wouldn't shut up.

A term of blank staring produced her first positive idea. Perhaps the children were as hungry as the dog. If she filled the kitchen with the smell of food, if it could possibly compete with the enveloping stench…the children might come to her.

The refrigerator's offerings matched that of the pantry in scope. Blinking into the fridge light, she chose a package of hamburger.

Despite a small thrill of discomfort every time she made a loud noise, Leila banged pots and pans onto the stove as she worked to alert the children. The silence continued and as pasta boiled and hamburger browned she wondered if she had really seen a little girl earlier.

Road weariness gripped her as she stirred the hamburger until her hand relaxed on the spatula and her eyes lost their focus. The drive eastward pulled her back into its embrace. Her long drive had soothed even as she clung to the twin pressures of the need for flight and the worry over how much gas she could afford. The alien landscape of desert and prairie, so different from lush Northern California, whispered to her. Here you can get lost. This vast emptiness will defeat him.

The first time she attempted escape he tracked her down, hauled her back to their house, and beat her. The last thing she heard before she passed out were his threats to kill her if she ever ran away again.

Spare, flat Nevada contradicted him, assuring her he couldn't find her. Farther on, the salt flats of Utah assured her freedom. The red rock spires tempted her to awe. The grind of driving through endless western Wyoming dulled her into complacency.

Cheyenne, so sudden in the long prairie, reminded her a flight due east along I-80's major arterial flow lacked subtlety. She turned north on I-25, began making turns at random. A dearth of population emphasized the variety of the landscape. One year of her childhood—maybe when she was eleven or twelve—she read every Western she could get her hands on. For the first time, the vocabulary in those books made sense. Butte, outcropping, escarpment, box canyon, ridge…and the smell of burning hamburger refocused her into the present.

Leila flicked the stove off, combined hamburger with pasta and sauce, and served dinner for one. Hopefully, she left a stack of plates and forks beside the food.

Hunger redeemed the loneliness of the meal. Subsisting on jerky, trail mix, and coffee for the last two days gave her an appetite. When she realized she could eat no more, Leila sighed. The food aromas had failed to produce children.

Only after the dishwater cooled under her hands did she hear a sound. A soft scraping of the top plate's removal. The clink of a spoon against the pan of food left on the table. Leila froze for a second, then consciously released the tension in her shoulders.

A moment of thought and a gulp against the lump in her throat prepared her. She hummed the first song she remembered from childhood. The lullaby made her hesitate again when she recognized it. Hush little baby, don't say a word… Her earliest memory of mother's love and comfort in a comfortable home invited just the behavior this child displayed—utter silence.

Last dish done, she pulled the drainer plug and turned. The little ghost girl sat on her knees to position herself high enough on the bench to eat. She hunched over the plate and shoveled food into her mouth with both fork and fingers, jaw moving fast.

Muscle moved under the skin of her forearms, clearly visible with her movements. No baby fat, Leila thought. Finger-shaped bruises marred the pale skin. Her tangled, mousy-blonde hair hung into the spaghetti sauce.

CHAPTER TWO

The silent girl scraped her plate and swung away from the table.

"Wait," Leila said.

Her command froze the girl in place, head down, the tangled hair falling across her cheek hiding her eyes.

Leila couldn't stomach the idea of spending the night alone in this quiet, smelly house haunted by a child or children silent as death. What would make the girl stay in the kitchen? She glanced around, noticed the absence of anything child-related. No toys on the floor. No artwork on the fridge.

"Would you like to play with me?" Leila asked.

The girl rewarded her by not leaving.

"Stay there," she said.

The dog padded to the girl and sat, pressed against her side. The girl rested her hand on the dog's neck. Girl and dog melded into a sculpture of stillness as she searched the kitchen for something to do—paper and crayons in the drawers? No. Play-doh? No.

Pressure to amuse the girl spawned an idea. In the pantry she found elbow macaroni and, as she turned away, a box of food coloring caught her eye.

"We're going to make something beautiful," Leila said, and sat at the table. She patted the bench next to her and invited the girl over. No movement.

"Come sit with me. I won't hurt you. We're just going to make a necklace," she continued, patting the bench again.

The girl looked up, not quite meeting her eyes, but didn't move until the dog came over to Leila. She petted its head, trying to demonstrate how gentle she would be. The girl, her motions mechanical and slow, moved to the opposite bench.

When the girl seated herself Leila tore open the box with a little too much force. The box resisted, then burst open, scattering macaroni everywhere. Some even hit the floor with bouncing pings.

"That's okay," Leila said when the girl jumped. "Now later on we're going to need some string but right now we'll just play with these."

She put a drop of green food coloring on an elbow and rubbed it in, wondering how long it would take to get the color off her fingers. Every time Leila moved the girl stiffened but Leila saw when she spoke in a low, sing-song voice, the girl relaxed a little. She filled the silence by narrating her actions.

"Now the macaroni is all green. It looks pretty, doesn't it? We can make them different colors with this dye. Here, let's make a red one."

From her peripheral vision Leila watched the girl watch her. Now she leaned ever so slightly over the table, focused on Leila's fingers.

"We're going to make them in three colors. Green, red, and blue. We could use the yellow, too, but it wouldn't show up so well."

Leila pushed the first three dry ones across the table and the girl swayed back as her hand crossed some invisible line on the table. Leila kept chattering. The girl fingered the macaroni before her.

"What's your name?" She asked, slipping the question into the conversation. She paused. The girl looked up and met her eyes but made no sound.

"It's okay if you don't want to tell me your name. I don't mind. Do you have brothers or sisters? Where are they?"

They played a little longer but her questions reminded Leila of her duty to find out if other children lived here. Bill had said "children," not "child."

"I'm going to call for your brother or sister to come to dinner," she told the little girl, and drew in a deep breath.

Fear gripped her more strongly than ever. Chills tingled up and down her spine and a feeling of threat pressed in at her from every direction. For a split second, she saw herself from above, her natural height disguised by rounded back and slumped shoulders, holding her breath. Even her usually exuberant hair looked flat and lifeless.

"Never mind. I'll go search the house."

She looked down at the girl, puzzling over leaving the little thing alone while she went off. It didn't feel right.

"Come with me," she said.

The girl looked up, vision focused somewhere around Leila's left cheekbone, and looked back to the macaroni.

"Come on, you can show me your house," Leila said.

21

The girl turned a macaroni in her fingers and Leila understood it was more interesting than she. With a sigh, she turned away.

***

At the entry to the living room she hesitated, unable to force herself into the unknown. Doubts swam into her consciousness. She wondered what was the matter with her and the thought she might be losing her mind raised its ugly head.

The light falling from the kitchen door gave her a pathway halfway into the living room but also kept her from seeing beyond it. Leila imagined the gloom as a sort of blindness creeping up on her. This incremental blindness would dim her vision even as she fought to believe she could still see.

She longed for light. With an effort, she reached out and slid her palm up and down the dark wall of the living room. Her heart skipped a beat when she first made contact with the pebbled surface. It did not feel like the backs of spiders. Self-reflection failed her. Why would I expect it to feel like—and even in her own thoughts she could not say, "The backs of spiders."

No wall switch revealed itself. The absence meant one thing: she needed to walk into the room, fumble around, perhaps bump into evil things, all in order to light a room she really didn't, after all, want to see. Only the thought of more children kept her facing the dark. She stood, balanced between fear and the need to find the children, and told herself how childish and stupid she was being to cringe at the dark.

The dog rescued her. It padded up, claws clicking on the tile, and leaned its warm, heavy body against her thigh. She walked into the gloom. Nothing bad happened and she told herself she was being a baby.

The mocking words she threw at herself sounded like Stu. She hated herself for bringing him with her when she left. Half a dozen shuffling steps brought the far side of the living room into dim view. The white of a lamp shade hung in the air, supported on a stand invisible in the poor light.

Leila fumbled below the shade until her fingers met the ridges of the switch. She expected disappointment when she twisted. It would click and the room remain dark and the terror come back. Instead, light blinded her.

Piecemeal furniture, clearly chosen for comfort, not style, populated the room. On the walls, painted a light earth tone, hung several examples of art Leila's California sensibilities termed kitschy. Three horses running ahead of a storm. A cowboy in an oversized hat, lined face in close-up and eyes staring back at the viewer. Some other landscape with a frame imitating a lariat. The bookshelf bulged with books and papers.

Dust lay heavy over the room. A fuzzy coat of it covered the bookshelves. The furniture groaned under its weight. On the carpet, Leila saw one brighter strip of color—a track from the staircase in the corner to the kitchen door where the dust had been scuffed off.

Leila examined the mundane room. She could not understand what had spooked her or even remember with clarity the dark fears of a moment before.

"You can't handle a dark room? What an idiot," she muttered.

Her self-mockery burned her with its acidity.

"Let's go upstairs, dog."

The dog looked up at her and showed her front teeth in what Leila assumed to be a grin.

She stopped again at the foot of the stairs. Bare boards, nail heads visible, composed the risers. No carpeting, no tile, it looked like someone never finished the house, starting right here. The sight unnerved her. She looked for a railing to hold for security. Not there. Just naked walls covered in unfinished sheet rock. And—she knew it before she looked up—no light above the landing. With a sigh she started up. The dog dashed ahead, impatient with her halting progress.

The second step groaned and her heart jumped when, from upstairs, an answering groan of a door swinging shut greeted the noise. After that she needed to force herself to put her weight down, lift herself up. With each step upward her fear sharpened. She paused at the landing to regroup. Unbidden images of insanity crowded into her mind. She thought she heard a woman screaming. She gasped and her sinuses protested at the ferocity of the smell.

Only the knowledge that the dog preceded her got her up the second flight as the pressure of fear and the horrible odor continued to assault her. The stairs opened to a hallway which ran the length of the house. At the end, a window let in the gloom of the dying day.

All the doors opened to the left. Leila thought back to the view of the house's exterior and understood. The second story was only half the width of the first. She stopped at the first door.

"Hello? I'm coming in?"

No response. She opened the door. A bare bulb lighted the

room. Unfinished walls complemented the plywood floor. To the left, a huddle of blankets showed where a child slept. Leila's cheekbones felt tight with her effort to not cry at the lonely sight.

To the right, a closet door hung cracked open. Dog claws clicked on plywood behind her. It brushed past her leg and nosed the closet door open a crack more.

"Sophie, go away!" A child whispered the command.

The dog backed out, turned its head and looked at Leila. Was it asking her for help? Or just telling her what she already knew—a child was hidden in the closet. Now with a firmer purpose, she opened the door. A dirty, bare foot poked out of an impressive pile of clothes.

"It's okay," Leila said. "I'm not going to hurt you."

No response. Not even a toe twitch.

She studied the situation while her back tingled from being turned to the darkness of the hallway.

The dog lay down, muzzle pointed at the closet, alert eyes turning from her to where the child hid and its great, furry ears cupped forward. She took a page from the dog's book, placed her back to the closet's door jamb, and slid to the filthy floor.

"Hi, I'm Leila. Your father..." She thought better of talking about Bill. "I came here to take care of you."

Even with her back against the closet door jamb her neck still tingled with the sensation of being watched. She wanted so badly to get out of the house, away from these silent children, the stink, the dirt...But instead she had to sit here and somehow make contact with the child hiding under a pile of dirty clothes.

"I want—I want..." The pitch of her voice started rising, so she stopped and tried again. Sharing her anxiety certainly would not reassure this child.

"I made dinner. Are you hungry?"

No response.

"Your sister ate. I think she liked it."

The clothing shifted a little. A crumpled, striped shirt rolled half a turn down the top of the pile and one dark eye stared back at her from the hole left by the shirt.

"I made pasta with tomato sauce and hamburger. It's not fancy but it tasted good."

More movement rewarded her.

"After dinner, I played a game with your sister. We dyed macaroni to make a necklace, but I couldn't find any string."

"Is there any left?" The child spoke in a clear soprano. The reply sounded sweet as a chorus of hand bells to Leila's starved ears.

"Yes! There's more food coloring, and lots of little elbows but— "

"No. Food. Is there any food left?"

She took a moment to mock herself for her misunderstanding before answering. "Yes! There's plenty of food. I didn't know how much to make because your—because I didn't know how many people would be eating."

"Oh. Okay."

A tectonic disturbance in the clothes revealed a boy. As soon as his face became visible the dog whined and started to crawl into the closet, tail wagging.

"Good girl, Sophie. Good girl." He reached out and scratched the top of the dog's head and her tail went into high gear.

Leila wanted to curl up and whimper when he turned his face to the light. His left cheek was covered in the darkest, angriest bruise she had ever seen. The bruise invited her imagination to see what sort of blow could so mar a boy's face.

"She plays hide and seek with us," the boy said.

A rush of gratitude filled Leila. The information, offered without prying, gave her a different mental image to concentrate on.

"And her name is Sophie."

Leila felt relieved to have a name for someone in the household. "What's your name?"

"I'm Sleet."

He stared at her as if daring her to comment so she shrugged instead.

"And your sister? What's her name?"

"She's Storm. Is she still downstairs?"

Leila nodded. She and Sleet, without words, both got off the floor. Sophie jumped to her feet, too, turned one quick circle in place, and barked. The sharp noise made Leila's heart seem to miss a beat it jumped so hard.

"All right, all right!" Sleet looked at Leila. "You didn't let her out, did you?"

"Is that what—oh. No. I'm so sorry, Sophie."

Thinking back, she realized Sophie had been dancing and going to the door while she played with the Storm.

"I've never had a dog before," she told Sleet.

"Well, dogs need to go outside to do their business." He

sounded stern.

Sophie dashed down the stairs ahead of them. Sleet led Leila. He stopped on the third stair up and put his hand out to stop her, too. When he looked back at her, the bruise on his face combined with the shadows in the stairwell to give him a grotesque appearance. Only his pleading expression stopped her from backing up a step.

"Is he really gone?" Sleet whispered.

Leila nodded, but his expression didn't change.

"He's really gone," she said, and realized she, too whispered.

Sleet turned back, took a deep breath, and committed his foot to the second stair. It squeaked. He flinched, paused to listen, and continued into the living room.

***

Storm still played in the kitchen. The colored macaroni marched in straight, color-segregated lines along the table. She acknowledged their presence by looking up, face blank, and went back to her play. Silence permeated the kitchen. Leila stared at the careful lines of macaroni and realized her complete ignorance about children. She didn't even know if this was normal behavior.

Stu had often told friends he was "too big a kid to have kids." Leila braced herself when the line came out. Somehow he always found a way to hurt her without their company noticing after he said things like that. He would grab her hand in a show of companionship and then squeeze hard as if he wanted to crush the delicate bones together. Or he would reach behind her as if to pat her on the ass and pinch her instead. She schooled herself to remain expressionless before the audience. If she flinched, it went

28

poorly for her when company left. A year or so into their marriage, Leila stopped longing for children. She feared for any child Stu ever managed to father.

A shrill bark from the door returned Leila to the present. She sympathized with Sophie's bladder and hurried to let her out. The door wouldn't open. Sleet rescued her.

"You have to sort of lift it while you're pulling on it," he said.

She did as he suggested and the door groaned open. Sophie dashed out with a wiggle and a sweep of the tail and something wonderful happened.

The fresh air of the high prairie evening pushed past Leila's face and rushed inside. Her mood lifted, her eyes opened a fraction wider, and she straightened her shoulders. Leila stood in the open door and leaned toward the clean, sharp blackness of full night. The air—much colder than Leila thought it had any right to be—brushed her face and brought to her the wild scent of the prairie.

Eyes closed, face lifted to the breeze, Leila stood braced against the open door until she started shivering from the sharpness of the wind.

"I can't believe how cold it got," she said as she swung the door shut.

An unfamiliar voice an octave lower than Sleet's answered her.

"It's because of the elevation."

She jumped, turned, and shrieked at the same time.

In her imagination, some unholy amalgam of Stu and Bill Colvin stood behind her, explaining about elevation. When she came down, facing the voice, she saw another boy stood in the doorway from kitchen to living room. Much larger and taller than Sleet, this boy stood, feet braced and strong jaw clenched and stared at her.

"I'm Sunray," the boy said. "But everyone calls me Ray. Who're you?"

"You'd know if..." Sleet began.

"How many of you are there in this house?" Leila spoke over him.

The unpleasant thumping of fright in her chest made her question loud and rude. Silence followed the question.

After the children all exchanged glances, Ray spoke.

"What you see is what you get."

"Okay," Leila said. "I'm sorry. I didn't mean to yell like that."

Ray gave her a nod—one slow dip of the chin while his eyes never left hers. Sleet actually smiled a little—a twitching up of the lips on the unbruised side of his face. Storm said nothing.

"So...I'm sorry, but...I'll introduce myself. I'm Leila and I'm here to take care of you. Storm and Sleet and, and Ray."

Again, the nod from Ray. Sleet, whose glance kept returning to the food on the table, gave up on the halting conversation and served himself.

"So...how old are you kids?"

Ray continued to stare, his upper lip twitching. Leila interpreted the expression to mean her question was intrusive.

"I'm twenty-five," Leila said. "I've never spent much time with kids so I can't tell how old you are."

"And I'm the only one speaking here now that Sleet has his

mouth full," said Ray, and reached out with his foot and kicked at Sleet's seat. The half-hearted violence failed to slow the rate at which Sleet shoveled food into his mouth.

"So I'm thirteen," Ray said. "Sleet here is ten. And Storm is three."

Leila thanked him and thought of another question.

"What did you mean about the elevation?"

"Where did you come from?" Ray asked.

"How do you know I'm not from somewhere around here?"

Ray snorted and shook his head. She shivered when he eyed her up and down, then thought about her clothes. She couldn't remember what she was wearing and didn't want to self-consciously look down to check. She knew the clothes would be prissy and feminine in a sleek sort of way because Stu shopped with her and made her buy what he liked.

She gave up and looked down. A pastel blue silk shirt with faux pearl buttons. Dark blue jeans, some sort of designer label, that had pinched her mercilessly as she drove the Buick east. And flats. She couldn't remember what the women she had seen in town wore but she did have an impression blue pastel wasn't on the palette.

"I stick out like a sore thumb, don't I?"

Sleet answered this time.

"No. Definitely not."

"You're right. I just drove in from California," Leila said.

"Which is at sea level," Ray said, sounding pedantic. "The elevation, you know?"

The tone of his voice made Leila feel like apologizing. The

31

urge frightened her.

"So what?" She asked.

"So this ranch, here in Wy-O-Ming, is at 6500 feet elevation. Do you know what a mile is?" Ray's voice, now openly hostile, drove her to her emotional knees.

She shook her head, mute, despite knowing how many feet composed a mile.

"That means the air here is much thinner than where you live. There's less air to hold heat. So when the sun goes down, it gets cold real quick."

Blinking away a film of tears, Leila reverted to familiar behavior.

"Do you want some dinner?"

Ray gave her another laconic nod and went to the table.

"It's cold," he said as he served himself.

"I could heat it up for you. Do you want me to?"

"Yeah. Do that."

She served a plate and set it in the microwave, all the while keeping up an internal dialogue entirely composed of insults to herself for bowing to the ill temper of a thirteen-year-old.

CHAPTER THREE

After two days of driving, a job hunt, and coping with an awful house and strange children exhaustion clouded Leila's thoughts. Leila's foggy mental state allowed a downward spiral into self-hatred. Today had been her second day of driving east like the Furies were pursuing her. She wanted to sleep with a longing so strong it felt spiritual. But the house and its attendant stink and filth pressed in on her.

Finding a place to sleep became her only ambition. She longed to go sleep in the Buick but her conscience struggled through the fog in her head and informed her she couldn't leave the children alone in the house overnight. She needed to...

Leila felt a hand on her arm. She startled awake, half rising from the bench at the kitchen table. Her forehead hurt where it had rested on the grain of the rough-hewn wood. Sleet stood by her.

"You need to go to bed," he said, sounding far more stern than his ten years should allow.

"I don't know where to sleep." Her statement sounded whiny in her ears.

"You can sleep in Storm's room," Sleet said.

When she asked he explained, as if she were rather young and perhaps stupid, that Storm's room was next to his.

"No. Oh no. I'm not sleeping up there..." The bench bumped her calves and stopped her from backing any farther. "I'll just...I'll just look around."

Sleet and Storm looked up at her from the table, their big eyes made even more solemn by their thin faces. Leila wanted to thank them over and over for staying with her when she fell asleep at the table. She wanted even more for them to sleep in the same room with her. When she found a place.

"You'll wait for me, right?" she asked.

Sleet nodded. Storm just stared.

A hallway opened to the right of the doorway to the living room. She muzzily wondered if it had been there all along. Now, Leila saw it as her last great hope for somewhere to sleep. The colors in the house faded to sepia through the lens of her exhaustion.

The first door to the left opened into a bathroom which stank of desertion. The naked toilet paper holder complimented the empty towel bars. Likewise, no shower curtain hung from the bar. The filth on the toilet seat didn't prepare her for the sight of a forest of fuzz growing in the water. Leila shuddered and flushed. The fuzz waved briskly in the swirling water but clung to the sides of the bowl.

"Let there be a bedroom," she pleaded as she exited the bathroom.

Down from the bathroom two closed doors faced each other across the hall. Leila checked the left one. A laundry room. The door to the right opened onto the master bedroom. A king-sized bed filled most of one side of the room. The other side, to the left of the door, boasted open floor space, an antique roll-top desk, and a couple of sitting chairs.

Silver-striped maroon wallpaper covered the walls. The curtains and bedspread matched. In contrast with the rest of the house, this place looked comfortable, and she hated it. The room felt private and wholly owned. She couldn't imagine sleeping here. She had to sleep here. Her skin crawled when she thought of sliding between the sheets.

The master bath, done in greens and blues just as deep in hue as the maroon, looked lovely. Seashells were scattered to either side of the sink. Fish swam in the shower curtain. The shower was tiled and double-sized with two shower heads.

A slight scuffing noise from the door announced Sleet and Storm.

"Are you going to sleep in here?" asked Sleet.

Leila nodded.

"We're going upstairs, then."

"There's room for all of us here. Let's all...let's have a sleepover together," Leila said.

"Here?"

She nodded.

Storm began to back away from the door, held only by her brother's hand in hers. Sleet gave her a look which reminded her of Ray—disbelief combined with disdain.

"We're not allowed in there."

His flat statement invoked more feelings than Leila could cope with. Disappointment asked her to burst into tears of the silent, self-pitying sort she perfected during her marriage. Fear told her to beg and cajole. She automatically tamped down a flare of anger—the sort Stu would have punished her for.

The conflict turned her into a woman stuck in neutral, hands down in the middle of the room, shoulders slumped, face blank. The children turned and left.

Leila studied the bed. She couldn't sleep there and she felt too tired to question why. The fluffy bedspread clung to the sheet as she dragged it away, her grip firm on a hank of the bottom corner. She and the bedspread ended up in a heap under the window at the far end of the room from the master bed. The image of dirty dishes stabbed through her brain. She hadn't washed up before lying down. Guilt and fear instilled under Stu's tutelage stabbed through her brain just before she fell into sleep like a rock falling into a well.

A mess of tangled dreams grabbed her throughout the night. Stu came looking for her but although she could see him, he couldn't find her. Stu's baby-innocent face shifted into the craggy, square outlines of Bill's face and surged straight toward her in a wave of fury.

Leila grew smaller as Bill neared and in terror she looked for a place to hide. Children surrounded her on all sides but when she tried to hide among them they forced her forward. His hot breath on her face reduced her to cowering and moaning in terror.

Something hit the back of her head, her eyes flew open, and reality came back accompanied by a rush of relief. In her struggle to avoid Bill's wrath she had thrashed against the leg of one of the sitting chairs. She turned away from it and saw a dark shape looming above her.

She threw herself back and hit her head again, this time harder, just as recognition set in. The dog, Sophie, muzzle pointed, ears up.

"Go away! Go," she whispered in fury, afraid to speak louder lest she awaken the house.

Sophie whuffed one more breath of warm air on her face, turned, and left. She spent a few minutes puzzling over her fear of waking a house up. In the darkness the nonsense thought still grew in her imagination until she shuddered and pulled the comforter over her head and shivered until she slept again.

She became aware she was sleeping and knew that a woman in a white dress sat by her. She could see the glow of the dress against her closed eyelids. The woman earnestly explained something to Leila, over and over, but she whispered and Leila couldn't understand what she was saying. She dreamed she awakened and saw Sleet standing by the door, watching her but he was both Sleet and a different boy, in the way of dreams.

***

Leila woke in the morning with only the awareness that by the light she had slept in. Stu's alarm would go off any minute and he would be furious about the absence of coffee. The bedspread bound her arms and she fought it a moment until true wakefulness arrived and Stu was not by her side and he never would be again and she relaxed against the pillow and smiled so widely that she could feel the expression in her cheeks.

The house seemed prosaic, its filth empty of the malice she felt last night. She stumbled down the hall feeling pleased about everything but the scum on her teeth. Awakening to a life

37

without Stu gave bounce to her steps.

Sophie sat at the front door. The dog's anxious expression as she waited earned her forgiveness for the scare she had given Leila in the night.

"We'll both go out," she said, and scruffed her hands through the fur on Sophie's neck.

She stopped just outside the door, shocked into delighted insensibility by beauty. The air, far cooler than she expected for a June day, possessed a clarity which made what she remembered of humid California air seem soupy. The land and sky lay against each other like familiar lovers.

A scrim of dew covered everything and Leila lifted her head to inhale deeply. An earthy, spicy scent hit her nostrils and buoyed her further. She searched for the source of the scent, wandering beyond her car as it grew stronger. Her nose drew her to a sage bush and she crushed one of the tiny, pointed leaves in her hand. The scent penetrated to her lungs and she stood straighter and thought, for the first time, that she could do this. Whatever this was.

For the first time in her life she realized the importance, in all this empty land, of orienting herself. No street signs or directions indicating where to turn left would be of any use if she got lost.

She faced the sunrise and lifted her face, eyes closed, to the growing light. East. Opening her eyes, she saw the road coming toward the house. She turned north and saw a steep rise of land leading to a ridge running east-west behind the house. The way up to the ridge looked uninviting, studded with ankle-twisting rocks and gray-green sage bushes half as tall as Leila.

The house loomed before her as she turned west. She stood in the same place as yesterday when Bill's truck roared away in a cloud of dust. Her enthusiasm for the day clouded over as she considered the building which somehow both hunched and loomed.

The view south offered a surprise. She looked down and over a valley stretching miles—how many she could not tell in the clear air. Something about standing here near the top of the ridge with so much open air sparked her imagination. She thought she could feel what it would be like to be freed of gravity and fly out over the spacious landscape. Her cheeks hurt from smiling twice in such a short period of time.

Only the cold air seeping through her wrinkled silk blouse stopped her from staying much longer. She needed some things— a change of clothes, a toothbrush, a hairbrush. And a shower, for god's sake.

Fetching what she wanted took some rummaging. On the morning of her departure had thrown things more or less at random into the Buick's spacious back seat. Not everything she had packed made sense now. She grimaced when she saw the old prayer book her Uncle Murray had given her at her Bat Mitzvah, wondering what on earth had possessed her to bring it. And yet...she glanced over her shoulder at the house and juggled the clothes and toiletries to free a hand for the book.

As she crossed the driveway the house rose up to meet her like a dark hole in the perfection of the day. She looked at it and smelled the foulness of the air, heard the dusty quiet, tasted it like mold on her tongue.

***

Showering in the master bathroom felt weird. She kept turning, feeling eyes on her naked body, anticipating her own startle and scream. She decided enduring the creepy feeling was worth it once it was over and she was dressed in clean clothes. The morning's sense of hope returned and she looked forward to breakfast with Sleet and Storm and then, grudgingly, included Ray on the list.

She noticed what she had missed on her trip to the car. Clean dishes crowded the drying rack. Someone had washed the last of the plates and the pot after she stumbled off to bed.

When the sautéing onions reached the point of translucence all three children arrived as if the scent were a cue for congregation. Sophie scratched at the door and Leila hurried to let her in, wanting to look out over that southern expanse again and feel the clean air on her face. The fresh air invited her to state the reason for her good mood. She dared for the first time to tell herself she was free.

"Whatcha cookin'?" Ray wanted to know.

"Omelets! Mushroom, onion, and green peppers with cheese."

Leila felt wary of holding a conversation with him, but the innocent question lulled her.

"Why no ham?" Ray didn't sound disappointed, or curious. The question instead sounded like an accusation.

Leila's whole body stiffened. The spatula stopped moving. What could she tell him? Her instinct, a cringing apology, felt wrong in the morning light pouring through the window over the sink. She reached for the uplifting sense of freedom and told herself this boy was not Stu. She had always been talking back to Stu in her head. Now she could say those things. Whatever she wanted. She was free, after all.

"You don't have to eat it if you don't like the way I cooked it."

She grinned while she looked at Ray. The expression sprang from astonishment at her bravery. Ray studied her.

"Fair enough," he said, and went to sit at the table.

Also at the table, Sleet announced his fondest dream for the morning.

"I hope you're making lots. I'm starving."

From the corner of her eye, Leila could see Storm still playing with the colored macaroni at the table, baby fingers lining each one up just so.

"Ray? Sleet? Is there any string or something around here?"

The beaten eggs hit the pan just right, bubbling up but not burning on the bottom and Leila gave herself a little shout of joy and relief. Stu was so particular—and she cut herself off, her heart leaping again at the realization he was not here and would not be. She could burn the eggs all she liked but it still felt nice to get the heat right first time on a new stove.

"Um." Ray's deep voice sounded better when uncertain. "There's some fishing line?"

She had only a vague idea what fishing line might be.

"Let's see it, then," she said.

Sleet got up and walked to the far end of the counter and pulled open a drawer. He lifted a spool of translucent green line and handed it to her, carefully closing the drawer without slamming it. Leila knew the feeling. Leave no mark. Make no sound.

"This is perfect if you can make knots in it?"

Ray laughed and the flash of sympathy she felt when he sounded uncertain dissipated at his mocking tone. She didn't understand and she cringed. Sleet rescued her.

"It's sort of for tying knots," he said. "Haven't you ever been fishing?"

"Oh, no." The innocence of his question made her want to explain. "See, where I grew up..." She thought of the Bay Area, the long, straight canyons of concrete which substituted for streams, and gave up. "We don't really have anywhere to fish."

The eggs needed a minute to cook through. Pulling some of the line off the spool, she tried to yank it in half and thought she might have cut her fingers.

"Ow! We need scissors."

Ray chuckled. Leila glared. Ray returned to the drawer and withdrew a folding knife, unfolded it with a click to reveal a very sharp-looking blade with a curve at the end, and came at her.

Leila backed one step, a step which lost her all the momentum gained by glaring at Ray. He gave her a look equally composed of pity and disdain, flipped the knife in his hand so quickly she missed how he did it, and handed it to her, handle-first, with a slight bow.

By the time she sweated through tying a macaroni onto one end of the line, the smell of the eggs reminded her to concentrate on cooking. She set the toy down.

"Here. One of you boys show Storm how to string the macaroni so she can have a necklace."

She concentrated for a few minutes on the omelets, feeling more and more proud over how they turned out. Sliding the first one onto a plate she turned.

Ray and Sleet were sitting on the bench to either side of Storm. All three of their dishwater blonde heads bent low over the fishing line.

"That's good," Ray said. "Now pick up another one."

Leila froze, plate of food forgotten.

Storm carefully reached for a macaroni, body tense with concentration. Her fingers hovered over a blue, then went to a red one. The little fingers made a careful pincer motion and brought the red macaroni up. Sleet held the end of the line steady as she approached it, jabbed it at the line, and missed. Leila held her breath.

"Nah," Sleet said. "Hold it still. I'll help."

The macaroni-holding fingers still weaved and bobbed. Ray reached over and put his largish fingers around Storm's tiny wrist, covering some of the fingerprint bruises on her arm. Together, he and Sleet helped her string the macaroni. All three watched it drop to the end of the line.

"Perfect," said Ray.

Leila turned back to the stove, banged a pan unnecessarily, and turned back to the perfect scene.

"Who wants the first one?"

"Give it to me," Ray said.

Bitterness against the querulous boy rose into her mouth and she wished she had just given the food to thin little Storm. She handed the plate and a fork to Ray and turned back to the stove, feeling depressed over the evaporation of the beautiful thing she just witnessed. Her emotional sea change did not go unnoticed. Sleet came to her elbow and spoke in a stage whisper.

"You can't just give her food like that. It needs to be cut up. And cooled. And you gave her too much. Sometimes when there's food she doesn't stop eating and she throws up."

"Oh," her reply started as a polite response to Sleet's offering of information, then became a cry of pain on Storm's behalf. "Oh!" She leaned her forehead against a cabinet and stayed like that until tears began to fall into the rest of the omelet mixture.

The kids devoured their omelets by the time hers cooked through. She saw all three of them bent over the macaroni necklace again as she went to sit down. The passage of the tears left her quiet inside. She ate slowly and watched the kids at play. Instead of feeling touched by their solicitous treatment of Storm, Leila looked at them for the first time with a dispassionate eye.

Storm, protected by the hovering wings of her brothers' bent bodies, still wore the simple white nightgown of last night. In the sunlight Leila observed its gray hue, the many stains on the front and sleeves, and the places it looked sheer from wear. Storm's shoulder-length hair tangled and oiled its way along one side of her face.

Sleet's hair fell over one eye as he leaned in to guide Storm's macaroni-holding hand. Another little pasta twirled down the length of fishing line and he brushed the hair away. The filth and tangle showed less in shorter hair but clearly he needed a bath and a cut, too. His clothes looked in better shape than Storm's nightgown but…

Ray's hair stuck straight up all over his head in jagged clumps. It appeared someone, perhaps a blind person, had attacked him with shears of some sort. He extended his arm to attract Storm's attention to a stray macaroni and the cuff on his long-sleeved plaid shirt pulled up halfway to his elbow. Leila wanted to peek under the table to see if his pant legs showed too much shin but restrained herself. She knew they probably did.

"All right!" Leila sounded too bright, too excited. The kids jumped in unison when her exclamation broke the silence.

"Sorry. But seriously. After I clean up the kitchen, I want to give Storm a bath."

"Good luck with that one," Ray said.

At the same time, Sleet spoke up.

"I'll clean the kitchen for you."

"That's all right, Sleet. I can do it," Ray offered.

"But you got to do it last night! Now it's my turn." As he spoke, Sleet glanced over his shoulder at the uneaten portion of Storm's omelet on the counter.

Leila tried to remember if she had seen the leftovers from last night in the fridge when she went hunting for ingredients. Surely a child would have shoved a Tupperware straight into the fridge…so, no, she hadn't dug around one for eggs this morning.

"I'll make more food at lunch," she said.

The announcement elicited a grin from Sleet and a nod from Ray. The small signs of approval warmed and reassured her.

45

CHAPTER FOUR

When the last macaroni slid onto the fishing line, Leila tied the ends. She reached to place the necklace over Storm's head and the little girl swayed backward with a quick, boxing-style fade. Again, Leila felt sick.

"Sweetie, I'm not going to hurt you," she said.

Storm's eyes stayed focused on Leila's hands. Leila recalled Ray saying the girl was three and despite her dearth of experience, she knew three-year-olds were supposed to talk. The realization pounded home the fact that she needed to take it slowly. She tried another tack.

"Look. It's a necklace. It's supposed to go over your head and hang around your neck."

Leila demonstrated, sliding the necklace over her head. Storm reached out one hand toward the necklace, palm to the floor, fingers splayed, and opened and closed the hand. Leila smiled a little and took the necklace off. Storm wouldn't take it from her hand so she set it on the table between them. After a few seconds of struggling, Storm got the necklace on. It dangled halfway to her bellybutton.

"That's right! It looks really nice on you," Leila said.

Storm looked up from the necklace to Leila, wide, dark-blue eyes scanning, scanning.

"Now it's bath time. Let's trot ourselves into the bathroom and get clean."

Leila rose from the table. Storm got up and followed. At the door, she paused and looked back at Sleet. He nodded at her.

"It's okay, Storm. You can go with her. Go on!"

At this permission, Storm trotted down the hall behind Leila to the bathroom. Leila surveyed the room. No towels. Filthy tub. More than filthy toilet. No washcloths. Nothing. Another thing occurred to her. Storm's clothes must be upstairs. Leila sighed, feeling the shreds of last night's unreasoning fear.

"Never mind, Storm. Go play. I'll come get you after this is fixed."

She flipped the wall switch in the laundry room and her mind reeled a little at the juxtaposition between plenty and filth she should have expected. A wash tub sat next to an expensive washer/dryer set. All three were covered in a thick scrim of dust. Linens and towels lay stacked and folded on open shelving but on the floor, everywhere on the floor, piles of rank clothing scattered like the husks of old, dead things. Taking up the rest of the large room, a black gun safe stood facing south. She waded through the dirty clothes and shook whole dust bunnies from a towel and washcloth, turned to leave, and almost ran over Storm. Leila shook her head, not understanding why the girl had followed.

They marched back to the bathroom where Leila knelt to scrub out the tub, wondering all the while how she had ended up in a bizarre parody of worship in someone else's house in the middle of Wyoming. She raised up on her knees, stretching to reach the last corner, when something firmly goosed her butt. She practically levitated from the floor as she spun. A Broadway play's

47

worth of emotions ran through her before she hit the ground again—shock, terror, fury—and landed to find Sophie grinning up at her, tail wagging with joy.

"That. Was not. A good. Joke," she grated at the dog.

Storm stood and stared, one filthy finger in her mouth.

The tub cleaned, toiletries borrowed from the supply in the master bath, and towel located, she faced the problem of acquiring clean clothes for the girl who still hung around Leila's knees.

Her reluctance to simply walk up the stairs and search Storm's room ashamed her with its intensity. Everything she had seen of the second floor made her skin crawl just thinking about it.

"Storm?" The girl met her eyes. "Do you have clean clothes in your bedroom?"

No response. No expression, just that unwavering gaze.

"Okay. Fine."

Flushed from scrubbing the tub, Leila felt the omnipresent dirt and disorder beating her down. She imagined sitting back, letting the children stay in their unkempt state. She could cook meals and make sure they didn't die in their father's absence and walk away when he came home, fifteen hundred dollars richer. The uninvited thought made her head pound with rising pressure and finally frightened her so much she stopped thinking altogether. She couldn't believe how attractive the thought was and wondered who she really was to be able to think such a thing. On mental auto-pilot, she reverted to her simple goal. Give Storm a bath.

In the kitchen, Sleet lingered over washing the last pan. He ran the rag around and around, watching soap bubbles chase each other.

"Sleet? Could you go get me some clean clothes for Storm?"

"Yeah…but I don't know if— "

"If she's got clean clothes, just get me some, okay?" She interrupted. The thought of giving up on the children, her intimate knowledge of the idea's momentary attraction, frayed her nerves. She breathed deeply and watched him walk off, each step paced and deliberate.

After a bit Sleet returned with clothes and offered them to Leila, eyes averted. She took them and examined each one. A yellow t-shirt. Blue pants with a stretchy waistband and a yellow flower embroidered on one leg. And underwear, she noted, feeling proud of Sleet for remembering.

"Great! Thank you, Sleet."

***

Storm again padded after Leila into the bathroom. Water rushed over Leila's left hand as she fussed with the temperature before stopping the drain. She turned to Storm.

"Okay. Off with the nightgown."

Storm studied her, then turned back to watch the water splash and bubble into the tub.

"Come here, Storm." It occurred to her to wonder if the girl could hear.

The girl shuffled a few inches closer to Leila, still focused on the running water. A few inches brought her close enough.

"Look. You need a bath. We've got to get this filthy nightgown off…" Leila reached down from her seat on the toilet

49

lid and grabbed the hem of the gown.

Storm tried to step back but could not because Leila held the hem. The girl stumbled, swayed, eyes wide and fixed on Leila's face. For a moment, she feared the girl would fall backward. As soon as Storm regained her balance, a startling feat for a child so young, Leila released the nightgown and Storm darted out of the bathroom and down the hall. Leila's dismay turned into determination not to lose this battle and she shot from her seat in pursuit.

The struggle renewed when Leila caught Storm at the bottom of the stairs. She snatched the tiny, fleeing figure mid-step and lifted her higher than she intended.

"Shit! You're so light," Leila said, then gave up on speech as Storm began to flail.

Storm's creative and skilled struggles extended the walk back to the bathroom. She twisted, kicked, pushed with her hands against Leila's arms, and tried to sunfish her way out. Back in the bathroom, Leila held her with one arm around her waist while she tried to peel the nightgown up with the other.

"It's okay. I'm not going to hurt you! Just. Hold. Still."

When the nightgown reached Storm's thighs the fight went into high gear. One baby-arm flailed, Leila felt a searing pain in the side of her head, and the girl rose up in the air as she used her new grip on Leila's hair to draw their faces together. As Leila began to yield to the pain from her pulled hair, Storm started snapping at her face.

Aside from grunting with effort, Storm made no sound. Completely unnerved by this silent ferocity, Leila attempted to disengage. She reached across her body to grab Storm's arm, focused on releasing the grip on her hair, and Storm bit her forearm. Leila yelled at the sharp pain and heard outside the bathroom door, an answering set of giggles.

"Get her off me! Help! Get her off!"

Sleet and Ray popped around the corner and, still giggling, pried their sister off Leila. Sleet grabbed her face and, with a pincer-motion on her cheeks, got her teeth unclenched. Ray forced her fingers open one by one until Leila's hair came free— one way or another. Quite a bit, strung between the girl's fingers, went with Storm. Her brothers each grabbed a hand and they led her, still stiff with fury, out of the bathroom. The tub began to overflow.

Leila spun the tap off and sat and shook.

***

Again, she thought of the money in the envelope, the Buick waiting in the drive. Fifteen hundred dollars of distance from Stu and these horrible children and this horrible house. Her arm throbbed. The spot on her head where so much hair recently parted ways with her burned. And her heart hurt for Storm. The effort to bathe her ended only with terror, with fury. Her own use of physical force, in retrospect, made her feel as dirty as the nightgown.

The light from the bulb overhead dimmed as though a cloud had passed over it. In her abstracted misery and doubt, Leila did not notice when dread overtook her.

"I can't do this," she growled in a deep, gritty voice. "I shouldn't have to put up with these brats."

51

Heat surged through her. She rose to her full height from her habitual slouch. Each step she took toward the kitchen filled her with a sense of righteous rage, confirming her purpose. The envelope, stuffed among a dusty collection of cookbooks on top of the fridge, came down heavy in her hand. Her perception of the world around her narrowed to the envelope, the door, the car outside.

A vague disquiet bubbled up. What would the children do without her? The superheated pressure inside her batted away the idea, urging her to just leave. She looked at the dust on the envelope again and hated everything.

She took one step on numb legs toward the door before a cold, blue light transformed the kitchen. The hatred coiled and hissed within her just as cold descended. Where before the house had seemed unusually chilly for the summer, now she sensed the breath of the arctic itself exhaling onto her back. She shivered and wrapped her arms around herself. There had been heat inside her, she remembered. She reached for it, longing for that hot purpose.

Colder, colder. Hugging herself, stripped of rational thought, Leila knew something watched her. The cold spoke to her, suggested the idea it would go with her—all the way to sunny Mexico. She would never be warm again if she left the children.

The money dragged at her arm. So heavy. She raised it, pulled open the envelope and studied the contents. Freedom. A second cold fact occurred to her. She had nowhere to go. Nothing to do. No place on earth. Friendless, parentless Leila. She tried to remember places she dreamed about during her marriage. Beautiful places. But her brain felt stuffed with cotton. A great blankness hovered.

The last of the proud stiffness left her shoulders and she resumed her habitual slump. "I can't do it," she said. "I can't leave."

The cold backed off a little but her fingers still felt icy around her grip on the envelope. She threw it back onto the fridge where it tumbled behind the cookbooks, safely out of sight.

The cold lifted degree by degree. Fatigue filled Leila. She sank onto one of the benches and sighed, noticing a nasty taste in her mouth.

"What. The hell. Was that?" She shivered with fear. The sound of her voice reminded her of that other grating sound which had come from her mouth when she had called the children "brats." Something foul had come from her mouth and now she had the aftertaste to prove it. She tried to make sense of what happened. The disgust, the rage, speaking in a strange voice, the cold, the sense that something watched her. Reviewing it pushed her toward hysteria.

***

In an effort toward self-preservation, she shoved the memory and its attendant questions aside just as Sophie wandered in. The dog idly snuffled the kitchen floor, nose swinging from side to side and nostrils flaring. Leila embraced the dog's gentle search for crumbs with gratitude that she could focus on the mundane.

"Are you hungry again?"

Sophie looked up, shook her head with vigor, and stared.

Leila was contemplating rewarding the dog with hamburger for being her only friend on earth when a light knock sounded on

53

the front door. Sophie ran to the door and began barking, each great doggy shout punctuated by raising up with both front paws off the floor and then shouting again when her paws hit the tile. The noise was unspeakable and Leila's instant reaction was to cringe away from the door, convinced for a moment Stu had found her.

But Stu never knocked so lightly in his life. With great force of will, Leila chose to believe the knock did not herald her husband's arrival. She considered her options while moving to the door and realized she had only two. To open or not to open.

Sophie ceased her racket when Leila put a hand on her head, instead pointing the way to the doorknob with her nose and setting her tail into metronome wagging mode. The dog's attitude soothed Leila enough to struggle the door open, remembering to lift and pull.

The door swung free and Leila let out a brief, strangled scream. The figure of a man, a black cutout against the sky, was standing at the door, hand raised in a fist. The scream died when she realized the intent of the fist. To deliver another light knock to the door. She hoped it wasn't a very big scream.

"Sorry! Sorry ma'am—I didn't mean to scare you..."

Although Leila couldn't see his face—backlit as it was with the sky—his voice sounded like regret. Sophie broke the tableaux, nuzzling Leila's hand and then trotting forward, tail waving. The man lowered his arm to ruffle the fur on her head and neck, then looked up at Leila in concern.

Leila opened and closed her mouth several times as her vision adjusted to the lighting. The man's eyes were too far apart and his lips too thin for a handsome man. But his face was all muscle over bone with a topping of dirt and Leila felt herself blush. She looked down and her gaze caught at his belt buckle, an improbably large, shiny affair with elaborate engraving. Then she realized where she was staring and her blush grew even deeper.

"Are you okay?" He asked.

Leila completed her dying fish act with an effort.

"You did startle me. Sorry." And realizing how strange her unexplained presence must seem—" I'm Leila. Mr. Colvin hired me to watch the kids?"

Her simplistic explanation was queered by the complexity of reality. The man's eyes flicked over Leila's shoulder to the empty kitchen, then returned to Leila's face. He nodded.

"Again, I'm sorry to startle you. I'm the hand, Jimmy."

"Jimmy the Hand?" The words were out before Leila could edit them.

He started laughing. He doubled over with it and all Leila could see was the complex topography of the top of his hat as he gasped, hands on the dirty blue-jeans covering his knees. She had never imagined a cowboy hat could look so—so genuine, so right. Leila found herself staring at his hat and apologizing with a growing sense of anger over his unexplained hilarity.

"I'm sorry. I'm really sorry. I don't know why I said that. It came out all wrong."

"Jimmy the hand, yes," the man gasped. "Yeah. I'm the gangster who watches the horses."

"Oh." The large part of Leila which believed she was being laughed at, not with, retreated. "That's right...that guy in the

55

hardware store said there were horses."

"Yes, ma'am. Good ones, too. Would you like to take a look?"

"I've always wanted a horse."

Leila had been one of those young girls who had gone through a phase where she believed owning a horse would cure all her problems. She sketched fanciful horse heads in her junior high notebooks and collected horse figurines and read books about horses. The Bay Area, however, was not a haven for horses—at least not the middle-class areas where Leila lived.

The children she considered leaving minutes earlier now weighed heavier in the balance than the joyful idea of spending time with light-hearted Jimmy and a bunch of horses.

"I can't. I've got to stay with the children."

"Well, bring 'em along!"

The shame of the failed bath stopped Leila from agreeing to anything on the children's behalf.

"I'll ask them…maybe tomorrow?"

"Sure! Any time. Just look for my truck."

Jimmy made his way back to a battered red truck with Sophie dancing circles around his legs as if he were a bowlegged, stork-like Pied Piper.

***

Three pairs of eyes stared at Leila when she turned back to the kitchen. Somehow the children knew just when to materialize—apparently out of thin air.

"What'd Jimmy want?" Ray said.

"I guess just to invite us to see the horses?"

"Huh. He never does that when Dad's here."

Her brain stimulated by the interaction with Jimmy, she saw Ray's mention of his father provided an opening.

"Speaking of your Dad...do you know how long he'll be gone?"

Leila didn't know what answer to hope for. A short time? So she could get out of here? A long time? So she could try to help these children? Ray's answer, though, provided her nothing but worry.

"No idea." Ray's clipped tone provided her no clues to his feelings.

Another question occurred to her but she couldn't figure out how to ask them what happened to their mother. "Do you have a mother" was just stupid. Everyone is born to some mother. But asking where she was could open up a depth of pain in these children she couldn't even stand to imagine.

"Okaaaaay," she said, playing for time.

She realized she needed the children on her side and that she didn't know what to do. The answer came to her as she stared at their faces—Storm's face intent on the necklace, Sleet's face looking to her for direction, and Ray's closed-down expression.

"Okay! Everyone sit down. We're going to have a...a council meeting." She almost said "family council," and felt glad she stopped herself.

Sleet hopped onto the bench. Storm, already seated, continued to play with the necklace. Ray stared, unmoving.

"What? You don't want to be a part of the decision-making process?" Leila said.

She made eye contact. Held it. Slowly, he sat down.

"There's nothing to talk about," said Ray.

"But couldn't we—" Sleet began. Ray cut him off.

"No. Whatever. No."

Sleet gave a one-shouldered shrug and looked down.

"Okay!" Leila said.

"You said that already," Ray pointed out. "Twice."

Leila felt hope begin to grind to a halt. The initiative lost, she wondered what to say.

"Look. Here's the situation. I'm here to take care of you three for...for a while. I don't know how long. And..."

Her sentence stalled. She couldn't decide what to say until she realized only the truth would do.

"And frankly? You don't look very well cared for right now."

Sleet snorted and Leila smiled.

"But here's the thing. I've never taken care of children before. And—and I really screwed up already this morning."

Ray stopped digging dirt off the table with his fingernail and looked up at her, his steady gaze unnerving.

"Well, so. You tried to tell me, Ray, before I started with the bath. And I didn't listen. Now I'm listening. What...how...what do you kids need?"

Sleet began to cry. His complexion lightened where the tears tracked down his face, cleaning as they flowed.

Ray looked away.

"Maybe that was the wrong question. I'm sorry," she said.

She piled through questions, looking for the right one, and still preoccupied with the bath. She really wanted to get Storm clean and dressed in something nice. Those pants Sleet brought down with the little flower on the leg, for instance…she held them again in her imagination, saw Storm in them, and felt profoundly stupid.

"Sleet." He raised his chin a little, met her eyes. "Sleet, those clothes you brought me? They don't fit her, do they?"

"No," he replied, the word almost inaudible.

"We need to go shopping," Leila said, and sensed fifteen hundred dollars evaporating like dew on a sunny day.

"Why don't you just go yourself?" Sleet wanted to know. He looked shaken by her words.

"No, no," Ray said. "She can't go by herself. How's she going to know what to buy? We should all go."

"But…" Sleet leaned over and hissed at his brother, "I don't think we should all leave— "

Ray twisted a little on the bench and before she understood his intent he backhanded Sleet across the cheek.

Leila yelled as if Ray's hand had connected with her face.

"Don't do that!" Two steps brought her into Ray's proximity.

Although tall for his age, she still outsized him when they both stood. She raised her hand to him, her rage infusing her arm with new-found strength. Ray turned his face up to her, a one-sided grin twisting his face oddly. Outside the door, Sophie's bark brought Leila back to herself.

"I was…" she said, and lowered her hand.

The kitchen felt cold as ice. She opened the door for Sophie. Warmth and sunlight pranced in along with the dog. She left the door open despite her perennial worry Stu might arrive at any moment and take the house by force.

Leila opened her mouth to apologize to Ray but the words wouldn't come. She switched gears, moving to distract, to smooth over. Her urge to deflect the conflict proved unnecessary. She looked up from her study of the floor tiles to see Ray leaving the house.

"Where are you going?" She called after him.

"Shopping," he yelled back, the sarcasm dripping.

He walked with head high, feet moving confidently over the rocky ground. Sleet followed with all the stoop-shouldered reluctance of a man walking to a loved one's funeral. Sophie rushed out after the boys.

Leila shrugged and fished the envelope back off the fridge, then looked around for Storm. The girl had made it as far as the door jamb, then stopped. Now she grabbed onto the frame with a starfish sucker grip.

"C'mon, Storm, let's go for a ride in the car," Leila encouraged.

The girl gave no response.

Leila suppressed her first impulse to pick her up, shivering at the idea of forcing the child to do anything, ever. She walked around the girl in the door and studied her from a new perspective.

The sight of Storm's face in direct, natural light stunned her brain into peace. Her unnatural thinness showed what most toddlers' fat-rounded faces hide—the shape adulthood would bring. Leila saw that in the sun her eyes were dark blue, almost violet. Her high cheekbones, wide brow, and pointed chin made a perfectly-weighted frame for those beautiful eyes. Despite the dirt, her skin almost glowed in its fairness.

60

"Oh, Storm," Leila said. "You're beautiful! Let's go show the world how beautiful you are."

Storm didn't move, just stared at the car where Sleet stood, leaning against the open door as Ray piled Leila's things around in the back seat.

Leila got down on her knees in front of Storm and opened her arms.

"Come on," she said. "It'll be okay. Come on, I'll carry you."

Storm pressed her lips together and swayed back. Sophie responded to Leila's entreaties instead, trotting over with sinuous grace and getting one good facial lick in before she could stand up.

Leila tried walking away from Storm, calling her to come to the car. Perhaps the threat of being left alone in the house would get her out the door. Sophie followed her halfway then turned, looked at the girl, and rushed back. The dog nudged Storm's hand where it clung, dislodging it, and started licking at her face.

"See?" Leila said. "Sophie is coming, too. We're all going."

Sophie whipped around at her name and stood, shoulders as high as the girl's armpit. Storm placed an arm over the dog's back and to Leila's relief, they began mincing across the drive, Sophie tip-toeing at one-quarter speed to accommodate the girl's small steps.

Leila hurried ahead of them. She had not planned to bring Sophie and now room in the car would be scarce. Everything left in the back seat needed to go in the trunk.

Storm appeared to have no idea how to get into a car. Leila recalled Bill's huge, red truck. Of course she wouldn't know. Ray

61

lifted her in, taking care to not hit her head, then leaned in and began fiddling with the recalcitrant middle lap-belt before climbing in to sit beside her. Sleet walked around to the other side and opened the front passenger door. Sophie leaped in to take the co-pilot's seat, her movement smooth as flowing water.

Leila did a final check—seat belts on, dog securely ensconced, and noticed the gaping front door of the house.

"Aw, damn," Leila said. "We left the door open."

"I'll get it," Sleet said. His voice sounded sticky with tears.

At the front door he grabbed the handle, then leaned inside, and shouted something into the house. With the car doors shut, Leila couldn't hear the words.

CHAPTER FIVE

Leila's spotty memory of the previous day's drive in to the ranch did nothing to prepare her for the drive out which revealed wonder upon wonder. A range of mountains, jagged and blue, defined the distance to the west.

"Look at them," Leila said. "They're huge!"

"The Owl Creek Mountains," Ray said.

No fencing lined the road, giving her the sense they were part of the prairie around them. They drove between a ridge and a stream-bed where the field was spotted with rocks the size of small cars. In the stream bed grew bushes with burnished, mahogany-colored stems—the brightest color in a landscape of tans and rusty red and struggling green.

"What are those bushes? I've never seen anything that color before?"

"Willow," Ray said. "It loves water."

The car topped a ridge and a valley of immeasurable proportions opened before them. The road cut straight across the valley and Leila sped up, then braked so hard she went into a skid. She reversed until her window came even with the animal she had spotted. There, standing still as stones, was a solitary deer-like creature. Its hide was tan on top, white on bottom, and it had horns unlike any Leila had ever seen before. They sprouted, thick

HEATHER M^CLOUD

and ridged, from the animal's forehead, tapered a bit, and then each split into two up-curving spikes. The animal gave her a lucent gaze and then sprang off at a tangent from the road. Leila had never seen anything move so fast.

"What was that?"

"People call them antelopes," Ray said.

She knew he mocked her but listened anyway.

"But they're not, really. Mom said they're 'sposed to be called pronghorns."

Sleet sucked in a breath when Ray said the word "mom." Leila held hers.

"So...your mom. Did she teach you lots of things like that?"

"Yeah, we were homeschooled," Ray said, but his voice slowed with hesitancy.

"What about now? Where's your mom?"

"She's gone."

Leila identified the finality in his tone. No more information on mom would be forthcoming, but one more question begged to be asked.

"Is your mom the one that named all of you?"

"Yeah," Ray breathed out the answer, then fell into obstinate silence.

"Why are they supposed to be called pronghorns instead of antelopes?"

"They're not antelopes," Ray said. "They're actually closely related to goats."

"But it doesn't look like a goat," Leila said. "It looks like—like..." She couldn't remember the name of the African antelope it resembled.

"Yeah. It looks like the antelope family. That's because of convergent evolution. You know what that is, right?"

"Uh."

"Right. The idea is that— "

Leila interrupted, knowing she shouldn't ask but needing to anyway. Her question turned Ray into someone else, someone educated to be engaged with the world.

"Your mother taught you all of this?"

She might as well have turned a switch and shut the back seat off. In the rearview mirror, Ray's expression hardened into immobility. Sleet turned to face out the window, shoulders hunched.

"Okay," she said. "Okay. I'm sorry."

They reached the highway just after a prairie dog town. Leila spoke again to the back seat, asking for the nearest store. The answer only came after a silence which filled the car with the sound of the idling engine and gusts of wind.

"Well," Ray's voice sounded rusty. He cleared his throat. "Jesus Saves Thrift Store is in town here and there's a Walmart in Riverton."

At the word "Riverton" Sleet began to snivel again.

Leila did not want to buy the children second-hand clothes. She had always despised the smell of thrift stores, a smell composed of abandonment and desperation in equal parts. But when she asked, Ray informed her Riverton lay over an hour away.

***

The town of Elk Crossing appeared to have never been told of life beyond the highway bisecting it. The stores faced that one strip or, creatively, were located on the same block but facing a side street. Jesus Saves Thrift Shop lay one block beyond the first street light. Leila pulled into the last parallel parking space in front of it. For a moment she sat and considered with dismay the sight of actual adult people sauntering past on the sidewalk.

"Okay!" She twisted in the driver's seat to look at the children while she spoke. "We'll just…"

She saw the children, then, as someone else might see them. Sunlight fell on Sleet, drawing out a dark green color around the blue-black bruise which marred his face. Storm looked stubborn again—or still. The dirt on her nightgown appeared ready to grow legs and attack something. Ray's clothes pulled and bunched every time he moved. And none of them wore shoes.

"I…" Leila said. "I don't know…"

Sleet spoke up for the first time since leaving the house.

"It's all right. We can just stay in the car."

Leila, on the verge of tears, apologized in a whisper.

She rolled down each window half way—a compromise between the mild summer heat and the wind. Every motion she made slowed and stiffened with the force of her self-hatred.

"I'm sorry," she said again. "I'll hurry."

In Ray's eyes, she thought she saw a reflection of her feelings. He understood her self-hatred and agreed. Sleet rescued her with his mild response.

"No hurry," he said.

The store resembled what she feared. Clothes crowded

together in circular racks. Racks placed too closely together. Poor lighting. The used-clothing smell. Sensory overload produced by clashing color and pattern combined with the burden of finding clothes which fit to make the task feel impossible.

"Hi!"

The bright greeting made Leila jump a little. She looked over the clothes to a counter halfway down the length of the store. A woman as tall as Leila leaned toward her, smiling.

"How are ya?" The woman asked, but didn't wait for an answer. "I'm Cindy! And you're new in town. What can I help you with?"

Leila noted the other shoppers tuning in to Cindy's greeting. Self-consciousness warred with relief. She chose relief and broke into a smile.

"Leila," she said, and stuck out her hand. Cindy shook firmly.

"So what can I do for you?"

"I'm looking for clothes for…" What to call them? "…for three children. Three, ten, and sort of a big thirteen."

"Boys? Girls?"

"The little one's a girl."

"Do you know sizes?"

Leila blushed and looked at her flats.

Cindy touched her arm, eliciting a flinch, and withdrew her hand with a frown.

"Look, Leila. We'll find something, okay? But I've got to know where to start looking. Did you bring them?"

"In the car," Leila said without thinking.

Cindy trotted toward the front door, drawing Leila in her

wake, and yelled over her shoulder.

"I'll be right back, everyone!"

Leila wanted to protest. This Cindy woman had taken over her shopping trip. And so quickly. But she didn't know how to stop the woman.

Sophie had her head out the window, looking toward the storefront. She growled, low and long, when she saw Cindy. Leila thought, with relief, the woman would turn back then. But without breaking stride she simply made for the driver's side of the car. Her dodge failed. Sophie's head popped back into the car and she bounded across to the driver's seat, stuck her head back out, and growled again, ears flat. Cindy stopped.

"Your...dog?"

Leila damned herself even as the social requirement to "be nice" took over.

"Sophie! Stop growling at the nice lady."

Sophie paid no mind so Leila went and stood by her head, rubbing her ears back into relaxation.

"It's all right," Leila said, half to Cindy and half to the dog.

Cindy edged around Leila and Sophie and peered in the back window. The bruise on Sleet's face presented itself to the window. Slowly he turned and looked up at the woman, then looked down immediately. Storm toyed with her macaroni necklace—the feeble colors of the macaroni drab against her gray nightgown. Ray sat and stared ahead, unwilling to participate in the examination. Even with his hands quiet in his lap the sleeves of his plaid shirt pulled halfway to his elbows.

Leila saw them as if for the first time again through Cindy's

68

eyes and felt deep shame. The condition of Storm's hair alone spoke volumes about the children and their caretaker. It never occurred to her to beg this woman's help. Years of enforced isolation had trained that urge out of her.

Without a word, Cindy turned, beckoned Leila back to the store. When the door swung shut she whirled and looked at Leila with an expression that killed any protests Leila may have been just about to utter. The expression on her face—equal parts rage and disgust—pinned Leila to the spot.

Cindy nodded once, glanced out the window at the car, and turned to the racks of clothing. Leila's mind squirmed, trying to fight its way out of her emotional haze. It tried to warn her of something—something bad—and she pushed it away, afraid to face more disaster, knowing she would only freeze up again.

"This will fit the oldest boy," Cindy said, and lifted a shirt from the rack. "He wasn't standing up so I can't be sure of the inseam, but I'm thinking he's a 29 waist. There are a few jeans that size over there…" She gestured at a rack toward the back of the store, and watched Leila until she started in the indicated direction.

Leila threaded her way through the bulging racks of clothes. She found the indicated rack and pushed one hanger after another past her. The handwritten labels showed no particular effort at order.

She glanced up to check Cindy's progress on Ray's shirts and saw the woman back at the counter handling a phone call. Again her brain stirred, a sluggish reptile attempting to respond to a sharp stick. Her emotional temperature stilled the beast back into

69

hibernation.

***

Content with three pairs of jeans for Ray, Leila wandered until she found the toddler section and began sorting through clothes for Storm. Sleet she left until last because she felt most unsure of his size. She soon realized Storm's clothes presented a problem, too. Although the height of a toddler, she would swim in most of these things, her thin body unable to fill out to expectations.

The bell above the door rang and the reptile in her brain stirred again, reminding her of all the times she had known Stu was about to hurt her even before he entered the room.

At that thought, she became certain Stu really had walked in. Long seconds passed as she wrestled fear in an effort to convince herself to look up. Finally, by dint of telling herself only small children hid from their fears under the covers, she convinced herself to look up from the footy pajamas in her hands. A big man edged in her direction, his wide shoulders out of place among the close racks. Brown uniform. Shiny gold accessories. A cop.

Leila tried to still her growing panic, telling herself nothing was wrong, she'd done nothing wrong. The cop squeezed between two racks and looked straight at her, his eyes slightly squinted in a face almost as weathered as Bill's. To the right, Cindy watched until the cop crossed some line of distance which gave him permission to speak.

"Ma'am?"

She looked around, hoping with a fervency approaching prayer that he was talking to someone else. No one presented themselves as alternate targets and she looked back toward the

70

cop. She couldn't meet his eyes. Instead, her gaze skittered up his pants, landed on the butt of the gun, kept going until she hit the left cheekbone, and stayed there.

His second "ma'am" sounded more demanding.

"Yes?" Her lips felt numb.

"Are those your children in the car?"

"Yes" and "no" both out of the question, Leila stayed dumb. She began to shake, the footy pajamas shaking along with her hand until she appeared to be flagging someone down.

The cop's face changed, the deep wrinkles around his eyes rearranging themselves into something less like agricultural furrows.

"Cindy! I need a chair."

He reached out and took the pajamas from her. She had trouble getting her fingers to release the fabric.

"Breathe, ma'am. You need to take a breath."

Leila obeyed and felt her eyes maybe bulged a bit less. She didn't understand what was bothering her so profoundly. The proximity of a large man obviously had something to do with it. She knew enough to understand that having a large man so close might bother her for a long time to come—a gift from Stu—but the uniform frightened her as well as the question the cop had asked.

A metal folding chair scraped on the concrete behind her and when the cop took one step closer she collapsed backward. The cop got down on one knee, looked at her with a frown. Her brain tried to distract her by making note of unimportant details like the breadth of his forehead and a faded scar across his left cheek.

"Normally, this is the point where I would ask, 'Is there a problem?' But I'm going to skip that part." The left side of his mouth twitched at his own humor.

Even within her panic, Leila appreciated his effort.

"Thank you," she whispered, and took a deep breath.

"Good. That's better. You just keep breathing."

He stayed there on one knee while Leila took breath after breath. The numbness receded from her lips and her peripheral vision returned. When he shifted his weight a little, the light from one of the bare fluorescents flashed the gold of his name plate across her face. "STEVENS" it announced.

Eventually silence and breathing and staring at this cop's face moved from boring through uncomfortable followed by unbearable. Leila found she wanted to talk.

"The kids in the car. They're not mine."

Her declaration, though, sounded wrong—like a lie of the foulest sort.

"Okay. No. They're kids I'm babysitting."

That feeble word—babysitting—also felt wrong. She tried again.

"Their father hired me to take care of them."

Closer. Taking care sounded right.

"And you left them in the car because..." Stevens said, leading her on.

"Because they're barefoot. I wasn't thinking. I mean, I've never had kids before and I just wanted to get them some clothes."

He nodded and stayed silent.

"I didn't realize how bad they looked. I don't know why I didn't notice. I couldn't leave them alone and they need clothes. And I looked at them. When we got here? I couldn't bring them in."

Stevens let another few long moments of silence pass before he spoke.

"Well, that makes sense. Before you finish your shopping—and I don't want to keep you long in case the car gets too hot—I just need to ask you a couple of questions."

Leila nodded. She felt done with the panic, done with the speaking. And she longed to rush out to the children and check on them.

"Name?"

"Leila Stein."

He held up the little flip notebook to show her the name.

"No," she said, and spelled her name correctly for him, fearing to correct a man with power. But he nodded and thanked her, crossing out and rewriting without a change in his placid attitude.

"Address?"

Her mind ran in helpless circles at that one.

"I don't have one. Are you going to put my name in a computer?"

At this question he did frown.

"Just the one law enforcement uses," he said.

Her panic returned. An image of Stu hunched over his computer in the den stabbed into her like the beginning of a migraine. Again she tipped into panic. It locked her muscles, narrowed her vision to a tunnel, and caught the breath in her throat. She wondered if she were going to pass out. Little black spots meandered through her field of vision.

"Ms. Stein, you need to breathe."

His voice sounded very far away.

"Breathe!"

She took a shuddering breath and refocused into the present. Through the black spots still clouding her vision she saw a worried cop bending over her.

"Ms. Stein, I would appreciate it if you wouldn't do that again. It scares me."

His statement, so far from stereotypical as to be absurd, and the woozy feeling in her head combined to make her giggle. The sound shocked her.

"I'm sorry!" She said. "I'm sorry. I'm not laughing at you. I just…"

Stevens glanced away from her, bit his lower lip, and looked angry when he looked back. The little dimple on his chin deepened and the crow's feet around his eyes took on a life of their own.

Leila cringed.

"Don't," he snapped. "Don't apologize when you haven't done something wrong."

She nodded, eyes glassed over.

"Who asked you to watch these children?"

"Bill Colvin."

He thanked her, stood straight and looked at her for a long minute.

"Bill's ranch is a ways out," he said. "And I've delayed your

74

shopping. I think the kids need some ice cream."

He offered her a hand. She noticed more scars on it—two running jagged through the coarse hairs on the back of his hand and a thick one on his thumb.

"I'm—I'm sorry?" She said, and winced. "No! I'm sorry I didn't mean..."

He withdrew his hand and let it hang naturally over the butt of the gun.

"Ms. Stein."

"I'm trying," Leila said. The words still sounded like an apology. "I hadn't realized I apologize so much."

Standing from the chair challenged her numb legs a little but she managed. Leila considered the cop's comment about ice cream as she trailed behind him. He stopped at the counter where Cindy stood and pretended to busy herself with something besides staring.

"Cindy," Stevens said. "Do me a favor and find some clothes for the kids."

"You bet, Cole. I'll have them ready when you come back from ice cream," she said, and then blushed a little, looking down.

"Right," Stevens said, drawing out the word. "I don't suppose asking you to stay off the phone would do anything?"

She laughed at his tone.

"I figured," he said, and sighed.

"Ice cream shop's over on the corner of Third and Elk Street," Stevens told her on their way out the door. "Can you find it? There's no point in following me. I just walked over."

Her confusion gave way to disbelief. "You're buying the kids ice cream?"

"Is there a problem with that?"

"No," she said. "No. And I know where it is."

***

Outside, Sophie's shaggy head still protruded from the window. Her sides heaved with her panting and Leila felt for her. The kids didn't look uncomfortable, though. They didn't even look bored. In fact, Leila thought they looked blank.

Sophie spotted Leila and her ears flattened and she wagged with enthusiasm. The big dog's tail overflowed the front seat. Sleet brushed it out of his face and smiled at Leila—just a tiny softening of his lips.

Her emotions lifted like a kite in an updraft at Sleet's smile. She couldn't wait to get back in the car and be with them. The sensation reminded her of the way she had felt when she first met Stu and she wondered if she were falling in love with the idea of being a parent to these children. She remembered trying to tell Stevens she was just the babysitter—how wrong it felt. Now she turned in the seat and looked at each of them for a moment. She returned Sleet's smile. Her glance brushed the curve of Storm's soft baby cheek. Ray lifted one eyebrow at her and, yes, even him, she loved him. For the first time in a very long time Leila felt determined to act. A statement formed in her brain. "I will keep them safe forever." A shock of joy lit up her interior landscape and she embraced the words and the joy.

Elk Crossing had apparently changed while she was talking with Stevens. It seemed lighter and more beautiful to her than the dull-edged, pedestrian little town she had driven through. A block to the south, Stevens stood on the sidewalk and her light mood astonished her with a little jolt of pleasure in seeing someone she knew.

Stevens bought the ice cream. He insisted. The cashier called him "Cole" just as Cindy had and caught Leila's questioning glance at his name tag.

"It's my first name," he said. "I grew up around here."

"So they never…"

"Nope! No one ever got used to calling me 'Sherriff Stevens.'" He appeared unfazed by the apparent lack of respect.

On the way out the door, Leila commented they had bought one cone too many. "There are five of us."

Cole just grinned. He juggled four cones in his big hands and, after handing one to each of the children, he turned to Sophie. The dog made short work of the treat—devouring the whole thing in two crazed-looking bites.

The children's ice cream consumption methods fascinated Leila. Ray took judiciously-sized bites out of his from the top down. Sleet licked the cone round and round in circles, careful never to let a melting runnel make its way to his fingers. Storm more or less buried her face in the ice cream, never looking up.

Leila kept her sigh at the sight internal, swearing to herself she would find a way to bathe the girl. Her arm still smarted from the Storm's bite. And when she looked down, she saw a tiny spot of blood clotted there.

She and Cole watched while the kids ate until their own cones started to melt. The two rested on the hood of the car as they ate. Cole's vanilla cone disappeared almost as fast as Sophie's and then he just looked around at the fine day while she consumed hers more slowly.

"You're new here," Cole said as he watched a bird wheel through the sky above them.

Leila nodded. "Yeah. Got here yesterday."

"And got a job the same day," Cole said. "That's not the easiest thing usually."

"I was...lucky." Under the warm sun and far from the house, the insistent dread she often felt there seemed silly. She wondered what her problem was.

"I'm glad," Cole said. "So Bill thought he'd get someone to watch the kids while he was out on the ranch all day..." He trailed off, toying with the thought.

"No. He left on vacation the minute I got there. It was weird. He took me to the house and just, well, just left."

"Huh," Cole grunted.

As she sat there on the hood of her Buick, the chocolate ice cream cold on her tongue, the sun warm on her face, Leila was struck by how happy she felt. She couldn't remember feeling this happy before. She looked back at the kids to reassure herself it was all real and saw Storm's head drooped down to her chest, the remainder of her cone still in one hand. Sleet had the look of a businessman late for an appointment. He looked at Leila, looked around at the road out of town, shifted in his seat.

"Damn! I've got to get them home. They're wearing out."

Cole frowned and muttered something Leila didn't catch.

She thanked him for the ice cream and drove back to the thrift store where the clothes Cole had requested lay piled on the counter. Leila glared at Cindy and paid for the clothes while trying to not touch the other woman's hand.

CHAPTER SIX

By the time Leila shoved the old Buick into park she was suffering from sugar crash, emotional let-down, and old-fashioned exhaustion.

Sleet sprang from the car before she even switched off the engine and sprinted to the house. Leila didn't even jump when he slammed the car door. The trek from car to house—normally about 30 feet—looked miles long and the only reward would be entering a stinking house which gave her the shivers.

Sophie danced from foot to foot in the front seat. Ray and Storm didn't move from the backseat. Leila turned and saw Storm still slumped over the remains of her cone. Ray sat beside her, one arm around her shoulder.

"Her head kept falling over," he said.

Leila gave a little internal wail of protest against the absence of rest, the presence of duty.

"I'll come get her," she told Ray.

Sophie ran off into the brush to pee as soon as she opened the door for her. Then, half climbing into the back seat, she pulled Storm's limp body to her chest. The girl asleep weighed twice as much as she had this morning at bath time. She stirred only once during Leila's trudge to the house. A rock turned under Leila's foot and she staggered. Storm jerked in response and her eyes flew open, locked onto Leila's face, and softly closed again.

Ray ran ahead to open the sticky front door. The rank, oily smell of the house rushed out to greet her, running its cold, heavy tendrils over her hair. She felt instantly filthy.

After plunking Storm, all disorganized limbs and lolling head, onto the love seat to finish her nap, Leila turned for the bedroom for her own nap. The pounding of feet down the stairs stopped her. Sleet appeared on the landing, launched himself down the second flight, and skidded to a stop before her, eyes wide.

"I'm so hungry!"

Leila almost groaned. Only years of training under Stu's rough tutelage kept her from making a sound of protest. She went to make lunch, passing Sleet on his way back upstairs with a full glass of water, a sight which made her realize her tongue felt swollen with thirst.

Somehow in her haze, Leila got sandwiches put together—a heaped plate of them as she remembered the children's constant clamor for more food. She went to bed, wondering at her fatigue, and then tallying up the time since Stu had let her leave the house for hours by herself.

Sophie woke her up later with a couple of licks to the face. Leila grinned at the sensation even before she opened her eyes.

"All right, all right, I'm awake," she told the dog.

She rolled onto her back, spent a few minutes staring blankly at the ceiling while fending off Sophie's affectionate muzzle. For those few minutes, she basked in the wonder of her good mood. She felt…light. Simple things like the texture on the ceiling looked beautiful. Lying on the floor in a nest of blankets, she thought about nothing and enjoyed everything.

The words of her intention came to her as wakefulness returned. She repeated the morning's resolution to herself, that she would keep them safe forever.

Her left arm, the one Storm bit, twinged when she lifted her arms to straighten her hair. But that sort of nagging pain featured so much in her life with Stu that she paid it no mind, just fluffed the wavy, brunette mass into place as she strode down the hall.

The kitchen stood empty, clothes still on the table in a heap. After letting Sophie out, she automatically began sorting by size and folding into three piles as she considered the implications of her resolution for the first time. She tried to picture a way to get the children out of the house and into her care. Obviously, she could simply call social services...For the first time she realized there was no phone in the house. She shrugged off the increased feeling of isolation and continued thinking. No social worker in her right mind would let her keep the children. Calling social services wouldn't work.

Maybe the tactic she used with Stu would work here, too. They could all run away from this house. They could go someplace no one would ever find them. Mexico, maybe. Belize. The idea warmed her. To be away from this house where she felt watched by something unseen and where Bill would sooner or later return appealed greatly.

Hard on the heels of that idea came a sudden, compelling conviction that they were all in danger. Terrible danger. It loomed in her mind, clouded her thoughts, and sped her heart.

A high, keening sound, a human siren of anguish, filled the

house as if in response to her thought. She dropped a half-folded shirt and started for the stairs at a run.

The orange light of evening slanted through the living room, making her shadow jerk and billow across the north wall. The keening stopped just as she made the bottom stair and Leila stopped, too. The silence felt just as threatening as the sound and the irrational fear of going upstairs gripped her, as strong as a physical force pushing her back toward the kitchen.

"Hello?" Leila whispered up the stairs. She meant to call out but instead the word sounded like an invitation to the force which pushed her away.

A scream answered her whisper. The sound was more than what a terrified child should be able to wrench out. But the reality of the cry burst the bubble of fear around Leila and she tackled the naked steps into darkness two at a time. With each step upward the air grew colder and something chittered about the wrongness in the back of her mind. The last stair and then she stood in the dim hallway, the only light coming from the window at the far end. Something moved across the light and she screamed.

A looming black figure stood between her and the source of the screaming. The hulking cutout of a person, it shambled toward her. The screaming went on, louder now, and ragged. Leila started backpedaling, wanting to go back down the stairs but afraid to turn her back to the faceless thing coming toward her and hanging on to a thin determination to answer the need of the screamer. She backed until her heels hung over the lip of the top stair and still the figure kept coming.

Leila whimpered. As if in response to the weak sound, the screaming from down the hall cut off. The figure before her turned toward the silence and in the half light from the far window Leila made out a face. Dull of eye and slack of muscle, the face still looked like Ray's.

Grasping the thread of determination which had carried her up the stairwell, Leila forced herself to remember her resolution to protect these children.

"Ray?" Her voice squeaked out.

The head turned toward her again, the eyes seeming to look beyond her, beyond the wall behind her.

"Ray. It's Leila. Ray."

Her eyes were adjusting. She could see his face now, a little, could even see a silvery scar running down one cheekbone which must only show under certain light. She could not look away. Ray stood still long enough for Leila to feel her breath begin to slow.

"Ray," her voice came out stronger this time. "Are you all right?"

He blinked. Blinked again, and only then focused on her.

"I...I locked them in the room." Ray informed her in a wondering voice.

Leila didn't know what room he referred to but didn't let that lack stop her.

"Okay. Can we let them out now?" Leila spoke to him in a tender sing-song usually reserved for fretful babies and threatening dogs.

Ray's voice dropped into another key and grated across the next words. "They're bad. Bad children."

In concert with Ray's grating voice, a series of strong urges washed over her. She saw herself running from the house.

She saw herself barring the doors with the children still inside because they are all poisoned, evil children.

In the midst of a vivid vision of setting the house ablaze, something touched her shoulder. She hunched up, away from the touch. The flames called to her with their purifying brightness. Someone shook her shoulder, hard. Her eyes snapped back into focus and Ray's eyes stared into hers. He looked different— concerned, frightened.

From down the hallway there came the sound of sobbing. She couldn't imagine that Sleet sounded like that—so young. Storm was crying, but not crying as Leila imagined a child in pain would cry. She was crying like someone had died, in quiet, endless sobs. Leila forced her attention back to Ray.

"Ray? We need to go let them out."

She forced herself to step forward. Ray turned, decisively, and walked down the hall to the third door. He reached to draw a bolt mounted high on the door frame and then hesitated. Leila reached over his shoulder, impatient to rescue the children, and forced the door open.

Diffuse northern light glowed from the window in the room. Storm huddled on the bare floor. Sleet crouched beside her with his arms around her. They both stared at the west wall. Leila looked, saw nothing but blank, stained sheetrock. The room contained no furnishings, no decoration. The window. The bare floor. The closet door. That was all.

"Hey, guys." Leila pitched her voice low.

Sleet turned slowly to face her and she saw tracks where his tears had washed some of the dirt off the right side of his face. The bruise on the left side shone where tears had also run.

"Help me," Sleet said.

Leila stepped past Ray into the room and felt a wave of vertigo. It reminded her of a fun house she once explored as a child, a room where none of the walls were at the right angle and the ceiling was not square. The smell was much stronger. Once on a still, warm day in California a crazy-haired homeless woman sat next to her. The smell of this woman's body, of shit and dirt and stress and misery had made her gag like she gagged now. She grasped the doorframe as black and silver concentric circles took up residence in the center of her vision.

"Help me," Sleet repeated.

Leila took a deep breath of the foul air, squeezed her eyes shut, and forced herself to walk across the room. She stumbled to Storm, limp and sobbing in Sleet's arms.

"I can't carry her," Sleet apologized.

Leila lifted the little girl and stumbled back into the hall where Ray waited.

Leila wanted to hit him, to beat him within an inch of his life. He must have seen the anger before she smothered it because he shrank back.

"I'm sorry. They were being bad."

Leila turned, shifted Storm's limp form to one arm, and wrapped the other around Sleet, drawing him close against her front.

"Come downstairs with us," she told Ray. It was as close as she could come to accepting his apology.

***

Leila sat at the kitchen table and cradled Storm. Sleet sat close by her and Ray hovered around the door to the living room, kicking one foot against the door frame over and over.

"What was that, Ray? What happened up there?"

Her voice brought an immediate response. From the front door. Sophie started whining and scratching at the door. Ray hurried across the kitchen and opened the front door Sophie came inside, tail high, paws mincing across the floor like a dancer's trained feet, all power disguised by precision.

Ray closed the front door and stood facing it, silent, and Leila opened her mouth to ask him again.

Sleet interrupted, his speech thickened a little as if his tongue were dry.

"It's not his fault," he said. "Things…happen."

Leila shivered at the way he said it. Sleet's statement reminded her of the old adage "shit happens" but that wasn't the way it sounded when Sleet said it. In Leila's mind, the word "things" swam with dark shapes impossible to make out but still threatening. After a long pause, Leila agreed.

"They do seem to."

With her agreement, the anger she felt clenched in her chest melted away.

"Ray," she said, "come sit with us."

Ray's shoulders dropped a few inches. When he turned from facing the door, Leila's heart sped a little, half expecting to see the slack face and staring eyes from upstairs. But it was Ray—just

87

Ray—who looked at her.

Storm's shivering began to subside. Leila held her even closer, glad for the warmth of her body. With twilight coming on, the gloom in the house deepened. Leila's mood matched and she struggled to comprehend and cope. She reached for the positive feelings of earlier in the day.

"Look, everyone. We've got some things to talk about. Hard things," she said.

The boys nodded, watched her face.

"See, I want…I'm going to…"

Tears took the place of words as she stared at the scarred table. She wanted this so desperately—to save the children and to care for them forever. But they had to want that, too. She needed them on her side and believed, young as they were, they deserved a choice.

"When I came here?"

They nodded again.

"I was running away. From my husband. He…didn't treat me well."

She reviewed her words and understood them to be inadequate.

"Truth is…he beat me. A lot. And other things. And, and, I was afraid he would kill me?" Her voice rose in pitch. She stopped to gather her strength.

"So you ran away," Ray filled the silence for her.

"Yes. And I ended up here."

Sleet picked up her suggestion.

"You think we should run away," he said.

"Yes!"

"No," Ray said.

"Why not?" Leila asked.

"Because…" Sleet began slowly.

"Because no," Ray said. "We can't leave. We won't leave."

Leila toyed with giving in to despair, the familiar emotion inviting her with its habitual energy. But of all things, uncertainty blocked the way to despair. What would she do if she gave up? No answer. What would it take to go forward? She didn't know. But she could see the next step forward so she took it.

"If we don't leave, we'll be right here when he comes back," she said.

Sleet's face paled.

"That's the way it has to be," Ray said. Underneath the toughness of his voice Leila heard despair matching her own.

"Look," she tried again. "I can get custody of the three of you. I can try, you know?"

Sleet appeared close to tears. Ray laid his hand on his brother's shoulder, shook it gently, like a reminder.

"No," Sleet said. "We can't leave."

"I—I want to. I want to…" The more they resisted, the more Leila became convinced her half-formed desire to be a mother to these children was true and right. She simply did not have the words to explain.

"You want us to be safe," Ray said. "But it's impossible. He's coming back. And we have to stay here. That's all."

He sounded sick. And now Sleet did start to cry.

Storm's body began to weigh heavy in Leila's arms. She looked down at the girl and saw she had fallen asleep. Her relaxed form radiated heat against Leila's chest as if Storm's guardedness while awake kept her from sharing even her body heat with another. The trusting warmth gave her courage to try one more time.

"All right. But what if I made sure he never came back?"

Sleet spoke up in a small voice choked with sobs.

"You mean, like, killing him?"

"Yeah, right, you couldn't pull that off," Ray said. "He's too tough."

Their sincerity as they discussed killing their father gave Leila pause. She shook her head and told herself to focus on what was real and important.

"I actually meant trying to get him arrested, not dead," she said.

Ray snorted. "Riiiiight. And then when he gets out?" He wandered out of the kitchen.

"Is dinner soon?" Sleet asked.

Storm weighed too much to hold any longer. When Leila stood to go put her down, the girl's body tensed. She squirmed around until she could grab Leila's arm and neck. The force of her barnacle grasp contradicted Leila's feeling that nothing would change, nothing could be changed.

Eventually Storm woke up, gazed into Leila's face sleepily. Leila stared back, overcome with a feeling of tenderness. Then Storm's eyes opened fully, consciousness returning. Her face took on the guarded look so habitual that Leila hadn't even noticed it until sleep erased it, and she slipped from Leila's arms onto the ground and padded off.

***

She made dinner to a disquieting symphony composed of her dismal thoughts, conflicted emotions, and a growing conviction that something was in the house with her, watching her, perhaps crouched behind her...

Her memories of the day frayed under the weight of the black eyes behind her. She refused to turn. To turn would be to acknowledge something were there, to give a name to the wrongness of the house. Instead she tried to turn her thoughts back to practical matters and confronted loss and confusion. At one brief point during the day she had been buoyed by her decision to care. Now that purpose lay lifeless, crushed by the grim reality of the children. Her attempt to infuse them with her hope had only exposed the fragile emotions for what they were— a stupid dream. For a few moments she hated them. She hated Storm for slipping away the moment she realized she clung to Leila. She hated Sleet for his apparently hopeful question—you mean, like, killing him? She particularly hated Ray for his bitter, honest appraisal of their chances, which were none.

With the hatred came visions of violence. Cold raked her shoulders, froze the sockets of her arms into place. Dinner started to burn as, more detailed than mere imagination, she saw herself running the children down and beating some sense into them.

Like a drowning woman she reached for something to steady her and as if in answer she heard the wind beating at the side of the house. She couldn't stand the thought of turning her back on the house to go open the front door. As if the cold in her bones was more than her imagination, she found her movements slowed and stiffened. Still, she fought the sensation and turned toward the blank rectangle of the entry to the living room. She backed up until she could see the door knob in her peripheral vision. She lifted and pulled at the front door and the prairie rushed in, all at once.

Leila gasped at the clean, cool air brushing her face and smelled the richness of the open land with its myriad hardy plants and animal life. The stark interior of the house lost its threatening aspect and became mundane. For a while she stood and shuddered as the cold left her body and the visions lost their power.

Even though she felt the open door with the kitchen light pouring out was an invitation to Stu and Bill to come right in, she left the door open. Better the prickle of familiar paranoia than...whatever that had been.

She and the children ate what she could salvage of their burned dinner in silence. Partway through the meal a sudden change in air pressure brought wind gusting into the house and the front door slammed angrily shut.

Leila made a strangled sound of terror, then jumped at the sound before she realized what made it. She bent, picked her fork up from the floor, and kept eating while her eyes filled with tears.

She got up to clear the dishes.

"Don't do that," Ray said.

"Yeah. We can do it," Sleet offered.

An edge of anger crept across Leila's consciousness again. The children's helpfulness reminded her how much she valued them. She didn't want to remember. They had just crushed her ideas for saving them, rendered her into a despairing heap, and now they offered to do the dishes? A feather of cold brushed her arm and she understood how tired she was.

"I'm going to bed," she said.

***

Although emotional exhaustion left her limp, the long afternoon nap did not allow for a deep sleep. She left the light on in the bedroom and drifted off after staring blankly for quite some time at the ridiculous wallpaper border of dusty pink roses on the maroon walls. No borderland separated her waking state from her dreams, only a sudden increase in irrationality let her know she was asleep.

A voice chanted. She recognized the voice as her own even though it wavered and slurred like a recording played back too slowly. "All wrong. All wrong," a mesmerizing repetition of two syllables which was now joined by other voices, one, then two, then a chorus, all chanting in somber unison.

Somewhere, far away, Leila thought she could hear a woman screaming. The scream admitted no sense of anger and no hope of self-defense. A simple, unending cry of agony. She smelled blood.

A door slammed, cutting off the scream but Leila knew it continued, always continued, and the chanting rose to an ear-splitting volume. Something about the voices sickened her as much as the tang of blood on her tongue and in her nostrils.

She tried to force herself awake but when she opened her eyes she knew she had dreamed them open. The room filled with haze, the light above her dimmed. Through the haze she saw Sleet's figure in the doorway peering at her. His clothes hung in tatters and she saw someone had been starving him and his hair fell to his shoulders in a dirty mass. He looked concerned, as if she were the one who needed pity, not he and she turned from the sight straight into the empty room upstairs and now Storm was screaming…

And so her night wore on.

At one point she stirred and opened her eyes. For some reason, the overhead light was off, yet light poured into her eyes. It took a moment to focus with her emotions numb from the abuse of her dreams. She stared into silvery light. The moon hung gibbous and bright outside the window. She felt awe and, comforted by the clean light, fell into a deeper sleep.

CHAPTER SEVEN

Leila became aware of her left arm even before she fully awoke. It throbbed and burned. A lot. She stirred and it hurt even more. Her eyes felt gritty when she opened them and the room swam with her dizziness and nausea.

She rubbed her eyes clear with her right hand, even that movement hurting her, and looked at the offending limb. Her hand was swollen into sausage fingers, the palm so fat her life line had disappeared. And her forearm—the area around Storm's bite marks was bright red and hot to the touch. Red lines crept up toward her elbow. She started shivering.

Leila remembered there was no phone in the house. Bill took the home's only phone with him in his pocket. She would have to make the long drive to Elk Crossing for help. She longed to simply lie back down but knew it was a bad choice. Drawing on the grit she developed while living with Stu, she forced herself to get up.

Standing took effort with her coordination gone and she had to grab the windowsill to keep from falling. The idea of getting her bra on was ridiculous with one hand which wouldn't work. And buttoning her blue jeans? Impossible.

In the kitchen Sleet looked hopeful, then frightened.

"You're sick," he said.

"I'm sick. I have to go find a doctor."

"What about breakfast?"

She staggered and put a hand on the table to brace herself, wishing with a sort of spiritual passion for a cell phone.

The morning she left California came back to her in Technicolor, more real than the kitchen around her. The palm tree, so green. Hibiscus, so red. She left it, of course, her phone. In her paranoia she thought it one more way for Stu to track her down.

"It's okay," Sleet offered. "We'll have sandwiches. We'll be okay."

Leila nodded, regretted it with a dry heave, and stumbled to the car in her pajamas.

The drive took over an hour and she saw nothing but the rutted road and, later, the center line on the highway. Then she wandered through town, unable to decide where to stop. Jesus Saves and the ice cream shop. The hardware store where she called Bill on her first day in town. The man there had been helpful. She parked at a crazy angle and stumbled inside. Somehow, the smell of bolts and fertilizer strengthened her. She made her way to the scarred counter where the same man who sent her to Bill in the first place stood.

"Doctor," she croaked at the man.

He dived around the end of the counter like the place was on fire. Leila's consciousness seemed to be snapping off and on like a camera shutter. She watched curiously as her perception changed the man's rapid movements into flashes and jerks.

"Hang on. I'll get you a chair."

"Doctor."

"Yes! I'm on it. But you've gotta sit down."

He got her a chair and went to the phone, frowning. Leila urged him mentally to hurry, meant to say something, something besides "doctor" and then she fell asleep.

"Can you walk?" A dim voice, wanting her to do something. She ignored it.

"Miss Stein!" This time more of a command but maybe she could ignore it.

"Miss Stein." Then someone shook her shoulder and she stiffened as the pain woke her.

Cole stood before her, towered, really, and frowned.

"They called the cops on me?"

His lips twitched in a small, wry smile.

"No. In this case I'm the ambulance, apparently. Now can you walk or do I need to carry you?"

"Walk." The idea of being slung in Cole's arms and carried to his cruiser did not appeal.

She managed the walk. Cole supported her on the right, and she slid limp into the cruiser.

"We'll be there in five," he said.

The clinic, a little boxy building which didn't fit Leila's idea of how it should look, came equipped with a nurse and wheelchair waiting outside.

Cole and the nurse poured Leila into the wheelchair and she slipped again into unconsciousness.

The prick of a needle in her arm made her stir and open her eyes in time to catch the tail end of a conversation.

"…ambulance takes an hour but she's got to be in Casper stat."

The woman's words filtered down into her brain. Casper. Ambulance. Then the woman saw Leila's eyes were open.

"You're going to be okay," she said. "But you need to be in the hospital for a while."

This presented a problem. Leila struggled to remember what the problem might be.

Casper. Ambulance. Hospital. The children!

"No," Leila said. "No hospital." She wondered if she had yelled in her urgency but couldn't tell.

The woman frowned at her. Leila squinted at her name tag. Sue Paddock, M.D.

"You, my dear, have cellulitis. Someone bit you. You're headed toward a nice, ripe case of septicemia. And you're dehydrated. You'll be fine in a couple of days, but you need to be in the hospital."

Leila shook her head, regretted it.

"No hospital. The children…"

"You'll just have to get someone to look after them, then. Just tell me who to call. I'll do it."

The argument was wearing Leila out. Panic at leaving the children was the only thing keeping her going.

"Cole. Sheriff." She needed someone on her side and his was the only friendly face she knew.

"He's in the waiting room, believe it or not," Dr. Paddock said. "I'll get him."

In a minute she heard footsteps coming back. She lifted her head.

"The children," she said to Cole.

98

"It's okay, Miss Stein. I'll find someone to take care of them until you get out," he said.

"No! No. Can't leave them." She understood they would be taken out of the house. And, with the perfect irrationality of the very ill, she was on their side. They should not leave the house. It felt wrong to leave the house. The house was sick and needed their help.

"Dr. Paddock says you could die if you don't get treatment," Cole said.

"Treat me here." She looked at the IV in her arm. "Here."

Cole looked at the doctor.

"She has a point," he said. "The children don't have anyone but her. Any chance..." He waved a hand at the examination room.

"Huh," said Paddock. "Well...all she really needs is hydration and IV antibiotics. If someone could run to the pharmacy in Casper...But I have to say, I have my reservations about this."

"How long would she have to stay here?" Cole wanted to know.

Paddock reached up and fiddled with the IV bag.

"It's ten now. Theoretically, we could get the antibiotics by noon if someone ran with their lights on? Half an hour to run the clindamycin...If she's feeling better with some hydration I suppose we could have her out of here by one."

"Can do," Cole said, and looked down at Leila. "I'll send someone to stay with the children."

Leila closed her eyes and slept without nightmares.

***

"Stick out your tongue," Dr. Paddock said.

Not awake enough to wonder, Leila obeyed.

"Good. Much better. How're you feeling?"

Leila blinked. The grit in her eyes had disappeared. The room no longer spun around her.

"Better?"

"You were really dehydrated," Paddock said. "I got two liters of normal saline in you before the deputy got back."

Leila wanted to know if she could go.

"Sit up."

When she did, Paddock wanted to know if she felt dizzy. She did not. After taking her blood pressure, the doctor nodded.

"Your blood pressure was very low when you came in. It's why you felt so weak and dizzy. I'll let you go, but you've got to promise me something."

"Anything."

"Take better care of yourself. Drink a lot of water. Water. Not pop or coffee. And you've got to fill this prescription and take it like it says. Every six hours no matter what."

"I'll do it."

"There's someone in the waiting room to drive you home."

A stranger? To drive her back to the house? She wanted to protest. But one look at Dr. Paddock's face changed her mind. Apparently the driver was not negotiable.

Stu controlled her every interaction for years. She wasn't used to meeting people, talking with them. But she had to get back to the children. She had been away too long already. And she sensed hesitation might be taken for physical weakness and keep her longer in the clinic. She stood straighter, and walked in the indicated direction.

Several groups of people sat in the waiting room. A mother and child combination. The toddler's nose ran with snot. A man with his thumb wrapped in a washcloth bleeding through in bright red. A woman, alone, coughing spasmodically. In the corner, almost hidden by a potted plant, a middle-aged man rose, his silvering hair dignifying an otherwise unremarkable face.

"Miss Stein?"

She nodded, tongue-tied.

"I'm Pastor Jim Weaver. Is it all right if I drive you home?"

The question, combined with the man's slender shoulders and calm demeanor, put Leila at ease.

"How will you get back to town?"

"Easy. My wife, Pat, is watching the kids so we'll ride back together."

Leila felt immediately sorry for the poor woman. She sympathized with walking into that house to care for those kids. They drove in the pastor's dusty car to pick up the Buick. On the way, he nodded at the square paper in Leila's hand.

"You need to stop at the pharmacy."

She thought of the packet full of money lying on top of the refrigerator and sighed with fatigue.

"I'll have to come back later and fill it."

He glanced at her pajamas.

"We'll fill it now. You can pay me back at church Sunday."

"I'm Jewish."

He gave her a wry smile. "Last I checked there were no

synagogues in Elk Crossing. Come pray with us. Bring the kids."

Leila nodded, still tired, and tired even farther by the man's insistence. She didn't want to go to a Christian church. She didn't want to offend this man, either.

The pastor's attempts at small talk on their drive out resembled a field of land mines for Leila. Her life presented no easy answers.

"What brings you here from California," for instance, produced cowering fear instead of an easy chat. He settled, after a while, on the weather.

As usual, the sight of the house slapped Leila into dread. She unfolded from the car and straightened, steeling herself against walking into that place.

"I'm sorry," she said. "The house smells really bad."

He assured her it was fine and, in gentlemanly fashion, went to open the door for her. He failed.

"You have to, um, sort of lift and push at the same time."

Once inside, she watched as the smell hit him. A small feeling of pleasure came over her as she saw someone else struggle to accommodate to the stench. She felt affirmed, as if his experience reinforced her own. Movement at the kitchen table drew Leila's attention. A small woman stood from the shadow across from where the light hit the table.

"Pat!" The pastor sounded glad to see his wife.

"Jim." Pat's voice, tense and low, sounded a bit ragged. "Start praying, Jim. Please."

He rushed to Pat and took her in his arms.

"What's wrong? Why am I praying?"

"I don't know. I don't know what's wrong. Something horrible," Pat said.

Leila could see her shaking in Jim's arms. An odd blend of satisfaction and fear swept through her, both the effect of seeing at least one other person felt the same way she did about the house.

Jim bent his head so his lips were close to the top of Pat's head and started muttering. Leila wondered if she was supposed to look away when someone broke into spontaneous prayer. They stood like that until Pat's shivering and Jim's muttering died away at the same time.

Finally, finally, they looked up at her.

"I am so sorry," Pat said. "I shouldn't have left you out. Come pray with us?"

Leila backed up a step without planning to.

"She's Jewish," Jim said.

"You're Jewish!" She sounded delighted, almost relieved.

"Uh, yeah?"

Pat stood straight now, little shoulders cradled in Jim's arms. She bore little resemblance to the shaken women they had walked in on.

"Do you have a prayer book with you?"

"Pat? What are you doing?" Jim wanted to know.

She waved off his question.

Irritated by her confusion, by Pat in general, and driven to find the kids, Leila brushed the question off.

"Where are the kids? Where's Sophie?"

"This was," Pat replied, "the worst babysitting experience of my life."

Leila laughed and liked Pat a little better.

"You don't know the half of it," Leila said.

Pat went still, looked at her, and Leila felt the woman actually saw her, Leila, a person. Stu had never looked at Leila that way. No one had, really. In California, people looked at each other like players in a vast video game.

"How are you feeling?" Pat wanted to know. "Are you up to a talk? I think we need to talk."

"Pat..." Jim said, halfway between warning and plea.

She batted his caution away from her and sat down at the table, waiting, square shouldered, for Leila to join her.

Leila's fatigue expanded to encompass Pat, the house, everything. She still didn't know where the kids were, whether they had eaten, anything. Two drives ruled her: make sure the kids were okay, and lie down. Her long training in mindless obedience, however, left her stuck between what she wanted and Pat's expectations. She stood and swayed and hated Pat for it.

"She needs to rest, not talk," Jim said, and pulled Pat to her feet.

Pat gave Leila that direct stare one more time.

"You shouldn't stay in this house," she said. "We've got to talk."

"Don't forget, Leila," Jim added. "Church at ten on Sunday!"

***

The minute the door slammed, Leila opened her mouth to call for the kids. They popped through the living room door before she could make a sound.

104

"Are they gone?" Ray wanted to know. He had a white-knuckled grip on Sophie's collar.

"We're not leaving, right?" Sleet asked.

Storm trailed after them, her right index finger in her mouth.

"You guys were hiding in there the entire time we were talking? Are you hungry? Did she feed you?"

"We're hungry," Sleet said. "We didn't know who it was so we stayed upstairs. Who was that, anyway?"

"And she didn't come looking for you?"

"Sophie wouldn't let her into the living room," Ray explained.

Leila pictured the scene without trouble. It had, after all, happened almost that way when she first entered the house.

"Let's make some food," Leila said.

"Are you all right?" Sleet wanted to know.

"I will be. After the antibiotics kick in, I think."

Leila realized she would not be able to stand long enough to cook around the same time the boys did. They came up with a solution which would never occurred to Leila.

"You tell us what to do and we'll do it."

She guided them through the steps necessary to prepare a late hot lunch, and then Sleet actually walked her to the bedroom.

"You'd be a great nurse," Leila told him.

"Nurses are girls," he said.

She slept.

Sickness gave her nightmares even more force and clarity. She stood in the kitchen in gloom, knowing wrongness, feeling panic for the children.

She labored toward the light switch through clinging

shadows, each dark swirl clawing at her legs, climbing toward her throat.

With relief, she reached the switch and flipped it. The click brought nothing but increasing blackness.

That was the wrong one, proclaimed a voice in her head, and it laughed at her.

She wanted to call for the children but with certainty knew if she opened her mouth the blackness would rise up and enter her mouth, fill her with its wrath and evil misery.

But the children. Something bad is happening. Something is wrong with them.

As soon as she thought it she realized the time had passed to help them. She opened her mouth to scream for them, to declare her sorrow and rage and guilt. The choking darkness rushed in.

She found herself in The Room upstairs. The children lay on the floor, their limbs at crazy angles to their bodies. She started backing toward the door.

She tripped over something which wasn't there. At the sound of her gasp and stumbling feet, the children rose up. They turned as one and came for her, slack faces and staring eyes aimed at her and through her and past her, their broken arms reaching for her, pleading for her to join them.

Sickness rose in her composed in equal parts of fear and longing. She knew their touch would complete the horror and transform her into one of them and she feared it and she longed to join them. It would be so easy to just give up. Storm reached her first, looked up at Leila, and opened her broken arms in a parody of a hug...

Leila woke up with a gasp and sat up in a convulsion of blankets and flailing, panicked arms. She gagged once and then sat, shivering from infection. Her lungs heaved breath at twice the rate they should have and her heart pounded in sympathy.

Unlike every other nightmare she had ever had, she did not feel relieved to wake up. Not here in this house. She focused on the practical, damning the absence of time pieces she chose to think it was time for an antibiotic.

At the kitchen sink she stared out at a landscape obscured by late dusk. She struggled with the child-proof cap and washed a pill down. Water tasted so good in her mouth. Only when she slaked her thirst did she notice the dimness in the kitchen mirrored that of her dream.

She stood there, hands braced on the kitchen sink, and cried. Fear of waking the house kept her sobs muffled.

"What's the matter with you?"

Leila whirled in fear of seeing a slack face, empty eyes. The sight of Ray's usual expression of disdain filled her with such relief that she threw her arms around him. He stood, stiff and unyielding, until she finished hugging him.

"You're not all right," he told her. "You're still sick."

"Is there a clock in this house? Watch? Anything?"

"Nope," he said. "Why?"

"How'm I supposed to know when to take my pills?"

"Huh. I don't know." Ray frowned.

He kept step with her as she made the weaving trip back to her room. He stopped at the door.

"How often are you supposed to take them?"

107

"Every six hours."

He leaned against the door frame, watched her walk back to the blankets on the floor.

"So that's four times a day," he said. "You just took one at dusk. You'll need one in the middle of the night, one at dawn, and one at noon. So what's the problem?"

"How do I know when it's midnight?" She thought she sounded like a whiny child.

"You can't tell?" Ray asked.

"Of course not! Wait—you can?"

"Yeah, I think so. Don't worry about it. We'll wake you up when it's time," Ray promised her.

Sleep snapped her up again. The relentless progression of nightmares gripped her until something soft hit her in the head and she startled upright with a screech. A crumpled towel lay near the head of the bed.

"Sorry," Sleet said from the doorway, "but you wouldn't wake up."

"You threw a towel at me?"

"Yeah, it's midnight."

In the kitchen, antibiotic taken in faith, Leila staggered as the floor seemed to writhe beneath her feet.

"You need to lie down again," Sleet said after a minute.

"I don't want to go back to sleep."

Sleet wanted to know what was wrong.

"Nothing," Leila told him.

He kept looking at her and the floor kept moving—just enough to keep her off balance.

108

"I keep having nightmares," Leila said.

"Oh ya, those," he said. "You'll get used to it."

She went back to bed. He stopped at the doorway and watched her cross to her nest.

"I'll be right back," he said.

He returned with Sophie and pointed at Leila.

"Go lie down," he said.

The big dog paced across the floor to Leila and sniffed her thoroughly, wrinkling her nose, and then licked her cheek once and lay down. Leila only dimly noticed when Sleet turned the bedroom light off.

A new nightmare feeling came over Leila. Stu stood over her—or maybe it was Bill. She couldn't get her eyes open far enough to check. She began to moan and thrash in protest and with a whuff of warm air, Sophie licked her cheek. Leila's eyes opened to the sight of the dog standing over her, safe, warm, real. She scratched the dog's neck in gratitude and with a sigh Sophie lay down again—closer this time. Leila threw an arm over the shaggy shoulders and slept.

CHAPTER EIGHT

Morning light warmed Leila's face. She woke bleary-eyed and looked immediately at her arm. The angry red which had been marching up her arm was now receding and turning pink. She looked next for Sophie, ready to thank the dog for her intervention, but she was gone.

Leila still swayed a little as she made breakfast but she hummed over the frying pan. The kids materialized as if the scent of food made them substantial. Leila enjoyed the idea that cooking for them was something of a magic trick.

Sleet wanted to know how she felt. Ray asked to look at her arm. Storm simply blinked sleepily and made a beeline for the food. Leila studied the kids as they ate and wondered for the first time how they amused themselves all day.

"Today," she said.

All three looked up.

"Today we're just going to relax and play."

Sleet grinned. Ray looked thoughtful.

Leila studied the kids for a minute.

"After baths," she added.

"How're you gonna..." Ray said, and nodded in Storm's direction.

"I don't know," Leila replied. "But you've got to admit, she really needs one."

She contemplated the question through the rest of breakfast. Sleet volunteered to clean up and put away the leftovers, leaving Leila free to execute her plan for Storm's bath. From the kitchen Leila collected a mixing bowl and a set of bright red measuring cups. In the pantry she found a dusty case of juice boxes and dumped the contents out of three.

"Come on, Storm," she said. "Let's go play a game."

As usual, Storm trotted obediently after Leila, although she paused at the bathroom door, site of their recent struggle.

"It's okay," Leila urged her. "I promise I won't hurt you."

The hesitation continued so Leila placed the mixing bowl with its brightly-colored contents on the floor, sat down on the floor herself, and began to play. By the time she built a tower with the juice boxes inside the mixing bowl, Storm had joined her.

Leila closed and locked the bathroom door, adjusted the temperature on the bath, and then took the mixing bowl and placed it in the tub.

"This is fun," Leila said. "The water is fun to play with."

She leaned over the tub and demonstrated, filling a measuring cup with water and dumping it into the mixing bowl. Storm leaned over the tub to watch. With a flash of joy, Leila saw when Storm caught on. A subtle shifting in the girl's face signaled the thought and Storm turned, grabbed the juice boxes, and floated them one by one in the rising water.

"That," Leila said, "was a great idea."

They played a while longer and then Leila took off her shoes.

"I'm going to get in the tub so I can reach the toys better," she

111

said.

Fully clothed, Leila stepped into the bath. As soon as she sat down she felt the cloth on her jeans tighten and cling to her.

Storm studied the situation. The muscles around her eyes tightened and she drew her hand back from the toys.

"Would you like to get in the water with me?"

A juice box bobbed closer to the edge and storm reached for it. Leila nudged it out of the way with her foot.

"Get in the tub and we'll play some more."

As before, Leila only saw the girl make her decision from the subtlest of changes in expression. Suddenly, she hiked up her nightgown and bellied over the side of the tub into the water.

Leila wanted to cheer but she restrained herself except for smiling.

They played, floating juice boxes, dumping water into and out of the mixing bowl. Storm even splashed a little, then looked horrified and guilty at the noise and mess.

"That's all right," Leila said. "You're supposed to splash in the tub."

Primed by experience, Leila tensed when it was time to get the nightgown off but Storm allowed her to slip the soaking cloth over her head. The soap presented the biggest challenge. Leila started with Storm's back. She trickled warm water down, then soaped up her hand. Storm stiffened with resistance when Leila first touched her with a soapy hand but after a little gentle rubbing of soap on dirty skin, the girl relaxed. From there the rest was finesse and soap and rinsing. Leila dreaded lying Storm down to wash her hair but even that went well.

112

When they got out, Leila handed Storm a towel and showed her how to dry off. Satisfaction warred with horror when she looked in the tub with its dark gray water. After helping Storm dress in her Jesus Saves clothes, she made a squelching, dripping trip to the bedroom and skinned off her jeans. She returned to the kitchen in time to find the boys exclaiming over their sister.

"You look great," Sleet said.

"Look at her hair," Ray said, and then, seeing Leila in the doorway, "how did you do it?"

"Soap," Leila replied. Sleet giggled but Ray just nodded his solemn nod.

"Two questions," Leila said. "Where's a hairbrush and who's next?"

Ray got it first.

"I'll find a hairbrush. Sleet can have a bath next."

Sleet stuck his tongue out at his brother and Ray charged up the stairs, away from bath time.

"Do a good job," Leila told Sleet. "Hair and face, too."

Leila stood Storm in front of her when Ray returned with the hairbrush and began to work out the tangles from the child's baby-fine hair. She crooned a song as she worked. The girl stood statue-still and let Leila work her way toward the matted hair on her scalp.

"Row, row, row your boat, gently down the stream…"

When Ray emerged from the bathroom, Leila decided her imagination was not playing tricks on her. Three clean children in the kitchen, smelling of soap and shampoo, definitely made the whole room smell better. Storm walked through the light from

113

the south-facing window and Leila gasped. Her hair glowed and sparked like a live thing.

"Your hair is so blonde," she told Storm.

***

Leila proposed an ice cream celebration of bath time, a proposal gladly endorsed by the boys. She was sorting through the contents of the freezer when Sophie began to bark and a knock sounded on the door.

She froze, realizing that in her happiness she had forgotten to fear Bill's return, to fear Stu finding her, for upwards of an hour. Ray peered toward the drive from the kitchen window.

"It's all right," he told Leila. "It's just Jimmy."

"Just me," Jimmy affirmed when she opened the door.

At the sight of his long face and wide-set eyes, Leila smiled. Here was one man who didn't stoke her fears. He took off his hat and scrubbed one hand through his sweaty hair, each movement deliberate, no motion wasted. Leila smiled more broadly at the sight of his hair, standing up at all angles around his head except where the hat band trained it to sit flat against his skull.

Still smiling, she turned to the kids. "You want to go look at some horses before we eat ice cream?"

"Nah," Ray replied for all of them. "You go ahead and—"

"I'll go," Sleet interrupted, and swung his legs over the bench.

"Are you sure, little brother?" Asked Ray.

"I wanna go," said Sleet. "Besides, someone should go with her." He tipped his head in Leila's direction.

"What," Jimmy asked, "I don't count as someone?" But he smiled as he said it.

114

"Nah," answered Ray, "you'll get all busy messing with the horses and she'll probably get trampled or something." He grinned crookedly at Jimmy, who laughed.

"Come on then," said Jimmy, and turned from the door.

As Sleet and Leila walked out Ray called after them. "Be careful, little brother!"

The wind, for a change, only brushed gently against Leila's face. She stopped halfway to Jimmy's battered green truck and gazed out across the southern valley. She still felt sick and weak, weaker with all the tub scrubbing she'd just done, but a few steps from the house left her feeling okay with that.

Half a mile out where the valley floor was at its lowest, a swathe of bright green showed vivid against the browns and tans and faded greens of the rest of the landscape. A herd of pronghorn grazed there and she remembered the marvel of seeing one up close.

"Beautiful, isn't it?" Jimmy said.

"Gorgeous," Leila agreed.

They piled into the truck and Jimmy drove them the quarter mile down the road to the barn. He drove the way he moved, slowly and deliberately. She appreciated the contrast to Bill's driving.

Jimmy swung an industrial-sized latch up from the double handles of the bay doors on the end of the barn, braced, and rolled one door open just wide enough to sidle through. They stepped into gloom.

A wide aisle with stalls flanking both sides ran the length of the barn. The place smelled wonderful to her.

"We've only got a few horses in here right now," Jimmy said as he walked along, "as everyone's out to pasture…"

Sleet paused at a stall, the top half of the door swung wide.

"Hey— "Jimmy said.

Sleet stood and peered into the stall. Whatever else Jimmy said was drowned out by a squeal. At the sound, Leila saw Sleet flinch, then stand a little taller. Jimmy started moving, fast, toward the stall. The screaming horse moved faster.

A dark head snaked over the half-door, ears pinned hard to its head. Light reflected off the white of its wide open eye as it stabbed its head toward Sleet, mouth open, teeth bared.

Sleet dodged but the horse moved faster. It missed Sleet's face by inches and closed its teeth on his shoulder. Leila saw his feet clear the ground as the horse lifted him and shook him.

Sleet screamed, making a noise much like the horse had, and then Jimmy was there, pounding on the horse's face and muzzle and yelling.

As suddenly as he attacked, the horse dropped Sleet and retreated to the far side of the stall. Sleet fell to the ground and lay curled there. Leila, who had been transfixed by the sudden violence, ran to him.

"Stay back," Jimmy yelled, and dragged Sleet away from the stall. A set of dull impacts shook the barn as the horse kicked its stall, making Leila flinch and see the point of Jimmy's warning.

Leila knelt in the soft ground of the barn and began tearing at Sleet's new shirt, trying to see his shoulder.

"I'm sorry," Jimmy said. "I thought he knew better."

Sleet's sobs wrenched his thin body. Unable to get his shirt off while he lay curled around himself, Leila changed plans.

"Let's get him back to the house," she said. Selfishly, she felt a pang at not getting to see the horses—except that one—and then felt ashamed.

Jimmy scooped Sleet up and carried him from the barn. Outside, Leila saw Jimmy's lips were pressed together, making a thin, white line across his face. She felt a familiar surge of fear. That expression—the male face under duress—looked so similar to Stu's in his furies. But Jimmy apologized again as he laid Sleet on the truck's bench seat. Leila realized this man's anger turned inward.

"It's okay," she said. "I don't know why he kept standing there."

She shifted Sleet's head as she climbed into the truck and laid it on her lap. She stroked his now-clean hair and cried with Sleet, whose sobs evoked such deep mourning that she found herself mourning along with him. At the house, Jimmy moved to pick Sleet up. The boy straightened, resistant.

"I can walk," he said.

Sleet stood for a moment, looking like a caricature of an old man, then straightened and walked toward the house.

"It's not your fault," Leila told Jimmy. For the first time, she felt sympathy for a man. His misery and his self-directed anger touched her. "Thank you for taking me to see the horses."

Jimmy nodded and swung himself back into the truck.

Inside, Ray's face clenched when he saw Sleet.

"What happened? What did you do?" Ray asked.

Leila ignored Ray.

"Let's get this shirt off and see how bad it is," she said.

"I'm fine," Sleet said. Now that he made it inside, he resumed his stoop-shouldered posture.

Leila huffed in. "You're not fine. That horse could have taken your head off," she said.

"Demon got you? Oh you shitting little idiot," Ray said. "What were you thinking?"

"Hey!" Leila snapped at Ray. "Watch your language."

Ray's tone wilted Sleet's posture even more.

I just thought...I thought that maybe," Sleet said. He sounded tired.

"Well you thought wrong. It was a stupid, stupid thing to do," Ray said.

"Enough!" Leila waved her hand at Ray.

She tugged Sleet's t-shirt up. The boy didn't resist but his posture didn't help, and neither did he, so she wrestled the shirt up and over his limp good arm and his head. The sight of Sleet's abdomen turned her stomach. Fading bruises covered a good portion of it. Somehow she had failed to extrapolate from the bruise on his face to what his clothing must cover. But she didn't wince or hesitate. She knew how much pity over a beating hurt.

The skin of Sleet's right shoulder was already darkening to deep purple and the horse's teeth had broken through in several places. Clotting blood stood in the horse tooth-shaped dents in his skin. She inhaled sharply at the sight.

Dully, Sleet turned and looked at the shoulder.

"No more'n what I deserve," he said.

"That's right," Ray confirmed.

The sight of Sleet's shoulder combined with knowing she was being left out of the loop frustrated Leila.

"What," she said to Ray, "are you talking about? And is there a first aid kit? Quit, for God's sake. Quit sniping at him and do something useful."

"This is useful," Ray said. "He's got to learn to stop being an idiot."

Anger flared in Leila, feeling strange and flooding her from toes to hair roots. The searing heat of it, the suddenness of reaching a flash point, the feeling of her face twisting, all the sensations were highlighted by their unfamiliarity.

"Get me. A first aid kit. Now."

She advanced a step toward him and saw Ray shrink before her eyes. The light of anger died in his face and she felt it rush into her, filling her to bursting. Making Ray cower felt good, felt just, and her fury strengthened her.

"There isn't one," Ray said.

She advanced another step, towering, furious.

"Then why didn't you fucking say that in the first place?" She asked.

Sophie began barking in loud, sharp exclamations. The explosive noise shook Leila from her fixation on Ray. She looked around at the dog, realized her arm was raised as if to strike something. Ray.

Sophie continued making noise, teeth bared, making little lunges toward Leila with each bark. The breath exhaled from each bark condensed in frosty puffs in front of the dog's muzzle. Slowly, Leila lowered her arm. The rage drained from her.

119

"Is it cold in here?" she asked.

Sophie gave her one last growl and turned away toward Sleet. As she turned, one paw slipped out from under her. Leila looked down and kept looking, unable to accept what she saw. A rime of frost covered the floor, accented by darker color where Sophie's claws had scratched through to the flagstone beneath.

"No," Leila groaned. "Oh no." She shook her head against the realization that the fear wasn't all in her own head, with the sense of presences unseen.

She looked around, wild-eyed at the children. Goosebumps covered Sleet's bare torso.

"It wasn't me!" Leila said, begging the children for understanding. "Something, something here in this house... Something is here."

A great screaming wail erupted in her mind. Her senses grew dim, confused. Distantly, she heard something clunk into the microwave. The sound reverberated in her bones. The hum and rush of the machine filled the kitchen and turned to swirls of smoky color before her eyes. The microwave's blower emitted the smell of meat. The smell took on texture, like pushing her fingers into raw meat gone gray in the refrigerator.

Leila rushed to the garbage can and vomited.

She knelt there, sobbing, retching. Future and past melded and swirled away. There was only this—the colors, the sounds, the smells confused and the sour bile coating her tongue.

Hands rescued her. A small hand, tentative, stroked the convulsing muscles of her back. Two more hands intervened, grabbing her shoulders from behind, steadying the racking sobs

120

which must have been her own though they were so distant. The hands radiated warmth like the glowing coils of an electric stove.

One more hand came to rest on her head, dove light, and began stroking her hair away from her face.

"We need to get her outside," Ray said, his voice level.

The anchoring hands tugged at her, urging her up, away from the trash can. She obediently rose. The front door opened and light, blessed, clean light, burst on her. Hands slipped into each of hers and pulled her toward the light.

A few minutes of deep breathing brought back the first tendrils of sanity creeping in from the clean air. Sunlight warmed her hair. The goose bumps on her arms receded into smooth flesh. She stood straighter, looked around.

Storm held her right hand, the little girl's face turned up when Leila looked down. Her smooth face held a hint of concern. On her left, Sleet stood and stared into the distance of the valley.

Ray walked out of the house with a glass of water. With reluctance, Leila released the children's hands and took the glass. Her mouth tasted foul. More sanity asserted itself with the prosaic act of swishing and spitting, then drinking with gratitude. Crying always made her thirsty.

"Keys," she told Ray. "Purse."

"You sure you're up to driving?" Ray asked.

"I need to see someone in town," she said. "Yeah, I can drive."

"No," Sleet said. "I'm not leaving."

Leila argued the point, and lost. Yes, they could stay there alone. They did it all the time. No, Ray explained, they weren't afraid—not much at least. Sleet assured her everything would be

121

fine. He would make the sandwiches this time and could she pick up some apples in town?

With the perfect irrationality of someone in emotional shock, the apples settled it for Leila. She would go by herself.

***

The sight of the first buildings at the edge of town reminded her she should check her face. What she saw was not encouraging. She had never been one of those dignified, pretty criers. And this time had been worse than most, producing swollen, red-rimmed eyes and bright spots on her cheeks. Her hair? Frightening.

Jesus Saves Thrift Store was closed. The hours posted on the door informed her they were open 8 a.m. to 5 p.m. Monday through Friday and 8 a.m. to 12 p.m. on Saturday. Closed on Sunday, of course. She had no idea what day of the week it was. She had no idea of the time, for that matter. Thinking of the time reminded her she had forgotten her antibiotics. She looked at the sun, as Ray had suggested, and saw it high overhead.

Sighing, she continued to the hardware store for the third time in a week—still with no intention of buying anything. The metallic ding of the bell above the door combined with the scent of the store to produce instant comfort. Fertilizer, nuts and bolts, wooden things. Randy emerged from one of the aisles. He smiled at the sight of her.

"You're better! How wonderful."

"I am better," Leila replied. "A lot."

Encouraged by the man's honest happiness at her recovery, Leila relaxed enough to say something honest.

122

"I came by for some other reason. But now that I'm here I realize I owe you thanks."

The man stopped some feet away and looked up at her. In his expression, Leila saw a shadow of some old trauma come and go from his face. She didn't know people well, but she knew trauma inside and out. It called to her.

"No, ma'am," he said. "I appreciate your thanks, but it's not necessary. Good enough that you're standing here. Now," he grinned at her and the last traces of remembered trauma passed from him, "can I help you find something?"

Leila laughed. With those simple words which harked back to every hardware store man anywhere, he brushed her embarrassment away and lightened her mood.

"You could help me find something," she said. "But it's nothing in here. I feel bad...I keep coming in here and asking—"

"You're not from Wyoming," he interrupted her.

"No," she said. "California."

"You've never been somewhere like this in the winter, I'll bet, too."

"Nope. Lived my whole life in California."

"I don't mean to pry, but are you going to be here long?" He asked.

Leila shivered, thought of the children, the house, Bill, and couldn't answer.

"Sorry, I'm prying. That's another thing we try not to do here is pry and now I'm getting ahead of myself.

"See, what I was trying to say is, you might have noticed not many people live here?"

Leila nodded.

"And everything is quite a distance from the next thing? You haven't been here in the winter, so you can't understand. But let me tell you, if we didn't all help each other? Any time it's needed? We'd all be dead."

"What, everyone?"

Leila hated herself for saying it, but she thought of Bill, and didn't buy his words.

"No, you're right. There're some bad apples in the bunch. And the rest of us? We help them, too. Enough philosophizing. What can I help you find?"

"Um, what day is it?"

"It's Saturday," he said.

Again her mood lifted, this time because the way he answered had held no judgment or mockery.

"Okay. That's good, I didn't miss church."

He nodded like this made perfect sense and waited for her to continue.

"So. I need to speak with the pastor's wife? I think her name is Pat? And I don't know which church or…"

He held up his hand.

"There's only one church in town," he said. "And only one pastor's wife named Pat."

He dialed the phone for her, just as he had when she first got into town. This time she noticed the last two fingers on his right hand were gone. She thought he noticed her staring. He said nothing.

Pastor Jim answered the phone and announced himself glad

she called. A fine sweat emerged on Leila's face when he said Pat was not home.

"But I'll give you her cell number," he said.

Leila grabbed a business card from the holder on the counter and a pen.

Pat answered her phone on the first ring.

"Leila! I'm so glad you called," she said. And then, lowering her voice, "When can you talk?"

"I drove in to talk."

"Good. I'll meet you at my house in five minutes. It's 510 Rawlins Street." She hung up before Leila could ask for directions.

The man across the counter pulled out a deteriorating phone book before she could ask. Leila stared at the cover, bright yellow where it wasn't torn and discolored. The book couldn't be more than half an inch wide.

"That's the Elk Crossing phone book? It's tiny!" She said.

"No. This is the phone book for Elk Crossing and all these towns."

He ran his finger down a list of a dozen names printed on the front of the book. Leila's eyes must have bulged a little, thinking of the two three inch books for San Jose. He chuckled at her expression, flipped the book open to a map, and showed her Rawlins Street.

"Here, take this," he said as she turned to go.

She turned back and he placed the phone book into her hands.

"I've got another around here somewhere," he said. "Also?" He held out the business card she had left on the counter, flipped it face up. "That's me, if you need anything. You know, directions, questions…we've even got shovels and square brackets around here."

She laughed with him and glanced at the card.

"Thank you. Thank you!"

Pat waited outside 510 Rawlins Street and arrived at the car door before Leila could get her seat belt unbuckled. Pat started talking the minute the car door opened.

"I'm so glad you came. Are you all right? I've been so worried about you. Did something happen?"

Pat's anxious, rapid-fire speech reversed the relaxation produced by talking with Randy.

"I need to sit down," Leila said.

"Of course. Let's get you comfortable and then we can talk. I'm sorry."

Jim and Pat lived in a little yellow house with white trim. Flowers bloomed in the yard. The bushes had all been trimmed and the grass was green.

"Your yard is beautiful."

"Thank you. Not many people garden around here what with the short season and the hail. But I miss it and I keep trying," Pat said.

Inside, Pat offered Leila coffee, which she accepted happily. The coffee pop burbled and Pat chattered.

Here in Pat's yellow house, in her small kitchen decorated with roosters, the idea there was something in the house lost its power. The last prickling at the back of her neck subsided. Still, Leila needed to talk about it to someone who might understand. She remembered Pat's face when they walked in the house yesterday. Pat set a mug of steaming coffee in front of Leila.

"What happened at that house?" Pat asked.

Leila decided she could love this woman. She hadn't known how to broach the topic.

"There's something in there," Leila said.

The words were an invitation, apparently, because her fear came rushing back along with an echo of the sick feeling from earlier. She got the mug back on the table before the coffee spilled.

"Yes, there is," Pat said. "What happened?"

"It's horrible. I got so angry. I'm never angry? And then I was angry at Ray and Sophie started barking—at me! —and I looked around. My...I...it was in the air, my arm, my fist. I was going to hit him, Pat, I really was. And I don't understand. It was like something got inside me and...then it was so cold. There was frost. Really, or I'm losing my mind. I saw frost."

The hair rose on Leila's arms at the memory evoked by her words. She wrapped her fingers around the mug for its warmth and solidity and looked pleadingly at Pat.

"I never caught a glimpse of the children," Pat said. "But Cindy said— "

"Cole asked her to not talk about it," Leila interrupted.

"That's never stopped Cindy," Pat said. She started to smile but her lips quivered and without warning her eyes filled with tears.

"What?" Leila asked. "What's the matter?"

"Oh. Oh Leila, I feel so awful. I'm so, so sorry."

Leila waited, feeling lost and a little afraid of Pat's mood swing. After a minute, Pat lifted her head and carefully blotted

127

her tears away from her mascara. She gave Leila a trembling smile.

"Sorry. I'm sorry. You must think I'm crazy. I just feel like I should have thought of those poor children. Someone should have thought of them.

"When Maria—their mother—when Maria disappeared…we should have checked on them…"

At first, Leila's big-city perspective kept her from understanding what Pat's guilt. Why would someone think to check? But she remembered what Randy had just told her.

The rules are different here. Someone should have checked on them.

"Why didn't someone check on them?"

"I suppose—no one ever thought of them much. I mean, you've got to see someone to think of them, right? And those kids—oh, they came to town some with Maria when she was around. But that family always kept to themselves. They homeschooled. And Maria wasn't like most people around here. She didn't really have any friends. Everyone thought she was a little weird."

Pat began to sniffle a little but now Leila's eagerness to hear more about the children's mother overrode her reserve.

"How was she weird?"

"Oh," Pat laughed a little, "She was like a hippy—came here from some university out east with her long hair and peace symbols. She was doing some research project on wildflowers of all things…And look at the weird names she gave the children."

Pat shook her head sharply and leaned over the table, her gaze

128

sharp and focused on Leila's eyes.

"This is all beside the point," Pat said. "The past, me feeling guilty. The real point is that you and the children need to get out."

Leila shook her head.

"The children won't leave. They just won't."

"The children are going to have to leave. You have to call protective services. Have to."

Leila shook her head, unable to explain the ferocity with which the children refused to leave, unable to explain—even to herself—her growing belief they were right to not leave.

"Okay," Pat said, seeing Leila's expression. "All right. Leave that aside for a second. What about the evil way the house feels? And smells? How can you..." she trailed off, took a deep breath, and tried again. "Look. There are Christians who see evil spirits behind every bush. Oh, that sounded awful. I never could hold with that type, though. I just never saw any reason to believe..."

"So you think there's an evil spirit in the house?" Leila heard herself say it. It sounded ridiculous here in Pat's kitchen. Pat shrugged and waved a hand.

"There's something wrong in that house. Very, very wrong. I'd say it's an evil spirit. Someone else might call it haunted. It doesn't matter... But yesterday afternoon? It was like something slimy was trying to crawl into my brain."

Leila nodded, understanding Pat's description too well for comfort.

"But the children won't leave!"

"Then you drag them out if you have to. Look. Jim and I can

129

find you a place to stay in town..."

Pat's words recalled for Leila the first attempt to bathe Storm, how wrong she felt afterwards to try and force a small, frightened child to do something against her will. She shook her head.

"No. We have to stay in the house until they're ready to leave."

"How long?" Pat asked.

"How long what?"

"How long will Bill be out of town?"

"I... I don't know," Leila said. The image of Bill returning while she was here in town tore a hole through her fragile peace.

"I've got to get back there," Leila said.

She stood and started gulping her coffee. Pat came around the table and put a restraining hand on Leila's arm.

"We haven't talked this through yet."

"I'm sorry," Leila said. "I just need to get back to them."

She grabbed her keys from the table, shaking Pat's hand off, and headed to the front door. Pat called to her from the front door when Leila was halfway to the car.

"Do you have a prayer book?"

Leila just shook her head, impatient with anything which slowed her return to the children.

CHAPTER NINE

She drove as fast as she dared, speeding on the short stretch of highway and slewing and skidding her way across the prairie on the dirt road. At one point a deer stepped out in front of her car along with her two fawns. She braked hard, the car slipped sideways and kept sliding toward the deer who, Leila could see through the passenger side window, had stopped to observe the strange phenomenon of a car moving sideways toward them. She swore and prayed at the same time. She had no control. The beautifully delicate fawns stared directly at her.

The car came to a stop just feet from the deer and then the mother decided to panic, springing into the air and dashing into the grass on the other side with fawns in hot pursuit. A whole herd of deer then materialized to chase the leader across the road, bunching and springing their way past the side of the Buick.

Leila drove more slowly. She didn't know what hitting a deer or antelope at forty miles per hour would do to her car, but it couldn't be good even aside from killing a thing of beauty. The close encounter with the herd reminded her what a strange, foreign world she lived in now where the outsider must always be the human.

The sight of the empty driveway comforted her when she

topped the last rise leading into the valley. In her imagination, all the way to the house, Bill's truck had been there. Her panic to return to the children subsided and she took a few minutes to grip the steering wheel and contemplate the house. The longer she sat and remembered, the less she wanted to go inside. Pat's confirmation of her feeling that something was in the house shook her as if it had just been said.

The front door opened and Ray started to pick his way across the rocky ground toward her. Leila's mood lifted on seeing him, then plummeted even lower when she remembered she had almost hit him. Shame burned as she opened the car door with an apology forming.

Ray started speaking before the door was fully open. "You forgot your antibiotics. You've got to take them right now. I won't know how to time them if we get too far away from noon."

"I should have picked up a watch at the hardware store," Leila said.

"It's all right. You'll just have to take your next dose early."

He looked up at her, his facial expression neutral but his eyes looking, looking for something. She found she could speak.

"Ray. I'm sorry. I don't know what happened in there, but I think I almost hit you and I'm so sorry."

"Things happen," he said. His faint smile didn't make it much past his eyes, but it was there.

Walking into the house was easier with Ray at her side. At the kitchen table, Sleet held a slab of steak to his shoulder. He pulled it away when Leila asked to see and it didn't look a whole lot worse.

"Where's Storm?" Leila wanted to know.

Sleet started with his expressive one-shouldered shrug and then quit with a wince.

"I think she went upstairs," he said.

"You forgot these again," Ray said, and put down a glass of water and an antibiotic tablet before her on the table.

Sleet had the meat on his shoulder again.

"Does it hurt bad?" Leila asked.

Again, Sleet began to raise his shoulder and changed his mind.

"It's not great," he said. "I've had worse, though. I'm fine."

Leila recalled the collection of bruises on his abdomen, all in different stages of healing. Questions occurred to her, questions which began to seem urgent in light of the events of the day.

"We need to talk," Leila said.

The boys looked at each other, seeming to exchange information telepathically. Sleet sighed.

"Fine," Ray said. "Talk."

"Not in here. Let's go outside. Ray? Would you get Storm and bring her?"

Leila felt uncomfortable leaving the girl alone in the house.

"She'll be fine. Sophie's with her," Ray said.

"I really don't like to…" Sleet began, and trailed off.

She waited for Sleet to finish, then gave up. Navigating the strange new land of how these children thought, what they wanted, tired her. The boys trailed after her into what would be a front yard if anyone had cared. Instead, the prairie ran right up to the house with no demarcation.

Leila found a tuft of grass which looked softer than the

133

surrounding brush and sat, motioning the boys to sit with her. When they all settled, Leila found she didn't know where to start. There were so many reasons for reluctance. But the boys stared at her and Storm waited somewhere inside. She dove in.

"There are things I don't understand," she began. The warmth of the sun on her back reassured her.

"So...earlier? When I, when I yelled at Ray?"

Sleet nodded. Ray held perfectly still.

"I've never felt that angry before. I've really never felt angry before at all."

"Ever?" Sleet sounded disbelieving.

"Ever." Leila said.

"And then Sophie started barking at me. I didn't even realize I had raised my arm. You've got to believe me! I would never, never want to hit one of you. But I think I almost did. And there was frost! I swear there was frost..."

She started shivering. The boys sat silent and waited for her to get to the point.

"I'm afraid," she said. "I'm afraid to say it."

"That's good," Ray said. "It makes it more real if you talk about it."

"So you do feel it. Do you know why it's like this?"

Sleet looked down, found a small piece of foliage, and began to dismember it. Ray looked at her and shook his head.

"Didn't I just say it's bad to talk about it?"

Despite her frustration and fear, Leila gave Ray a wry grin. "Point to you, Ray. You never miss a trick, do you?"

Ray looked startled, then grinned back.

Leila sobered at another thought.

"Is it…your father…is it not his fault?"

Sleet began to shiver. "No!" He said. "He does it. He does it himself. The thing…it helps? But…"

"But I didn't hit Ray, did I?" Leila said.

"You didn't," Ray said. "But he does."

Leila's relief came from left field and bowled her over. She didn't want to be put in a position of excusing Bill's abuse. The feeling lived only for the short time it took Leila to realize she still had to get the boys to talk.

She bit her lip, hard, and forced herself back to the question. "Why?"

The boys looked at her, faces carefully blank.

"Why…" She couldn't make herself come right out and say it and she felt the boys' growing impatience with the conversation. The added pressure forced her words out in a rush.

"Why does the house feel so awful? Why the nightmares? Why do weird things happen? Why do I feel afraid all the time? Why can't we just leave?"

The boys shifted under the pressure of her questions and looked at each other. Sleet's face looked tight and strained. Ray's expression darkened toward anger.

"Maybe…" Sleet began.

"Don't," Ray said, "say another word." He turned to Leila. "It's none of your damn business. Quit trying to be so nice. Why can't you just—just go away?"

Pain exploded behind Leila's eyes and produced stinging tears. She could no longer see the boys' faces and didn't care to. Sleet's misery. Ray's reflexive anger.

"Fine. I can go away. I'll just run into town and call the social worker. And she'll come out here after I'm gone and drag you three from the house."

The silence of something precious being broken spread between them. Leila wiped the tears from her eyes and regretted her clearer vision when she saw their expressions. Ray looked like he might throw up. Sleet had gone pale with shock. He turned and looked at Ray and his face changed. His eyes pled with Ray. Then he clouded over with anger. She saw him choke back on the anger just as she had, and he changed back to pleading. Then the anger broke through again. Something in Ray snapped. He turned to Leila stiffly, as though every muscle in his body were resisting.

"Please. Don't. Do that."

A long silence followed, broken only by the sound of plant fiber tearing under Sleet's fingers.

"I'm going to go check on Storm," she said. Her joints protested as she pushed to her feet. She felt suddenly old and very, very tired.

Entering the dim, cool, and smelly house still felt like a slap in the face. The main floor of the house stood empty.

She went to the bottom of the stairs and could go no farther. A subtle, cold stream of air brushed against her face as she looked up into the dimness. It wafted the distinctive scent of the house even more strongly into her nostrils. She thought of roadkill, and sewage, and cheap perfume overlaying the last stages of illness. Her mind numb, she stood paralyzed at the bottom of the stairs and let despair roll over her. The utter silence of the house penetrated her brain, speaking to her of death and loneliness and failure.

She fantasized about carrying out her threat—leaving and making an anonymous call to social services on her way out of town. The thought remained fantasy. She would stick this out no matter what.

She had to make a conscious effort to unlock her knees and turn away from the stairs. As she turned, she thought she heard a voice, whispering, upstairs. The hair rose on her arms and neck and she felt despair. She went to the bedroom, curled up, and cried herself to sleep.

She awoke slowly, wondering why her brain felt so heavy. The awful talk with Ray and Sleet returned to her simultaneously with determination to make it right. She looked at the light and saw dinnertime approaching. As she walked down the hall toward the kitchen, she heard Ray's voice in the living room. Something strange in his tone stopped her to listen before she was seen. He paused, then began again in a low, gentle tone. She stood still and could practically feel her ears perking, reminding her of Sophie.

"'By it and with it and on it and in it,' said the Rat. 'It's brother and sister to me, and aunts, and company, and food and drink, and (naturally) washing. It's my world, and I don't want any other. What it hasn't got is not worth having, and what it doesn't know is not worth knowing.'"

She recognized the story from *The Wind in the Willows*. It evoked in her memory the quaint watercolor illustrations of the book she also had read as a child. Leaning her head against the wall, she wondered how she could have threatened to leave

HEATHER M^cLOUD

them—ever—and how she could apologize. She worried her lip with her teeth but the answer didn't come. The more she puzzled over her apology, the more anxiety she felt.

The children didn't notice her for a few seconds when she walked into the living room. Ray sat in the middle of the love seat, flanked by his brother and sister. All three of their heads bent close over the book. Her foot scuffed the carpet and they looked up as one. Sleet looked terrified, as though his go-to reaction to anything unexpected was fear. Ray's face was hard and closed as he looked up. Storm shrank back against the love seat and averted her eyes.

Leila walked within a couple of feet of them and sank to the floor.

"Would you please keep reading, Ray? I love this story."

He snapped the book closed and pressed his lips together. Leila quailed at the rejection but forced herself to not give up.

"Please, Ray. You read so beautifully. Read to me just a little?"

Finally, he opened the book again and Leila's heart settled.

***

She went to bed in a state of dread. The shadows in the room wobbled and kept forming up in her tired vision into something threatening solidity. Again she had asked the children if they would like to all sleep in the master bedroom with her. After all, their father might not allow them in but he wasn't here, was he? But they refused.

Once, Leila read that dreams occur during only a fraction of the time spent sleeping, that the remaining time is deep and peaceful. But after startling up from her cocoon of blankets for the fifth or sixth time, she decided all she did was dream and they were all nightmares.

Again she willed her eyes closed and sleep snapped her up in its jaws. She dreamed of the bedroom she lay in. Just as in waking life, she lay at the end of the room under the north window. Dread froze her where she lay. She couldn't turn away from staring at the dark space which represented the open door to the hall. Blackness, and something darker than blackness, emitted a growl so slow it sounded like gravel being rattled in a can.

Without transition or a change in light, Leila could suddenly see Sophie's form coming toward her, one step at a time. The dog moved as if her legs had extra joints. It required force of will, but Leila jerked her gaze away from the unnatural motion to look pleadingly at Sophie's eyes. Instead of the soft, intelligent gaze she expected from waking experience, empty sockets stared back at her. Shreds of black, rotting flesh hung from the sockets' edges and deep inside, flashes of white showed where the maggots worked. The dog kept coming for her.

Below her terror of the dog she mourned the animal she knew was lost forever, replaced by this lurching thing which had her destruction as its only goal.

Give up, something whispered in her ear. *So much easier if you just let it happen.*

She knew, then, the dog's bite would transform her into a being just like it and she would never be afraid again. It would be so easy. The urge to simply let the dog bite her was strong. She lay there, perfectly balanced between terror and submission.

"Do you have a prayer book?" Pat wanted to know.

139

With the sideways sensibility of dreams, Leila believed Pat's suggestion would solve everything.

She felt the dog's breath on her face, couldn't believe she had looked away. Leila screamed at the hot breath and at the knowledge she had waited too long to run away.

Her own scream woke her up. Sophie—real, warm, and looking concerned—stood over her. She licked Leila's face, quested over her body with her nose and paused, inhaling deeply, at Leila's neck and armpit. With a tentative wave of her tail, she then poked hard on Leila's arm with her muzzle.

"Thank you, Sophie. Good girl, good girl." She scrubbed her hands through the dog's thick fur. "I think I love you, dog. Isn't that strange? We haven't known each other long."

Sophie's tail went into high gear as Leila talked to her. The rest of the dream came back to her. Leila heaved out of the blankets, certain something horrible would happen very soon despite being awake.

She sorted through the meagre pile of possessions which had traveled with her from California. Each item which did not conceal the prayer book got tossed aside.

"I know it's here," she muttered. "Where is it?"

She remembered seeing the prayer book when she brought everything in and puzzling over how randomly she had packed the morning she fled Stu. Finally, she found it hiding half under a chair and covered with a dirty shirt. She picked it up and felt immediate relief from the emotional dregs of the nightmare.

The thick, dark-blue book's cover was embossed in gold lettering, first in Hebrew, then announcing in English: The

Authorized Daily Prayer Book by Joseph H. Hertz. She remembered her puzzlement upon receiving it from a distant relative the day of her Bat Mitzvah. The book did not represent a standard from her Reform upbringing and, being half in Hebrew, which she read poorly and understood not at all, and the other half in a sort of inaccessibly formal English, she had never done more than page through it once or twice.

Now she felt the weight of it as a promise. The conviction of her dream, that she must have this prayer book, echoed into waking life. She sat cross legged on her bed and placed the prayer book on her knees. Sophie lay down beside her with a sigh, furry back pressed against her leg. Leila opened the book to a random page.

"R. Simeon, the son of Menasya, said, these seven qualifications which the sages enumerated as becoming to the righteous…"

And on it went, in a dry sort of way. She turned back a hundred pages and tried again.

"Peace be unto you, ye ministering angels, messengers of the Most High, the supreme King of Kings, holy and blessed is He."

The last of the dream tattered and grew insubstantial. Peace, angles, holy, blessed, the words resonated and glowed at the edges as if newly minted. Sophie's back radiated warmth into her leg. Fatigue tugged at her and she lay back down without fighting. She still didn't turn off the lights, though.

A towel hit her in the head some time later.

"Shit!" Sleet said. "I missed."

Leila struggled up from a sleep, which, if not exactly peaceful, at least had not been horrifying.

"What do you mean, you missed?" Leila asked. "You got me right in the head."

"I'm sorry. I was aiming for the floor next to your head."

"You're right, you missed."

Sleet reminded her to take her antibiotics and then trotted off into the dark house. The fear returned during the dark trek to the light in the kitchen. She grasped at the edges of what she remembered reading in the prayer book. Something about peace. And angels. A week ago she would have sworn she didn't believe in angels. Now...

Dim speculations about whether angels really had glowing, white feathers on their wings (and whether they had wings) occupied her sleep fogged mind until she got back to bed.

She dreamed twice more that she remembered that night. Once, she dreamed someone standing over her bed but her eyelids wouldn't open. With an immense force of will she made them flutter a couple of times and caught a blurry image of Sleet staring at her, his face drawn thin and white as though he were under some huge strain. He appeared to be studying her as she slept and curiosity beckoned her to wake up and talk with him but sleep drew her eyelids closed again.

A small woman in white stood between her and the north window. She turned from the window, met Leila's gaze, and shrugged one shoulder just the way Sleet always did. She began glowing more and more brightly until the light woke Leila up and it was just the morning light coming through the window.

CHAPTER TEN

"Let's go to church this morning," Leila said.

The statement surprised the kids into putting down their forks. Ray chewed once and appeared to be considering the idea when Sleet kicked the table, his face drawn into an expression of distaste.

"Why do we have to go to church? Why can't you go to church and leave us here?"

"Pastor Jim invited us," Leila said. "So we might as well all go."

"I don't want to go. I want to stay here."

He had one shoulder hunched up toward his ear. The injured shoulder apparently hurt too much for hunching.

Ray nodded. "He's right. That's the stupidest idea I've ever heard."

Ray's tone hardened Leila's resolve to take everyone to church, despite her own awkward feelings over walking into a church for the first time.

"Look, Pastor Jim lent me some money for my antibiotics. I really need to go pay it back. He said we could all come to church and just pay him then. So we need to go."

"No," Ray said. "We don't."

He turned to Storm, who watched the proceedings from the kitchen table with two fingers in her mouth.

"Storm," Ray said. She turned to look at him. "Do you want to go to a place with a bunch of people you've never met and sit really still for an hour?"

Storm's eyes grew wide and her mouth stopped moving around her fingers. Leila wondered if she imagined the slightest possible shake of her head.

"All right!" Leila said. "I get the idea."

Ray walked to Sleet and grabbed his chin, turned the still-bruised side of his face to the light.

"Sleet. Do you want everyone staring at your face?"

"Stop!" Leila said. "You're right. I'm sorry. It didn't go so well the last time, did it?"

"No," Ray said. "It didn't."

"Except for the ice cream," Sleet said.

"But." Leila said. "There are reasons I need to go to town. Seriously."

"So go," Ray said, and Sleet nodded.

"I hate leaving you here," Leila said. "What if—what if Bill, your father, what if he comes back while I'm in town?"

"He's only been gone a couple of days," Sleet pleaded.

"We'll be fine, really," Ray said. For the first time that morning he dropped his antagonistic tone and Leila saw again the boy who had greeted her at the car and reminded her to take her pills.

On the drive to town, Leila felt relaxed enough to notice small things which brought joy to the moment. She worried a little about leaving the kids but knew it for the right decision. The crystal-clear air let the sun light the prairie with complete clarity.

144

A largish rock on the side of the road sparkled with reflected light. She almost stopped just to look at the rock. Pronghorns grazed at the side of the road. She slowed to watch them watch her.

Elk Crossing looked deserted. Not a car moved on the street, not a single person wandered the sidewalks. Within two blocks, Leila developed a fear that the people of the town had disappeared over night. Then a battered farm truck pulled out of a side street and made its dilapidated way down the street ahead of her.

She pulled over in front of the closed ice cream shop to consult her phone book. Elk Crossing Christian Church was listed on Fourth and Elm.

The church consisted of a taller middle section flanked by two one-story additions to each side. In front, an enclosed white signboard announced, "I WILL FEAR NO EVIL." Leila shivered. Smaller letters informed her the worship service began at 10:30 a.m. Leila guessed by the empty parking lot that she was very early.

She drove slowly around the silent town, looking for a place to stop and ask the time. Back on Third Street, she drove past shuttered businesses lined up door by door. One door had, in small, gold lettering, the word "SHERIFF."

That's the sheriff's office? A storefront between jewelry and western wear?

Bemused, she parked and went in. A large-boned, blonde woman looked up from her desk. A cubicle wall separated the desk from the rest of the office. The cramped space in which she worked made her seem even larger.

"Can I help you?" The woman asked.

"Yes. Do you have the time?"

"I've got all the time in the world, honey." The officer smiled at her own joke.

Leila liked her smile and gave her one back. Something about the woman made her feel comfortable.

"See, I don't have a watch and the house where I'm staying has no clocks...I'm just trying to go to church..."

"It's eight forty-two," said a male voice from the other side of the cubicle wall.

"Hey! Hands off, Cole," yelled the woman. "I've got this one covered."

"Nah," Cole replied, "I don't think you do." His head rose above the divider and he grinned. "Why, Leila Stein, imagine seeing you here."

Her good mood lifted further by being included in the banter, Leila grinned back.

"Come on back here and we'll discuss your urgent need for law enforcement intervention in the time-related department this morning," Cole said.

"Now," he said, "I want to apologize for my desk..."

They rounded the end of the wall. Cole's desk lay completely bare before her with the exception of a computer screen and a plate full of huevos rancheros accompanied by black coffee.

"Yeah," he said. "They say a clean desk is a sign of a diseased mind or something and I just wanted to assure you that it doesn't look like this most of the time..."

The officer sitting at the front desk snorted.

"None of your commentary, now, Deputy Williams!" He yelled. "Please, have a seat."

He pulled the desk chair out a little for Leila.

"Aren't you supposed to have two chairs in here?" Leila asked.

"We've got a little folding one but it's not very comfortable," he said.

He perched on the edge of the desk and picked up his breakfast.

"So…you have no watch?" He asked.

Leila shook her head. Something in the question put her on edge. She spent years with Stu dodging questions from law enforcement and having the big man perched above her evoked deep discomfort. She squared her shoulders and looked up at him.

"I don't have much of anything. No watch. No cell phone. I was in a hurry when I left California, and I wasn't thinking clearly."

"I thought that might be the case," he said, without emphasis.

Leila bristled a little. "So, what, I look like the type who can't pack for a trip properly?"

"No. You look like the type who didn't have very much time to get away."

He said it gently enough. Perhaps too gently.

"You know what? I just came in here for the time— "

"And you got it," Cole interrupted. "But you came to law enforcement so you're going to get a little more than the time of day from me."

He slipped off the desk and squatted next to her, his large frame filling the space between desk and wall. She was effectively

147

trapped. Her heart sped up and she could feel a nervous sweat begin under her arms.

Cole rose in a fluid motion from his squat to his full height and Leila flinched.

"Fuck." He said it softly but looked angry and Leila braced herself.

"Come on, let's go for a walk before church," he said.

Leila gave him two stiff nods, her wide eyes still watching his hands. They walked out.

Cole motioned with his head at Leila's Buick.

"You've got thirty days, you know," he said.

"Thirty days?"

"To get your plates changed."

"Oh."

They walked down the empty sidewalk in silence for a bit. Cole stayed several feet from her and moved deliberately. Leila's heart began to slow and she felt shame when she realized he had seen her panic.

They turned at the end of the block and started east. The sun lit Leila's face and reminded her of her earlier sense of peace. Cole cleared his throat.

"So, well, a lot of the time I let Deputy Williams do this," he said. "But I seem to have gotten involved."

His words made no sense so Leila let them slide off her as she pursued the peace which had so recently been hers.

"Look, you were a strange specimen, showing up here out of the blue with California plates and three children who look abused."

148

She stopped walking. His mention of the children felt threatening.

"So I ran your plates," he said.

Leila turned away from him, back toward the safety of the Buick. An overpowering urge to run swept through her.

Cole put one hand on her shoulder.

"No," he said. "With horses—with all animals, really—there are two instinctual reactions to danger. Fight. Or flight. But you're a person, Leila. You have a third option. Thought. Hang with me for a minute, okay?"

It took a minute for the sense of his words to penetrate the thick layer of emotion blanketing her.

"Okay," she said, and wondered what she just agreed to.

"So you came from Sunnyvale, California."

"Yeah."

"In the last two years, three calls were made to law enforcement concerning you. Two were made by your neighbors. One seems to have been placed by you."

"I don't want to listen to this. I can't listen to this. I need to go."

She would have backed away but his hand still lay heavy on her shoulder.

"Flight," he said. "That's flight. Now take a deep breath and think."

She did breathe. The air rushing into her lungs felt good and she realized holding her breath probably was a bad idea no matter what.

"Okay," Cole said. "That's good. Now, you ready for the next bit?"

She lifted her chin and met his eyes for the first time. The gesture was the closest she could come to consent.

"I need to know. Will your husband come looking for you if he finds out where you are?"

The pain, the terror, of her last failed escape attempt came back to her with a force great enough to make her feel dizzy. Cole's hand kept her upright.

"The last time?" Leila gasped for breath and started again. "The last time he said he would kill me. If I ran again."

Cole swore again, a low, meaningful word which summed up his feelings on the situation.

"But you're here," Cole said. "Now, I know this is hard, Leila, but you're doing great. Does anyone—I mean anyone at all—know where you are?"

"No. I mean, just some people here in town."

"You haven't called anyone and told them you're okay? You haven't been in contact with someone who might tell him?"

"No! I wouldn't, I mean, there isn't really anyone…"

And that had always been the nightmare, hadn't it? There wasn't anyone. Just her and Stu.

"Good—" Cole began. She cut him off.

"Not so good. See, he's a computer programmer."

Cole's shoulders slumped a little. She could feel it through the hand still holding her steady.

"Even in Elk Crossing you can't stay off the computer system forever," he said.

"No. You ran my plates…"

"Probably not anything to worry about. That system's fairly secure. But we have a lot to talk about," Cole said. "Let's walk some more."

They walked five more blocks. Cole increased his pace. By the time they stopped on a sidewalk that ran in front of a bunch of decent-looking little houses, Leila's breathing had picked up and her head had cleared.

"Wait here for a minute," Cole said.

He walked away from her, up to the house Leila stood outside, and unlocked the door. He reemerged in a couple of minutes with something in one of his big hands and a frown on his face.

"Here," he said, and handed Leila a not-very-ladylike watch.

"Oh!" Leila said. She wanted the watch very much, no matter how little it was likely it would fit her wrist, but she didn't feel sure she should take it.

"I shouldn't..."

"It's a cheap spare," Cole said. "Just take it."

When Cole had walked into the thrift shop Leila saw him as a threat. Just now he had been an interrogator. Friendly, yes, but still threatening. Now, for the first time, Leila realized he could be an ally. And she needed one.

"Thank you," she said. "Thank you. But...there's something else I need to talk with you about. Something important. Do you have time..."

This is hard, asking for help.

"Look at the watch," he said.

She checked the time.

"How did it get to be nine-thirty? I've got to go..." Leila

fretted. She promised she would go to church. But the real help might be right here.

"Come on back here to my house after church if there's something else," Cole said.

His offer broke her indecision and they walked back downtown in silence.

"You don't go to church?" Leila thought to ask Cole on the way back.

"No." He said.

"Pastor Jim seems really nice…"

"It's not him. It's the Big Guy."

"Ah."

***

Half the parking lot contained cars and trucks when she got back to the church. That felt okay but there were also knots of people standing and chatting outside the doors. Leila felt her stomach clench at the idea of interacting with a bunch of people she didn't know. For some reason, she hadn't pictured going to Pastor Jim's church as running a gauntlet of introductions she wouldn't remember and questions she didn't want to answer. She almost turned around and went back to Cole's house.

The announcement board still said "Fear No Evil," though, so she made it through the gauntlet of people outside the door by holding her head high.

Neither Pat nor Jim presented themselves in the foyer as she had hoped. Instead, the doors to the sanctuary were flanked by a well-dressed woman on the left and a slightly scruffier man on the right. The woman extended a hand to her even as the man handed her a program. They glanced at each other and the woman glared. The man withdrew the program. Leila wanted to laugh but restrained herself.

"Welcome to our church," the woman said, and grabbed Leila's tentatively extended hand. "You must be Leila."

Leila managed a smile despite the woman's mispronunciation of her name as "li-la" and the somehow unwelcome fact that the woman knew it in the first place. Leila's weak smile encouraged the woman to continue.

The woman introduced herself with a name Leila immediately forgot and went on talking. She tuned back in to the woman's chatter just as she asked a question.

"...but you didn't bring the children?"

The mention of the children sparked a protective feeling close to anger.

"No," she told the woman. "They're not here today."

Leila turned her back to the woman to accept a program from the man still standing behind her and thanked him. Without hesitation she turned and walked out of the church with head held high, her smile genuine this time.

Back at the station Officer Williams smiled when Leila walked in.

"Cole!" She said. "Your call!"

His genuine grin when he saw Leila assured her walking out of the church had been the right thing to do. She found herself grinning back.

"You just gave me time to finish my breakfast," Cole said.

"I'm sorry," Leila said. "It must have gotten cold over a stupid watch."

Cole's rewarding grin disappeared. Leila wanted to apologize again but didn't know what for.

"Change your mind about church?" he asked.

"There were, um, a lot of people there."

He nodded, a single sharp jerk of his head. They headed down the street with Cole in the lead and striding too fast for Leila to catch up.

At a corner he stopped and turned to her. "There was something you wanted to talk about," he said, still frowning.

Leila fought with her urge to run from the situation and her fear of bringing up a touchy subject with a man.

"I'm sorry," she said again. "But—I don't know? I don't know why you got so unhappy?"

Cole studied her, his gaze making Leila swallow hard. She forced herself to not look away. Something about his eyes…

"Do you know what I do when I'm not being a cop?" He asked.

She shook her head. The fear lodged in her throat made speaking difficult. Then she listened to what he had just said and heard the pain in his voice and realized his eyes showed the pain, too.

"What?" She asked, her voice scratchy.

"I train difficult horses. Horses with problems like biting, kicking, rearing, bucking. Bad horses."

"Okay…" She didn't see where this was going.

"Yeah, so sometimes someone brings me a horse they tried to cure themselves. And sometimes that 'cure' involved trying to beat the bad out of the horse."

Leila shivered but forced herself to stand still and listen.

"The horses like that? Well, they can act different ways. They're all afraid. Terrified. If you try to approach a horse like that they shy away. If they can, they'll run." He stopped talking.

"When I apologize for everything it reminds you of the horses shying away," she said.

Cole met her eyes for the first time since they left the station.

"Yeah," he said. "Leila, they're so beautiful. Horses are. But when they're broken like that...it makes me sick."

She fought the urge to say "sorry" again. Refraining made her feel like something had stuck in her throat. Cole resumed walking, this time more slowly. After half a block he spoke again.

"What did you want to talk about?"

She took a deep breath, preparing to speak, and couldn't. Stu, with her cooperation, had trained her to never talk about this sort of thing. But the kids were what mattered.

"The kids," she said. "I need to find a way to get custody. Before Bill comes back."

"Are you sure?" Cole asked.

"Of course! They can't live like that. They shouldn't live like that. You saw them."

"No. I meant are you sure you want custody. They won't be staying with their father any more," Cole said.

Leila stopped. Her heart pounded but she didn't know whether it was fear or anger driving it.

"You did more than run my plates," she said.

"That's right."

"You reported us to social services."

"Wrong," he said. "I reported Bill to social services. That's one of the things I needed to tell you. To expect Leslie to show up Monday morning."

"Oh my God. They'll take them away! Oh shit. What do I do? Oh. They can't—"

He grabbed her arm.

"Hey," he said.

She didn't respond, stood there, wide-eyed and stiff.

"Hey!" He shook her arm a little. "Talk to me. What's wrong?"

"Why did you do that? They can't leave the house!" Leila said too loudly.

"I'm an officer of the law," he said. "I am required, Leila, absolutely required, to report abuse. Now talk to me! Tell me why this is a bad thing."

She squashed her first instinct to run home to the kids that instant.

"I need to sit down."

"We're almost back at my house. Just…don't pass out on me or anything, okay?"

Cole sounded annoyed and Leila did not have to keep herself from apologizing. She ground her teeth and stared at the sidewalk. She saw the children's future hanging by a thread along with her own.

"Just—let's get to your house, okay? I really do need to sit down," Leila said.

After she and Cole walked into his house, Leila released the breath she hadn't realized she had been holding. The punishing stink in Bill's house accustomed her to bracing for the worst every time she walked inside.

The house smelled lemony, like furniture polish. The wood floor reflected sunlight from the south-facing windows into every corner of the modest living room. The room's neatness bordered on being stark.

"I'm going to get you some water," Cole said as Leila sank into a floral-print armchair which clashed with the rest of the furniture. "Do you want some coffee, too?"

She did want coffee, but not at the price of holding up their conversation, so she turned it down. The water tasted good. Panic always did make her mouth dry. She didn't wait for an invitation to start talking.

"Look. The kids won't leave the house. Believe me, I've tried." She paused to gather her thoughts.

"Why did you—" Cole began, but she kept going.

"The house is awful. Just awful. It's dark and scary and it smells really, really bad. It's filthy. So many bad things have happened to the children in that house…

"He's awful. Bill is. The kids are covered in bruises. Storm can't talk, or won't talk, and she's three! None of them act normal. I don't know what to do. I need to get custody of the kids. I need it now. No telling when Bill is coming back. And I'm afraid of him, but it'll kill me if I have to leave the kids with him…"

"Who's Storm?" Cole asked.

"Oh. The little girl. The kids have weird names. Ray is the oldest, then Sleet is ten. And then Storm. She's three. But the point is, the kids are weird about the house. They don't like to leave even for a trip to town. That's one of the reasons they're not with me now. If someone…" she couldn't go on. The thought of forcibly removing the kids made her stomach hurt.

Cole sighed and leaned back.

"It's a problem," he said. "It's any number of problems."

No reply came to Leila. Cole let the silence stretch, then shifted in his seat.

"Look. When Leslie—she's the social worker—when she shows up tomorrow, you and the kids need to work together. Make it clear to her that you want to be the children's guardian. And the kids need to let her know the same thing. There's nothing that can be done about keeping them in the house, but maybe we can talk Leslie into…" Cole trailed off.

"Thank you. Thanks for your help." Leila said.

"Don't thank me yet," he said. "This is a far cry from being worked out."

She wanted to tell him how long it had been since she had felt anyone was on her side, but felt pitiful even thinking it.

"Well," she said. "I've gotta get back and make the kids some lunch."

Cole walked her to the door and stopped with his hand on the handle.

"One more thing," he said.

Leila cocked her head, impatient to get back.

"I'm going to give you my numbers," he said. "I want a call if Bill shows up. And I definitely want a call if you see any sign of your husband."

Leila shook her head. "There's no phone."

158

"There's no phone? And you don't have a cell phone."

She stood by the door, waiting for him to open it.

"Get a cell phone," he said. "One of those ones that doesn't require a contract. Okay?"

"Yes. I'll do that."

CHAPTER ELEVEN

All three children exited the house as she pulled into the drive, picking their way across the rock collection that comprised the yard and over to her car. Not one of them wore shoes. Leila added that to her list of things to check before the dreaded Leslie showed up.

Sleet opened the car door for her, wincing a little as the weight of the door pulled against his injured shoulder.

Leila asked him whether he had taken any Tylenol at the same time that Ray reminded her to take her antibiotics. She grinned. Ray grinned. Sleet looked at them and shook his head, pretending to be put out by their levity.

Storm picked her careful way to Leila and, as she stood out of the car, lifted her face to make eye contact and raised her arms to be picked up. Astonishment froze everyone to the spot. Storm bounced a little on her toes, eyes still locked with Leila's.

She bent down slowly, put her hands around Storm's little ribcage, and lifted her up. Storm wrapped her arms around Leila's neck in a choke hold and looked down at her brothers with evident satisfaction. Leila's chest constricted and her eyes swam with tears.

"What's this?" Sleet asked.

Leila looked and saw he had retrieved the program from

Leila's aborted church-going. The picture on the front glowed in gentle pinks and yellows in the direct sunlight.

"It's just something I picked up at the church," Leila said. "I suppose we can throw it out."

"But it says 'fear no evil' on it," Sleet said.

"So don't throw it out. We'll look at it."

Once in the house, Leila noted how the stink made her skin and hair and lungs feel instantly filthy. With the thought of Leslie, she felt a drive to clean but Storm still clung to her neck, her vital, warm body pressed against Leila's chest. She squeezed Storm more tightly.

Sleet started speaking, his voice oddly halting as though he were wrenching each word up from some great distance.

"The Lord...is my...shep—shepherd. I lack..."

Leila craned her neck around Storm's limpet form to look. Sleet bent over the church program, frowning and moving his lips as he sounded out the words.

Ray plunked a glass of water and an antibiotic tablet down beside Leila and walked around the table to Sleet.

"Here, let me see," Ray said, and snatched the program out of Sleet's hands.

"Hey! I was reading that," Sleet said. "Give it back."

Sleet grabbed for it from his seated position and Ray danced out of the way, holding the program high. Sleet jumped to his feet and went after Ray.

"Come on! Give it back!"

Leila saw Sleet had no chance of retrieving the program given Ray's height advantage. Storm lifted her head from where she nestled against Leila's neck to watch the commotion. The touch of cold air on the sweaty place where the girl's head had laid emphasized for Leila the sweetness of the moment.

Sleet's voice began to take on a note of desperation as he jumped for the program Ray held just out of reach. Ray opened it and looked up, starting to read even as he dodged out of Sleet's way.

"Ray! Give that back to Sleet." Leila said. The deliberate teasing disturbed her, evoking memories she would rather lie quiet.

"I was just going to read it for him," Ray said.

"Sleet was reading it for himself," Leila said. "Now give it back."

"Yeah, but he was doing a lousy job of it," Ray replied.

Sleet stopped jumping for the program and dropped his hands to his sides, face radiating misery. Leila's face grew warm and she struggled to hold her temper in check. Still, her nostrils flared and her eyes narrowed at Ray.

"Give it back, Ray," she said.

"What if I don't?" Ray asked.

Leila recognized the quicksand a step too late to avoid it. Her flaring temper subsided, replaced with a little edge of panic. The idea of asking Leslie for custody of the kids when she couldn't even cope with Ray oppressed her.

"Your priorities, Ray? They need adjusting."

He stared at her, lips pressed together, chin high.

"Social services will be here tomorrow to check on us. Do you know what that means? Do you?"

Ray's face went white. Sleet sat down with all the control of a sack of potatoes dropping to the floor. Storm reacted to her brothers' shock by hiding her face against Leila's neck.

"Sorry," Leila said. "I didn't want to tell you that way. But here's the deal. I don't know if they will let us stay together. And I really don't think they'll let us stay in this house because your father is coming back— "

Sleet jumped to his feet and ran flat-out for the stairs.

"What?" Leila asked.

"Let him be," Ray said. "He has…things to deal with. What do we do?"

His stark plea for guidance, so unlike his usual tough façade, wrenched at Leila.

"I think…I think we've just got to lay it out, Ray. I don't know what to do, either. Do you want me to stay with you three?"

He winced. She couldn't tell why.

"Yeah. Yeah, we want you here."

"Fine. Then seeing as how I can't think of anything else to do, I'm going to clean the living room. Hey— "

Ray had already turned to go. He paused and looked over his shoulder.

"Do you have any ideas where that awful smell is coming from?"

He whipped his head around and walked stiff-legged out of the room. "No. No idea," he said so quietly she barely heard him.

***

Leila stood and rocked Storm and tried to think. The kitchen didn't look too bad—just needed some dusting. The living room

163

would require a deep cleaning...She knew she was avoiding the problems. She couldn't do anything about the scar on Ray's face or the bruise on Sleet's or how thin Storm was but she should do something about the smell. It seemed stronger upstairs. With that thought Leila could feel the house closing around her like a fist. Fear made her heart beat faster and brought a sheen of sweat to her upper lip.

"I can't go up there," Leila murmured to Storm. "I won't."

Her claustrophobic perception lifted. The house approved of her refusal and she hated it.

After Storm got tired of being held, Leila made lunch. After lunch she tackled the living room.

With none of the cleaning supplies she wanted in evidence, she started by dusting with a kitchen towel as she wished with all her might that the children would simply agree to move to town. But she had the impression only physical force could pry them out and it would leave her feeling violated to exert that force. The bitter memory of her first attempt to bathe Storm reinforced her conviction.

Dust soon clotted the dampened towel and filled the air. She sneezed, twice, and went to get the towel wet through.

Again, she wondered why the children so steadfastly refused to leave. It was as if they were addicted to the house, or in love with it, or...something else she couldn't imagine. Leila believed that, at least in the minds of children, there was a reason. The children's spirits had been twisted by a lifetime of abuse, neglect, and terror, but there was still a rightness about them which argued that their instincts had to be trusted.

164

A wet towel and thick dust makes mud. Leila wiped it away, rinsed the towel repeatedly, and still saw streaks on the bookcase, the arms of the chairs, the walls. She started wiping again and realized it was wasted effort because a third pass would be required after she vacuumed.

She turned to ask the boys where to find a vacuum cleaner but they had disappeared along with the plate of leftovers from lunch.

Storm and Sophie occupied the kitchen, Sophie lying on the floor, Storm sitting by her making patterns in the dog's thick fur with one hand. The other hand was up to her face, forefinger planted in her mouth. Tangles of hair decorated her cheeks and on the back of her head it was all frizzy where it had rested against the seat of the car.

"Where did your brothers go?" Leila asked Storm. She did not expect a reply, but she needed to hear the sound of her own voice in the dead silent house.

Storm looked at her with round, calm eyes. That finger was not in Storm's mouth to soothe worry, or it wasn't now. Perhaps she had been worried five or ten minutes ago and since forgotten her finger was there at all, now just a comforting warmth against her skin, a giving surface against her baby teeth. In contemplating the girl, Leila realized just how young she was and a rush of tenderness filled her.

"Are you tired? Do you need a nap?" Leila asked the first question that came to mind.

For the first time Storm responded to a direct question, shaking her head, a side-to-side movement which would have been perceptible only to one who had spent much time with her.

165

Leila rejoiced.

Sophie heaved to her feet and went to the front door. As Leila let the dog out she had another thought which made her heart skip a beat. What would happen to Sophie if they removed the kids? She couldn't imagine separating the dog from them. She wrenched her thoughts back toward the practical matter at hand.

"Would you like to help me vacuum?" Leila asked Storm. "Do you know where the vacuum is?"

Storm placed her hands on the floor, hoisted herself upward, and walked into the living room. She made a beeline to a door beside the staircase Leila hadn't noticed before.

An undersized, crouching thing, the door was not as tall as Leila and hardly wider than her shoulders. She decided she had not noticed it before because in addition to being untrimmed and painted the same color as the walls its only handle was a wooden knob sticking out, mushroom-like, from one edge of the panel. A dull pearl of paint marred the roundness of the knob, evidence of the haste or inexperience of the painter. The defect, once noticed, occupied all Leila's vision.

Fear came on her, sudden and complete. It pushed past the rational lens of consciousness into a place where feeling was all. On her left gaped the staircase from which a foul, cold air moved toward her. Facing her, the grimy panel of the new door. To the right stood Storm.

Aware but immobile, Leila stared at the horrid teardrop roundness of the paint drip, noting the slight tinge of grey on the outside edge where oily fingers had undoubtedly grasped it many times previously, and felt a nasty creeping presence on the staircase moving toward her. She could not look away from the door toward the staircase. Looking away from the door would be a mistake. Imagination failing, Leila could not describe what she feared. But the conviction there was something to fear consumed her.

Leila scrabbled against terror and changed her mind about vacuuming. She didn't need to open the door and find the vacuum. No amount of dust on the carpet could equal the importance of stopping the crouching thing on the stair. From her peripheral vision she noted Storm staring at her. The recent understanding between Leila and the little girl shredded in the stiff atmosphere.

Leila could see Storm turning into another threat. Unable to look away from the little door and unwilling to turn her head so her peripheral vision lost its glimpse of the stair, Leila imagined the girl changing, filling up with evil and advancing on her. The helpless feeling which had gripped her all the years of her marriage returned. If horror was inevitable, how much better to lie on the floor and choose suffering rather than fight a battle which certainly could not be won?

She fumbled for a positive thought from the prayer book and grabbed at the first thing which came to mind.

"Fear no evil," Leila said.

Lcila thrust out her hand, pushing through the threat-laden air in the girl's direction.

"Storm. Take my hand."

When the little hand slipped into her palm, Leila did not jump or scream as she wanted to. She closed her hand around Storm's and began to back them away from the staircase and the door. When they had backed away the length of a man's body, the fear snapped and lashed away into darkness.

In the kitchen, Leila sat at the table and lifted Storm into her lap. The church program still sat on the table. She picked it up and read. Her heart slowed with each word. By the time she reached the middle of the Psalm, Leila felt able to think again. She read the middle verse aloud.

"Even though I walk through the valley of the shadow of death, I fear no evil."

She stopped reading because Cole's lesson linked with the Psalm so firmly that it startled her.

"He said to think. I don't know what to think, though, Storm," Leila said. "None of this makes any sense. How could opening a door scare me so badly? Is there any point to this?"

She kept rambling while Storm snuggled against her chest, thinking aloud. Why is the house like this? Why are some places so frightening while others—like the kitchen—barely stirred the hair on her arms?

The girl's body jerked once, then relaxed into sleep just as Sophie scratched at the door to be let in. Leila clutched Storm to her chest and carried her into the living room where she laid her on the love seat before letting Sophie in. The dog nuzzled her hand in passing and flopped back onto the cool tile.

"It's hot for you, isn't it?" Leila asked the dog. "All that fur. Poor girl."

She reached down and, patting the dog, told herself to quit putting it off.

She stood again in front of the little door. Here was a nexus of fear. Leila reached into herself with a new sense of tendrils of thought fumbling for the truth of the situation. Again she was physically pushed back by the force of fear and anger and horror which came from the little space. She felt sick to her stomach, her heart pounded, her vision began to tunnel and her ears ring.

Leila forced herself to breathe, to accept the sensations as reality, however bizarre and unlikely. She stood outside herself and observed.

She felt a bead of sweat run down her face and feared if her heart beat much faster it would stop.

The urge to turn away pushed against her like a great physical need—thirst or hunger. She couldn't remember a single word she read from the prayer book the night before.

Her legs shook from the effort of forcing herself to stand within the fear. Hyperventilation threatened to lay her flat on the floor. She refused to turn away.

She pictured the prayer book in her hands, imagined the heft of it, the texture of the cover and the way the gold-embossed letters caught the light. She reached for the feeling reading it gave her the night before. The security and faith she longed for appeared at an impossible distance. But remembering they existed in some time, some place, helped.

Lcila reached out, grabbed the horrid little knob on the door before her, and pulled.

Her heart skipped a beat as the door swung open. Quickly, the time for anticipation and regret ended. Light streamed into the oddly-shaped space below the stairs. Dust, stirred by the movement of the door, waltzed briefly with itself and settled.

She looked around without stepping in. An unfinished board ran along the wall at eye level, holding a variety of cleaning products—rags, furniture polish, cleansers, ant killer, and more. A mop bucket sat, bottom up, in the middle of the space. Behind it Leila thought she could see the handle of an upright vacuum cleaner lurking in the farthest shadows.

She wondered why the terror would go away once she opened the door. Her fear, so real moments before, now felt a little foolish. But her heart still beat too fast. Her body believed in the experience even as her memory insisted on discounting it.

***

Leila's relief and let-down lasted only a moment. The vacuum cleaner occupied a space at least five feet from the door and going into the lightless room felt threatening. Sophie nuzzled the back of her knee and shouldered in beside Leila. The dog looked for all the world as though she were trying to figure out what Leila was staring at.

"Okay," Leila said. Sophie looked up at her, then returned to considering the interior of the storage room. "We've got to go get the vacuum cleaner. Sophie, you stay here and make sure the door stays open. I'll be right back."

She refused to repeat the scene of just a moment ago—a grown woman standing frozen outside a door, incapable of rational thought or movement—so she walked quickly into the room. Her second step carried her straight into something which caught in her hair and which, when she reached up to bat it away, turned out to be a pull cord for a bare bulb hanging from the ceiling. Yanking the cord flooded the room with friendly yellow light and revealed the sad circumstances of the cleaning equipment within. Everything lay covered in dust.

"Even the dust has dust on it in here," she commented, and giggled while she grabbed the vacuum cleaner.

Back in the living room with prize in hand, Leila closed the wretched little white door and unwrapped the cord. When she flipped the power switch the motor whined at a desperate pitch and produced little suction. Troubleshooting, never Leila's strong suit, luckily took only one step. Leila wrestled off the back cover and poked at the bulging bag inside. The debris had settled so firmly that Leila thought of time, pressure, and sand turning into sedimentary rock. She sighed. Anyone who kept such a neat cleaning closet would not put the vacuum cleaner bags anywhere but right in the same place where the cleaner itself was kept.

She marched to the door and yanked it back open without waiting to taste the fear. Right at head level on the left hand shelf was a box of bags.

As soon as Leila emerged with the box of vacuum cleaner bags, Sophie began dancing from paw to paw, head swinging and nostrils flaring. The dog danced up to her and nosed the box, whining faintly.

"What's up, Sophie?"

The dog ignored her, jabbing at the box with her muzzle. Curious, she set the box on the floor and stepped back to see what Sophie would do. The dog began to work the box over with her nose. At certain places she stopped, drew in an especially deep breath, and then exhaled. She inhaled so forcefully that Leila saw the cardboard side actually stick to her nostrils in one place. Then she started pushing the box with her nose and paws, scooting it over the dusty rug. The dog's clever antics amused Leila. A final shove knocked the box over on its side and now Sophie employed both forepaws, digging through the bags.

"All right, that's enough," Leila said.

Sophie ignored her. She dug all the bags out of the box, got down on both elbows and tried to stick her head inside, snuffling the entire time. Leila's amusement drifted back into curiosity. She pulled the box free, earning her a look of betrayal, and peered into it. A small book with a bright green cover was wedged into the bottom. When she pulled the book out Sophie began nosing it and whining. Leila sat on the couch and held the book so the dog could smell it to her heart's content. As the dog worked over the book, Leila held it and considered her prize.

"I'm sorry, Sophie."

Finally, Sophie satisfied herself with scenting the book and lay down at Leila's feet. She opened the unmarked cover to find the pages filled with careful hand writing. Vacuum cleaner forgotten, Leila leaned back and began to read the first entry, dated January 1 of the previous year.

CHAPTER TWELVE

January 1 — Bill is really doing well and I'm so glad. I can't believe how good he's been to us lately! I did talk to him, of course, after the last time, but I don't think that's what changed him? I don't know and right now I just don't care. This journal is from him for Christmas. I cried when I opened it. I can't believe he even thought of giving me this. It's like he's been sick and now he's getting better. For a long time now I haven't been able to remember why I fell in love with him or married him. This evening before bed we went through the dried flowers for the first time in ages and it was like old times. The pages and pages of beauty. But here I am sitting alone in the middle of the night, writing, writing. And I will hide this journal. A week or two of happiness is not enough to restore faith.

She lay the journal on her lap and stared across the room, not seeing the far wall instead this woman's life. Reasons to love Bill? The idea turned her stomach.

She thought back, and then back some more. All her memories of Stu stank of the knowledge of his brutality. For the first time, though, she forced herself to think—think about why she had married him, why she had stayed.

In her young life, Leila had a surfeit of loneliness. She remembered her childhood as one long dry spell with only her material needs satisfied. College had been a welcome opportunity to escape her unbearable parents. But she spent three semesters feeling out of step with every group on campus. The partiers, the studiers, the protesters...you name them, they all fell into groups where she failed to belong.

Stu stood out in her Intro to Sociology class as the other one who didn't fit. His square peg reasons differed from hers. She, the mouse, watched him in awe as he fought the ideas presented in class. On a day when they explored in-group out-group theory and marginalization of minorities, Stu exploded.

"You're all a bunch of damn liberals and this has nothing to do with real life."

At twenty-five, Stu carried himself straighter and spoke with more confidence than the eighteen and nineteen-year-olds who populated the class. Later, when he fished her from the depths of anonymity, he explained it hadn't occurred to him to go to college until he was almost twenty-one. The sociology class fulfilled his last core requirement before graduation and he hated it.

He adopted Leila as a welcome distraction from the class. In retrospect, she understood he controlled their every interaction from the first time he chose to sit beside her. She had welcomed the attention, sucked up every drop, and begged for more.

Leila startled at the pounding of feet on the stairs. She slipped the journal under her thigh as though she were guilty of something. Maybe the boys wouldn't appreciate her reading their mother's journal.

Sleet tore around the corner at the landing, skittered down the second flight, and jumped the last three stairs, coming to a skidding halt in the middle of the living room. He turned to face Leila, eyes wide.

"They're not going to take us away from here, right?" Sleet asked.

Leila sighed under the weight of the fear and sadness which rushed back into her. The distraction of finding the journal was over. Reading the mother's words would not change tomorrow's events.

"Sleet...I think they might."

"They can't! They just can't!" Sleet wailed.

Ray trudged down the last two stairs without bothering to avoid the squeaky one.

"We won't go," Ray said. Leila looked at him, then looked again. His drooping eyelids and the lines on his forehead made him look much older than his thirteen years.

"Why not?" Leila asked. "Even..." she swallowed and tried again. "Even if they didn't let you stay with me, wouldn't it be better to be away from this house?"

Sleet screeched an ear-splitting noise of frustration and fear. The vacuum cleaner's brief run hadn't woken Storm but Sleet's anguish did. She sat bolt upright, face tense, and looked like she wanted to cry. Leila wanted to cry, too. Anticipated grief wrenched at her and she felt suddenly tired in the face of Sleet's panic.

"Look at you," she said. "Have you looked in a mirror lately? The bruise on your face? Have you noticed how thin Storm is? What about the fact that she is three years old and doesn't talk?"

She paused, meaning to wait for a response but the rest of the

175

problem pressed on her.

"And look around you. Look at this damn house! Everything is filthy. You don't have beds or dressers. Hell, you don't even have carpeting in your rooms. And the place stinks. To high heaven. Does this look like a good place for children? Does it?"

The boys remained silent. They looked at the floor and shuffled a little. Finally, Ray looked at Sleet.

"We should tell her," Ray said.

"No!" Sleet's denial hissed through the air at Ray. "You're the one who always said not to!"

"Things have changed," Ray said. "What if someone tries to make us leave?"

"Then we don't go."

"What if we can't stop them?"

"But— "Sleet looked up at Leila as if realizing her presence for the first time. His eyebrows drew together and his eyes narrowed. He appeared for all the world ready to attack Leila.

"This is your fault," Sleet said to Leila. "I hate you. I wish you died years and years ago so you could never come here!"

She began crying even before the full force of his words sank into her consciousness. His tone of voice alone destroyed her equilibrium. When the meaning of his words penetrated her distress she covered her face with her hands and really let loose. Through her sobs she heard the boys' retreating back upstairs. Their desertion goaded her into deeper misery.

Storm curled into a fetal ball beside her. Leila hardly noticed, absorbed as she was in wailing and wiping at streams of tears.

She thought of leaving and the idea wrenched her in

unexpected ways. The kindness of Jim and Pat snagged at her consciousness. The competent good humor of the woman cop at the station threatened to comfort her. Doctor Paddock's insistence she take care of herself irritated her hold on self-pity.

Then Cole's face loomed. He asked again with equal parts frustration and concern whether she had any fight in her.

Sleet's words still ricocheted around her heart, hitting tender things and tearing them to bits but she knew then that even if the social worker took them she would fight to get them back.

Her sobbing eased and Storm's posture responded by relaxing a fraction. Leila reached out and began rubbing the girl's tense back.

"I'm sorry," Leila whispered. "I didn't mean to ruin your nap."

Storm relaxed incrementally as Leila kept rubbing her back. The meditative action relaxed Leila as well and her tears dried up. By the time Storm's back no longer felt tense, Leila floated in the calm aftermath of pain.

She looked at Storm's face. In relaxation, the girl looked more like a baby than a toddler with her lips pouched out and the veins showing under her eyelids.

"You're beautiful," Leila whispered to her. And then, without planning to, she said, "I love you."

Leila rose and headed for the stairs. Her heart thumped unpleasantly as she began to climb. She skipped the second stair and kept going despite the pressure to turn around and the growing unease. By the time she reached the landing and made the turn, the sensations associated with going upstairs pressed back at her like a giant, invisible hand trying to force her back down. Fear, anxiety, anger, depression, all were present in a hard wall of resistance. She stopped three steps from the top of the second flight.

A conviction grew in her that something horrible would happen if she continued up. Leila robed herself in thoughts of calm and determination.

"Fear no evil," she told the staircase, and then dipped her head in the direction of the terrible emotional storm and acknowledged it. Leila continued up. The sensations did not lessen, but her drive to avoid the unpleasantness disappeared and she overcame the last three stairs.

Children's voices muttered and overran each other in a rising and falling litany. Ray and Sleet's low tones kept Leila from making out anything but the occasional word but the tones and pattern of the conversation made the hair rise up on the back of Leila's neck.

Leila stood and listened. Unsurprisingly, the voices came from The Room—the bare room which somehow focused the feelings of evil in the house. The boys' location, combined with the odd quality of their conversation, convinced Leila that going back downstairs and cuddling with Storm was the right thing to do. She turned, felt a vast wind of discouragement before her, and remembered her purpose.

Leila accomplished the task of walking down the hall by focusing on the mechanics of moving each foot and leg. Pick up the foot, move the leg forward, put the foot down. Shift weight. Repeat. The process kept her sane all the way to the door of the room. Then the conversation resumed with more heat.

"…it be nice, just sometimes maybe?" Sleet asked.

"No! Not ever and you know why," Sleet replied to himself, sounding older, somehow, and more sincere.

"Come on," Ray broke in. "It's not like you have a choice."

Leila's eyes rested on the sliding lock set high on the outside of the door and she understood the solution. If she simply locked the door, Sleet's schizophrenic conversation with himself and Ray's cooperation would go away. She could go back downstairs and play with Storm.

She lifted her hand to the lock. In the process, her weight shifted and the floor let forth a tortured shriek. Beyond the door, she heard the closet door slam closed. The concussion of sound made her jump. By the time her feet met the floor again her heart resumed its pounding and she felt the nightmarish state lift.

She swung the door open, afraid the house might get to her again if she stood there any longer.

Sleet and Ray, both looking pale and determined, stood side by side and faced her.

"What are you doing up here?" Sleet asked. "You don't belong here!"

The room itself told her the same thing. The indescribably bad smell of the place flowed past her as a cold and gentle draft, caressing her face with filth. She looked down in an effort not to gag and the floor appeared to be undulating across the length of the bare room. Dizzy and nauseated, she could not remember the answer to Sleet's angry question.

Ray cocked his head a little as though listening.

"Grab the door frame and take a deep breath," he said. "Never

179

mind the smell. You'll get used to it. But if you hold your breath you'll pass out and we'll have to step over you to get out."

Ray's kind attempt at humor helped Leila get a grip on herself, as well as the door frame.

"Sleet, I know I've screwed things up," Leila said. "But, come on, are they really any more screwed up than they were before?"

"Yes," Sleet said. "You've ruined everything!"

His voice rose and the word "everything" came out as a ragged scream. Ray sighed. Sleet launched himself toward Leila, his face contorted as though he were still screaming.

Before Leila could step back from the door, Ray's hand shot out and grabbed the back of Sleet's neck, stopping the slight boy's lunge toward Leila. With a power which made the motion seem casual, Ray flexed his arm and threw Sleet sideways across the room.

Sleet cried out in surprise and hit the floor, just managing to break his fall with one hand before his face hit.

At the heavy thud of Sleet hitting the floor, several things happened at once. The familiar sound and vibration of a body hitting the floor wrenched Leila's consciousness backward to the many times it had been her abused body. Overwhelmed with the flashback to violence, she grabbed the door frame with all her might just as the closet door exploded outward and a shrieking apparition blurred toward Ray, hitting him in the back of the knees and crumpling him to the floor.

Leila screamed.

Ray swore viciously and rolled across the floor, fighting whatever had come from the closet. A confused overlayering of

180

sound added to the chaos—Ray, swearing like a sailor, Sleet's knees and palms hitting the floor as he scrambled toward the struggle, shrieking a protest over and over, "Don't hurt him, don't, don't hurt him, no…"

Sleet reached the struggle just as it ended. Motion too rapid for Leila's eyes to follow subsided into a tableaux of misery. Ray's body pinned a still figure to the floor. Sleet grabbed onto the hand protruding from under Ray and held it.

The door jamb guided Leila's suddenly limp body to the floor. Irrelevant thoughts flooded her, a mental commentary about how she seemed to be sitting on the ground and why was that?

"I think you can let him up now," Sleet told Ray.

Ray grunted his assent and half rolled off the smaller figure, who turned and locked eyes with Leila. Ray's vicious attacker was a little boy. Moreover, he looked like a smaller, thinner, paler version of Sleet. She wished Sleet would turn around so she could compare their faces but decided her first priority should be introducing herself. Gently. Her head still spun and light spots floated in her vision but Leila drew her knees to her chest and took a deep breath of the awful air.

"Hello. I'm Leila. Do you live here?"

The boy, still lying on the floor half under Ray, nodded. His long, shaggy hair stirred the dirt around on the floor.

"Ray? Why don't you let him up?" Leila asked.

Ray and the boy looked at each other for a long minute.

"Are you ready?" Ray asked him.

"Yes," the boy answered in a whisper.

Ray stood up and Leila caught a glimpse of the whole of the

boy's skinny body, ragged, too-small clothes, and pale, grimy skin. Then the boy skittered straight to the closet, whipped inside the door, and slammed it shut.

Sleet sighed.

"Sorry I threw you like that," Ray said to Sleet.

"S'allright," Sleet said. "I was out of hand."

Leila thought she now understood the stench in the room, the stench leaking out and poisoning the house, but understanding did not make it easier to bear. She began to gag as her adrenaline ebbed.

"Let's get her downstairs," Ray said.

Sleet went to Leila and squatted down next to her.

"I'm sorry for what I said."

Leila, a hand covering mouth and nose, nodded her forgiveness.

He held out his hand. Leila didn't really need his help to get up, but took it just to hold it. She struggled to rise gracefully while making it look like Sleet's slight weight helped.

At the landing, Leila glanced back up the stairs, uncertain if they really should be leaving.

Sleet pulled her forward. "He wants to be alone right now."

In the living room, Leila sat next to Storm's still-sleeping body and stared with unfocused eyes at the vacuum cleaner holding pride of place in the middle of the room. She sorted through her questions and came to a conclusion.

"I'm sorry, Sleet, Ray. I didn't understand."

Ray nodded his forgiveness. Sleet brushed the apology off with his signature one-shouldered shrug.

"Who is he, exactly?" Leila asked.

"My twin brother," Sleet said. "His name is Rain."

"How…" Leila swallowed and tried again. "How long has he…been in there?"

"Since— "Sleet began.

"—since Storm was a baby," Ray concluded for him.

"For goodness' sake, why?"

The boys stayed silent so Leila changed tack.

"Why didn't you tell me about him?"

"He didn't want us to," Sleet said.

"Rain…doesn't like to meet new people," Ray said.

"Obviously," Leila replied. "Anything else?"

"Dad told us not to tell anyone," Ray said.

He hung his head. Leila sighed.

"I see," she said. "Any more secrets you want to tell me about?"

Sleet's shoulders rose up toward his ears and he ducked his head. Ray looked Leila in the eyes and gave her a twisted travesty of a smile.

"Okay," she said. "Okay, I'm sorry."

Leila evaluated the failing light in the still-dirty living room.

"I'm going to make dinner," she said. "And then…do you think Rain would let me bring him some food?"

"He might?" Sleet said. "He likes food and he likes you."

"He likes me? He doesn't even know me." Leila said.

"No," Sleet said, his eyes wide with earnestness. "Sometimes he comes out at night? He says you've had a hard life and we should be nice to you."

"Seriously," Leila said, unsure whether to believe Sleet.

"Seriously," Ray replied.

Leila remembered the times she thought she dreamed of a skinny, ragged boy who looked like Sleet, and understood. For reasons she didn't understand, she did not feel intruded upon by the thought of Rain watching her sleep. She felt comforted, like someone was guarding over her, eyes filled with light-years of depth and sympathy.

Leila fried up steaks for dinner, whipped mashed potatoes, and candied carrots. She added peas for good measure. She piled a plate high, stacked a fork and steak knife on it, grabbed some napkins and a glass of water, and juggled everything toward the stairs. Ray stopped her at the kitchen door.

"Not the knife," he said.

She looked at the knife, thought of the shooting cannonball that was Rain when enraged, and allowed Ray to slip it off the plate.

She managed to forget the malevolence of the house all across the living room and up the first flight of stairs. As she made the turn at the dark landing, though, despair pounced on her. She believed he would never take the food from her.

She pictured his forceful removal from the closet, then from the room. He kicked and screamed and fought just the way she had the first time Stu raped her after beating her. She saw him breaking his nails trying to cling to door frames. A strangled sob tore its way out of her throat and wrenched at her sinuses. The plate wobbled, she smelled the food, and remembered the anticipation she had felt about doing something good for Rain.

Leila nodded her head in recognition of the situation and then glared up the stairs.

"I'm bringing a hungry boy food," she said. "And you won't stop me. She imagined Cole's voice, even and insistent, telling her to think. Then, the heft and color of her prayer book, it's feeling of pureness and hope. She couldn't remember the words she had read, so she invoked the feeling, instead, and her own words came. "Angels guard me and I will fear no evil."

Head high, eyes wide open, she started up the stairs.

The closed door to Rain's room suggested she knock. She juggled the plate and tapped twice.

"Rain? It's Leila. I've brought you some dinner."

No response. She opened the door and stepped into the room where the dim light of early evening filtered through the dirty glass of the north-facing window. Vertigo offered to take her rationality with its waving, reeling force.

She leaned against the door jamb to steady herself and kept her head high while she surveyed the dingy room. She noted the dust bunnies on the floor. A filthy window pane. A water stain on the wall across from the closet door. The knob on the closet which looked like dirty hands have touched it a million times.

She stepped into the room and began to talk.

"Rain? I made you a special dinner. I guess your brothers have been bringing you leftovers. But this is hot."

She waited to the tune of silence.

"Okay, so I'd really like to meet you when you're not busy fighting with Ray. If you don't want to talk right now, that's okay. But would you open the door enough to take the food from me?

185

It'll be better when it's hot."

More silence and the edges of despair started to tease her perceptions out of shape again.

"I'm going to come over to the closet now, Rain, and sit down next to the door. I have the food right here."

She sat with her back against the wall next to the closet door, stared without seeing at the water stain, and kept talking.

"I made steak, and mashed potatoes, and peas, and carrots. I don't know what kind of food you like but I hope there's something here you'll enjoy?"

Just as she was about to start talking again, a thin voice emanated from the closet.

"Did you say mashed potatoes?"

Her heart broke with sympathetic sorrow and with joy.

"Yes, Rain. There's mashed potatoes. Would you open the door so I can give them to you?"

The knob turned. Leila held her breath both against her hope and against the stench she knew would follow when the door opened.

Rain opened the door a crack. Leila turned her head slowly and saw the light from the room illuminate one eye and a strip of gleaming white cheek. A lock of his dark, shaggy hair trailed down. Leila smiled a little.

"I'm glad to see you, Rain."

His head inclined in a nod.

"Could you open the door far enough so I can get the plate in?"

He shook his head once. The closet door closed again. For a

186

moment silence reigned and Leila sat in gloom.

"I can't do it," Rain said.

"Oh, Rain. I'm so sorry," Leila said.

"Could you…maybe…just leave the plate on the floor?"

Leila considered and rejected feeling hurt as an option.

"I'll leave it right here," she said. "But…tomorrow? Do you think I could come spend some time talking with you?"

This time the silence stretched so long she feared she had asked too much.

"Yes," he finally said. "Now could you leave before the mashed potatoes get cold?"

She almost laughed.

"I'm setting the plate right here and going. You enjoy your dinner."

"Thank you," Rain said.

She made her way downstairs, fighting the urge to break into a run at each step. The sense something was watching her, ready to rush at her, almost overpowered her. She made the living room with her dignity intact.

The kids in the kitchen all stopped eating—even Storm—when she entered the room.

"Is he okay?" Sleet wanted to know.

Leila smiled.

"He's all right. He opened the door a little and we talked for a minute. I left the food for him."

"Duh," Ray said. "It's not in your hands any more."

Leila took the high ground and ignored his sarcasm.

"He opened the door while you were in the room?" Sleet

asked.

"Yeah. Just a crack."

"He really likes you," Sleet said, looking impressed.

Over her own plate of food, Leila started to droop and look forward to bed.

"Who's doing the dishes tonight?" She asked.

Ray and Sleet looked at each other.

"I think it's Sleet's turn," Ray said.

"Could you do them tonight?" Sleet asked Leila. "I'm really tired."

"Wait," Leila said. "One or the other of you has done the dishes every night since I got here…"

The boys watched her think through it. She figured it out after a minute.

"You were doing the dishes so you could sneak food to Rain. That's why I could never find the leftovers."

"You got it," Ray said.

The boys went back to scraping their plates, the situation solved. Leila initially heaved a sigh of resignation. Recent days, however, had made her begin to distrust that sense of resignation.

"What?" Ray asked.

Leila stopped shaking her head, unaware she had been doing it until he asked.

"No," Leila said. "You boys can keep doing the dishes. I'm cooking for you, and trying to clean— "she waved her hand in the direction of the lonely vacuum cleaner still standing in the living room.

Sleet looked downcast. Ray looked angry.

"Look," Leila said. "You do a lot to take care of Rain. I understand that. But that doesn't change the fact that you should help clean up after yourselves."

Inside, she shook. Standing up for a concept—even one so simple as doing the dishes—shook her to the core. Simultaneously, she believed it was the right thing for her and the children, so she stuck to it. Making this novel choice sent a small surge of happiness through her, like winning a race.

Ray locked eyes with her, his inner bully fighting her fragile determination. She lifted her chin and held his gaze. He broke first.

"Okay," Ray said. "We'll do them." He turned to Sleet. "But it is your turn."

Sleet began to protest. Before the squabble got out of hand, Leila stepped in.

"Who did them last night?"

"We did them together," Sleet said.

"Then you can do them together again tonight."

She marveled at the firm tone of her voice. The boys acquiesced with more grace than she expected.

Leila's fatigue demanded she go to bed but she dreaded more nightmares. Two things kept her from simply brewing coffee and pretending sleep is not necessary: her prayer book a chance to read the journal un disturbed.

She retrieved the journal and snuck off to the bedroom.

January 8 — He did it again. Yeah, Christmas was so nice. Two wee`ks of nice. Almost enough for me to remember. But he did it again. And the entire time the baby was screaming and I

189

couldn't go to her and I didn't want to scream but maybe I did. Thankfully I'm not hurt too bad and he didn't get to the boys. The baby is okay too. Gotta count my blessings. If only I could remember what they are. I can't think. I can't think. Please, God—but I don't know what to pray for. I'm trying to remember how I ended up here. What horrible fault of mine made me choose this? I wish I knew how to keep from making him so mad.

Leila put the journal down. The entry kept going, descending into a sort of madness of self-recrimination and misery but she couldn't read any more. She felt she knew this woman and wanted to reach out to her, put a hand on her shoulder, and assure her it wasn't her fault. Reading the journal held a mirror to her own life and she deeply understood for the first time that Stu's behavior hadn't been her fault, either.

The thought lightened her mood. She turned it over and over, looking at the idea from different angles, like a brilliant crystal in the sun. Aching for the children's mother, wondering what happened to her, but paradoxically freer with her new insight, Leila turned to her prayer book and began leafing through it.

The huge book contained so much material she couldn't settle on something to read. Eventually, looking at the table of contents occurred to her sleep-fogged brain. She read carefully down the two-page list, encountering words she didn't understand from her poor background—Shema, Amidah, Kiddush. Her persistence paid off some thirty entries down. "Night Prayer." She turned to page 996 and started reading. By the fourth line, she began to feel a surge of joy and thankfulness and recognition.

May it be thy will, O Lord my God and God of my fathers, to suffer me to lie down in peace and to let me rise up again in peace. Let not my thoughts trouble me, nor evil dreams, nor evil fancies, but let my rest be perfect before thee...

The words could have been written for her. But they had been written long ago for a whole group of people. Habitual loneliness diffused into a sense of connection.

...may Michael be at my right hand; Gabriel at my left; before me, Uriel; behind me, Raphael; and above my head the divine presence of God.

She lay down and sleep came quickly.□

191

CHAPTER THIRTEEN

Dreams approached. Repeatedly the swirling edges of terror crept up. They ate away at her sense of wellness and sent tendrils reaching deep into her sanity. This night she fought.

Stu's contorted face loomed above her. She grasped for the words of the prayer. Disconnected phrases came to her.

…nor evil fancies…lie down in peace…

Fighting to remember the sense of peace and unity and gratitude she experienced before lying down, she began to picture the words, to mutter them deep inside, to wrap herself in them. She focused on the feeling of security they gave her as she found herself transported to a twisted version of the living room where the walls warped into threatening shapes and doors she had never before noticed swung open onto darkness. She noticed she was asleep and the weight and warmth of her blanket became real. She slipped into deeper sleep.

Dreaming again, she thought she opened her eyes in the bedroom. Some strange attraction drew her to the living room. A pleasant sound, perhaps, or a feeling of safety. She rose up, and looking down, saw her body lying abandoned on the floor. Undisturbed, she floated toward the living room, moving without effort.

It was familiar in every detail: the sterility of a room which should have been the comfortable and friendly center of family life, the uncomfortable edge of fear leaking down from the north along the line formed by the stairwell and the door to the storage space, even the dust lay in her dream as she knew it in waking life.

A light shone from beneath the storage room door, light which both drew Leila to the door and made her afraid. There was no reason for light to be shining in that room but she had to open the door and see what was making it. Acting on a compulsion she fought at every step she approached the light and, wanting to scream, unlatched the door and drew it open.

The interior of the storage space glowed with a light which suggested the air itself emitted it. Light came from nowhere and illuminated everything, throwing no shadows. The mop bucket, still turned upside down, made a seat for a woman. She hunched with her near shoulder raised against the door. Slowly, she turned toward the door and Leila's urge to scream turned to pity. The thin woman with her fragile skin. The bruised hollows under her eyes suggested her stress and lack of sleep.

"What are you doing in here?" Leila asked her.

The woman straightened up and brushed her long brown hair behind her ear. In her other hand she held the journal.

"Oh. This is where you write, isn't it?" Leila asked.

The woman nodded and a ghost of a smile twitched at her lips.

"I'm sorry I disturbed you," Leila said.

The apology made perfect sense within the logic of the dream.

The apology earned Leila an ironic twist of one shoulder. She backed out of the room, closed the door, and walked back through

193

a more friendly darkness to the bedroom. She found her body, still posed in the abandon of sleep, and wondered how to get back into it. At the thought she found herself floating. She placed her dreamlike feet above the feet on the blankets and carefully began to lie down. Her dream-self melded with her body inch by inch and when her dream heart meshed with her body she was back inside herself and sank immediately back into sleep.

Sophie woke her in the morning, dancing and smiling her big doggy smile.

"Do you need to go out?" Leila asked her.

The smile got even bigger and she began whirling in circles.

"Okay, okay," Leila assured her.

Making her sleepy way to the front door, Leila reviewed the night with contentment. Although tension, violence, and terror still marred her dreams, she had fought them at every turn and won more rounds than she lost.

Sophie ran out the front door as soon as Leila wrestled it open. The early morning sunlight poured in and she lifted her face to it, eyes closed, and remembered meeting the kids' mother. The encounter continued to feel real even in the sunlight. She believed she could have touched that woman last night, and her flesh would have been solid.

Only after closing the door on the sunlight did she remember the threat that lay over them this morning.

A knot formed in her stomach so rapidly that she feared throwing up. She ran to the bedroom, grabbed Cole's watch, and checked the time. The hands read two forty-seven. Leila frowned and shook it. Still two forty-seven. She wanted to scream.

She went to the foot of the stairs and, defying her fear of making loud noises in the house, yelled for the kids to come down. Immediately, she knew she had made a mistake. Her panic over the impending visit of the social worker magnified ten-fold into a chest heaving anxiety attack. While she fought the sensation of suffocation, she heard pounding feet on the stairs and immediately felt certain her worst night terrors had come to life.

Ray popped around the corner on the landing, one gangly arm in his shirt, struggling to pull it over his head and charge down the stairs at the same time. His oddly-angled arms and bare torso showed just how much the boy had yet to grow despite how he towered over Sleet and Rain.

He's going to be a big man, Leila thought. With the observation came a flood of love for this difficult boy who still sometimes wanted to please. The tightness in her chest passed.

"What?" Ray asked. "What's the matter?"

"The watch stopped working," Leila said.

"So? They all do."

Leila wished she had a moment to process this new bit of information but the time—whatever it was—was pressing.

"So I think the social worker will be here around nine. But we don't know what time it is."

"Shit," said Ray.

"Ray, I know you can swear. You proved it when Rain attacked you. But please save it this morning, okay?"

"Yes, ma'am," he said, and sounded like he meant it.

Just then Sleet and Storm came down the stairs. Sleet held Storm's hand as if the little mountain goat turned girl needed help.

"Is she here?" Sleet asked, pausing halfway down the stairs.

"No. But we've got to get ready," Leila said. "How's Rain this morning?"

"He's scared," Sleet said. "And hungry."

Leila cooked breakfast while the boys bathed. She broke down and inexpertly made some of the bacon she found in the freezer, figuring something with a strong, pleasant smell might help. A little.

When breakfast was served the boys, now pink-skinned and tousle-haired, sat down with Storm. Leila piled a plate high with bacon and fried potatoes. A scratch at the door reminded her to let Sophie in and she, Sophie, and the plate of food headed upstairs to Rain.

At the bottom of the stairs, Leila paused and armed herself. The house, which she now thought of as a living thing, was already pushing her away from the stairs and she was sick of feeling bullied by it.

"I'm too busy for this," she announced to the empty stairwell.

In the kitchen, the sound of silverware scraping on plates ceased at her words.

"I will fear no evil," she said. "And you can't stop me."

The pressure of fear and despair continued unabated from the stairwell. Leila recalled how she wrapped herself in words of comfort and peace in her dreams. She did it again and then, ignoring the unpleasant sensations, marched up the stairs at good speed and used her momentum to carry her to the second floor.

She called out to Rain as she approached the door. He didn't reply, but he also didn't slam the closet door shut.

The door swung open to reveal Rain standing two feet from the closet door. The boy trembled from head to foot as he looked at Leila. She froze in place and watched him, feeling as though she were looking at herself during many of the moments of her life.

She held his gaze and smiled a little.

"Feels scary, doesn't it?" She asked.

He nodded, and swallowed hard.

"You're doing great, Rain. This is really, really impressive. I know it's hard to stand there. But you're doing great."

"Okay," Rain breathed. "What's for breakfast?"

"Bacon and fried potatoes. I brought lots."

"Ooooh. I love bacon."

They stood at an impasse, Rain doing all he could to not disappear into the closet. Leila feared walking toward him would be more than he could take. His nervous eyes flicked from the plate to her face and back to the plate.

"Rain? I want to give you this plate. If I walk toward you—very slowly—do you think you could just stand there?"

"I'll—I'll try."

"Good." She put all the warmth she could into the word. "You just hang on there and don't forget to breathe."

She lowered her eyes to his chest and took a slow, smooth step forward, working to bridge the eight-foot chasm between them. Rain's fists clenched. She could see the tendons in his wrists standing out.

"Come on, Rain. Breathe. Breathe in, breathe out."

197

She took another step and kept talking.

"You're being so, so brave. Just try to relax your shoulders a little."

Another small step.

"Wait!" Rain cried out.

Leila froze in place, looked back at his face. Tears trailed down his cheeks.

"Okay," she said. "Now what?"

"Just...could you just put it down?"

She laid the plate on the floor and backed away.

"You're very brave," she told him. "That was amazing. I'm going to let you eat in peace."

As she turned to leave, though, he stopped her with another plea to wait.

"Yes?"

He spoke in an urgent whisper.

"Don't tell her about me. Please don't."

Without considering the consequences, she answered his need.

"I won't tell them. I promise."

By the time she reached the bottom of the stairs she realized the foolishness of her promise, a promise she must keep if she hoped to ever help Rain recover.

The other children were almost done eating. Stress killed Leila's appetite, but as she walked past Sleet's plate she snatched a chuck of fried potato off and popped it in her mouth.

"Hey!" Sleet yelled in mock indignation. "That's was mine!"

Leila grinned and made a show of enjoying her stolen bite. She walked to Storm's end of the table and surprised them both by kissing the girl on the cheek. Ray smiled at them until he saw Leila looking, then turned back to his plate, covering his slip into good humor with a convincing scowl. Leila decided to reward him for the smile.

"Ray? You're the one who's so good at telling time. How close do you think we are to nine?"

He went to the front door and opened it. Sophie immediately slipped inside.

After squinting at the sun Ray gave them half an hour or so until nine.

"Fine." She tried to keep it light despite the way her chest tightened. "Why don't you boys brush your hair and clean up the dishes while I give Storm a bath?"

The boys agreed with a rapidity that suggested they, too, were trying to put the best face on the situation.

Storm climbed willingly into the bathtub without Leila having to get her jeans soaked. She fought a little at having her hair washed, but recovered quickly with the aid of her bath toys.

Just as she lifted the dripping girl from the tub, Sophie started her guard dog routine, rattling Leila's skull with her sharp, clipped barking. Storm's eyes grew round and she stiffened and lunged to cling to Leila's neck. Leila hurried to wrap a towel around the girl and made it to the kitchen where the boys stood wide-eyed, staring at the front door.

"Okay Sophie! That's enough!"

Leila clutched Storm in one arm, kneed past the furious dog, and fought the front door open just wide enough to stick her head

199

out. A large woman stood in the rocks before the front door. Leila first took in the woman's copious bosom trying to fight its way free of a floral patterned button-up shirt, and then noted the remarkable bags under the woman's tired eyes. These things were all she had time to notice before Sophie started to push her muzzle past Leila's knee, barking all the while.

"No, Sophie!" Leila yelled at the dog. "Get back."

Sophie wasn't having it.

The presumed social worker watched the dog fight to get to her with impassivity, apparently unconcerned by the offered prospect of being ripped to shreds. Feeling exasperated, embarrassed, and a little fearful for the woman, Leila met her eyes.

"Just give me a second," she said over the barking.

The woman nodded and Leila closed the door in her face. Sophie stopped barking as if a switch had been flipped and started waving her long tail and grinning at everyone. Leila considered yelling at the dog but settled for asking Ray to put her in the bedroom and close the door. Storm, still clinging to Leila's neck, began shivering.

"I'm sorry, baby," Leila said, and wrapped the girl more closely with the towel, making sure her wet head was covered, too.

Sleet stared at the door as if it were a monster.

"Sit down and take a breath. Passing out from anxiety isn't going to help."

He obeyed without back talk. Leila wrestled the door open again. The woman still stood there.

"I'm sorry," Leila said. "Please come in."

200

She stepped inside and Leila closed the door against the cool rush of morning air on Storm's undried body, noting as she did the way the woman's nostrils pinched as she drew her first breath of the air in the house.

After an awkward pause Leila remembered this woman didn't consider herself an enemy. "I'm Leila Stein," she said, and extended her hand.

"Leslie Eberhardt," the woman said, and they shook.

"Boys, would you come introduce yourselves?" Leila asked, seeing Ray was now back from the bedroom.

Ray looked at Sleet, sitting miserable and hunch-shouldered at the table, and stood up.

"I'm Ray," he said, and shook the woman's hand. "That's my brother, Sleet. I don't think he wants to shake your hand and we're not leaving this house, either."

Leslie's lips twitched in what might have been a suppressed smile.

"Ms. Eberhardt, would you like some coffee? You caught me getting Storm here out of the bath and I've got to go get her dressed?" Leila asked.

"Please, go take care of what you need to," Leslie said. "Coffee would be fine. And call me Leslie."

Leila asked Ray to make enough for both of them and hurried off to get Storm dry.

Back in the bathroom, it took more time than Leila planned to pry the limpet girl's arms off her neck long enough to get her dressed. Storm shivered the entire time, then clung back to Leila as soon as she picked Storm up again.

201

"Okay. It's all right, Storm. Shhh. It'll be all right," Leila said.

She carried the girl back to the kitchen in time to hear Ray talking.

"...we told him not to ride that horse, anyway."

A surge of adrenaline warmed Leila's face. Leslie looked up at Leila, who suspected the woman's blank eyes hid intelligence and—what? Compassion? Fatigue? Distaste?

"We were just discussing the bruise on Sleet's face," Leslie said.

"It's taking forever to heal," Leila said.

"How long ago did he have the accident?" Asked Leslie.

Leila frowned. "I don't know? Before I got here."

"And that was..."

"Um..."

Leila looked around the kitchen, trying to think how many days ago she arrived at the house. Nothing came to her except to tell the embarrassing truth.

"I feel like it's been months. But it couldn't be more than a week or so? I've lost count of the days."

"Would it help to look at a calendar?" Leslie asked.

Leila knew it wouldn't. Toward the end Stu hadn't allowed her any appointments, dates with friends, anything which took her out of the house. She stopped caring. So she had no idea what day she left. Early June. However, saying so would make her look like a real flake.

"Yes," Leila said. "A calendar might help."

Leslie looked around the kitchen.

"Is there one here?" She asked Leila.

"No. I don't know why, but as far as I can tell there isn't a calendar in the entire house."

"Huh. Well—" "Leslie drew out her phone. "We can use the one on my…that's weird."

Chills ran up Leila's spine.

"What?" Leila asked, afraid she knew the answer.

"My phone's gone dead," Leslie said. "I just charged it."

A shock of fear thrilled through Leila. Just days ago, it would have frozen her. Now, she repeated the mantra of Cole's advice.

"That's too bad," Leila said without emphasis.

Leslie looked around and Leila saw the thick, blonde hair on the backs of the woman's arms was standing up.

"Ray," Leila said, "Why don't you take your brother and sister to the living room and read them a story?"

Ray opened his mouth to protest and Leila cut him off with a flat-handed chopping gesture. With a nod, he pried Storm from around Leila's neck and carried her off with Sleet dragging his feet behind them.

Leila poured coffee and asked Leslie how she liked it.

After Leslie took the first sip, Leila sat down and leaned across the rough table.

"I know it looks bad," Leila said. "It is bad. But…the children and I have bonded fast and…you need to believe them when they say they won't leave. Please believe them."

Leslie sighed, coughed a little at the smell, and covered with another sip of coffee.

"Now Leila. What kids want isn't always what's best for them."

"But they can't leave!"

"They're leaving," Leslie said. "Today. While their father is gone."

Leila felt the temperature of the room plummet and again chose to think. Leslie shivered at the cold just after Leila noticed it. She crossed her arms over her chest and bowed her head.

"Is it cold in here?" Leila asked. "Let's step outside into the sun."

"Yes," Leslie said, and bolted for the door which Leila knew would not open for her.

Leila hurried after her, noting as she went the ice crystals forming in the coffee.

In the bedroom, Sophie barked once and Leila felt the darkness descending on her vision which heralded a really bad thing about to happen. She reached the door just as Leslie tried to open it and turned to Leila, despair on her face, when it wouldn't budge. She shouldered the woman aside, lifted and pulled, and the sunlight reflected off the tile and into Leila's eyes.

Leslie darted outside with unseemly speed. Leila fought the urge to run. Instead, she looked back and saw the children— Storm still wrapped around Ray—trying to come after them but caught in some dark well. They appeared to be moving in slow motion.

Leila rushed back in, grabbed a boy by each hand, and started for the trapezoid of sunlight. The boys' weights had increased exponentially. Dragging them forward seemed impossible and darkness thickened over her eyes again.

An almost overwhelming urge to lie down on the cold floor

and go to sleep swept over her. She gritted her teeth, tightened her grip, and dragged the children into the sunlight.

As soon as their bodies touched the light they began to move at a normal speed. Ray darted outside with a shivering Storm cradled in his arms but Sleet stood rooted in the doorway.

"Sleet, come on," she tried to shout. The words came out muffled and weak.

Meanwhile, the social worker had walked back to the door and peered inside at Leila's struggle. Sleet stepped out of the sun and moved away from her, looking like he were wading through deep water.

"Sleet!"

He opened his mouth slowly, slowly, and ground out a word.

"Soooooophieeee." His voice sounded like it had been slowed by a mechanical process, the tone half an octave lower.

The cold kept deepening. Through the ringing in her ears, she could hear Sophie barking and whimpering her protest.

In the back of her mind, a memory struggled to rise like a sprout pushing for the sun. She stepped into the shadow of the house.

"I will fear no evil," she told the cold darkness. "I will fear no evil."

She called upon the angels she wasn't sure she even believed in. "Michael at my...right hand—Gabriel...left hand... She pictured beings of light, of strength, of safety, surrounding her.

The pressure of evil on her mind and darkness against her eyes lifted. Sleet looked up at her, moving this time without effort.

"How did you do that?" He asked.

"We'll talk about it later," Leila said. "Do you feel okay with going to check on Rain?"

"Yeah. I think it's over."

"Good. I'll go get Sophie," Leila said. The dog's barking had subsided to a few discontented whimpers.

"What about the social worker?"

"You know what, Sleet? Sophie's more important."

He smiled at her and the psychological aftertaste of whatever had just happened faded.

"Okay," he said.

They split up in the living room. When Sophie heard her at the bedroom door she started barking again. Leila opened the door to a frantic dog. Too well-behaved to jump up, Sophie settled for bouncing up and down on her front paws and spinning in circles. Leila reached out to pet her and the dog stopped celebrating and got down to the serious business of scenting her all over for trouble or injury.

Ray stood in the yard and stared at Leslie's white sedan which housed the woman in question, all windows rolled tight. Leila and Sophie walked over and stared at the social worker through the side window. The woman paused, then rolled the window down a few inches.

"I'm sorry about—" Leila began.

Leslie cut her off. "What was that?"

Leila shifted her gaze away from her face to the plump hands gripping the steering wheel. She knew Leslie's hands would be shaking if not for that death grip.

"Well," Leila said. "That was the house. It gets—"

206

"—no! Never mind. I don't want to know." Leslie said. "In my nine years here I've seen cases which would turn your hair white." She reached up and fluffed her blonde curls. "Actually, they did turn my hair white. This is all from a bottle. But...that—whatever that was? That's not my line of work."

"So..." Leila said, trying to figure out what came next.

"So I still have to remove them," Leslie said.

She looked up from the steering wheel and Leila saw the distant, resigned look which met her when she opened the door this morning.

"Look." Someone hit that boy. Hard. That's no horseback riding injury. But..." Tears stood in Leslie's eyes and her voice shook. "I need your help. I can't go in there," she whispered. "Please, Leila. They're in danger. Please get them out. Now."

"No," Leila said. "No, I don't think so. This is something we have to work out on our own. I'm sorry."

The hound dog lines of Leslie's face deepened and she pressed her lips together until her lips paled despite the lipstick.

"Fine," Leslie said. "Then I believe the children are in immediate danger and I'm going to—to get Cole, I mean the sheriff, to remove them.

"Right. You think he'll be able to just going to waltz in there and make them leave?"

"He has to! It's his job."

Leslie spun the car around and pulled out in a cloud of dust that formed shapes Leila's disturbed subconscious interpreted as angry spirits billowing in the air.

CHAPTER FOURTEEN

Ray started walking over, paused when Storm kicked to be put down, and placed her on the ground.

"What are we going to do?" He asked.

"We'll figure it out, Ray. We have to figure it out."

"Right," he agreed, and knelt down in the dirt to help Storm pile rocks on top of each other. He murmured to her about a castle, and giants.

Leila stood and stared across the valley, inspired by the view as always. The peace of standing in the sun and listening to Ray and Storm play convinced her finding a solution would be possible.

Sleet emerged from the house and jogged over to her.

"What happened with the social worker?"

"She ran her off," Ray said, not bothering to look up from the castle.

"She ran her off?" Sleet repeated, looking at Leila for confirmation.

"I sort of told her I wouldn't bring you three to town," Leila said.

His grin showed all his teeth but Leila shook her head and met his eyes.

"I'm afraid I didn't do a very good job. She said she is going to ask the sheriff to come take you kids out of here."

"She's stupid, then," Ray said. "I told her we wouldn't go."

She suppressed the urge to ask Ray what he thought she should do.

"I've got to go to town," Leila thought out loud. "But I don't like the way the house is acting…"

"We'll be fine," Ray said. "Really. I'll take good care of everyone."

"I wish Rain would go outside," Leila said. "You could all go for a picnic or something…"

"He can't," Sleet said. "He just can't."

"I know," Leila said.

She marveled at the feeling of sadness her acknowledgement brought. For so long she had felt so little. Fear, yes, and despair. But even those emotions had been dull, as if she lived at a great distance from her own body. This acute sadness, fresh and new, gnawed at her. She welcomed it.

As she drove to town, Leila struggled to figure out what she would say to Cole, to Leslie. She searched for the right words but they failed her.

She topped the last rise before the dirt road met the highway outside town and shock traveled down her spine. Two cars headed up the hill toward her. She slammed on the brakes. The sheriff's patrol car led Leslie's sedan.

Leila pulled into the middle of the road and got out of the Buick. The patrol car stopped nose-to-nose with her and Cole unfolded out of it. All Leila's planning about thinking before she spoke and presenting strong arguments fled when she saw Cole's set jaw.

"You can't take them out of there," she said, almost yelling in her urgency.

Cole glanced back at Leslie's car. The social worker was just opening her door.

"Now, Leila, I have to if she says I have to."

"But— "

"No. I'm not going to stand here and argue. I know you hate this. But if things are as bad as Leslie just told me? It's the best thing."

Cole turned before Leila could say another word. Leslie just made it out of the car, saw him walking away, and got back in. Leila stood in the road a moment, thinking, then realized the situation didn't depend on her at all. Everything depended on what would happen at the house.

She turned the Buick around, considering getting it stuck in the ditch running alongside the road and deciding against it. Cole and Leslie started after her. At the house, she parked in the drive as close as she could get to the front door and jumped out of the car, holding herself back from running into the house. As soon as she got in the door she started yelling.

"Sophie! Come! Kids! Get down here!"

Her twin fears involved Sophie attacking Cole and getting herself shot and Cole finding the kids in Rain's room. The resolution of both fears involved gathering everyone—except Rain, of course—in the kitchen.

Sophie arrived first, panting and grinning when Leila praised her obedience. She inhaled to yell for the kids again but heard feet pounding down the stairs just as Cole knocked on the door and Sophie jumped up and began making an unholy amount of noise.

Hunched over to hold Sophie's collar, Leila crab walked to the door. Pulling the door open with only one hand proved impossible.

"Hang on," Leila yelled to Cole over Sophie's barking.

Ray reached her first and looked a question at her, then the door. She grimly nodded at him and dragged Sophie back a foot so he could pull it open. Cole stood there, looking relaxed.

Sophie kept barking at the sight of him and lunged against Leila, pulling her off balance. Cole reacted by squatting to the ground, hands at his sides and with one knee bracing in the gravel. Then he looked up at Leila from his supplicant position. For a split second Leila thought she saw pain in his face, then it was gone, and he mouthed words at her. She cocked her head, not understanding.

He shifted his gaze to the dog, then looked up at Leila, hands still loose and relaxed.

"Let. Her. Go." He mouthed again, and she understood, and raised her eyebrows.

He nodded, though, and reluctantly she released Sophie's collar. The dog stopped barking in favor of forward movement. In a single bound the dog stood before him. Cole didn't move. Sophie stopped short, lowered her muzzle, and sniffed at Cole's right hand, still hanging at his side. Slowly he turned his hand over. She licked his palm and he ran his hand over her neck and shoulder. Her tail started waving—a sedate pendulum of pleasure.

211

Cole stood, wincing a little. Leila heard one of his knees pop and winced in sympathy.

"Old riding accident," Cole said, and invited himself into the house.

The kids, clustered on the far side of the trestle table, watched him with their best poker faces. If it had been a competition, though, Storm would have won.

Cole sat at the table, straddling the bench. Sophie accompanied him, crowding his outside knee in a bid for more affection. He rested a hand on her withers and lifted his head. Leila saw his nostrils flare as he scented the room. He stiffened and one side of his lip curled just a little, then his face settled into a peaceable expression again.

"I didn't introduce myself when we had ice cream," he said to the kids. "I'm Cole."

Their stony stares promised no response so Leila stepped over to them.

"This is Ray," she said, and gestured to the gangly boy at her side.

"This is Sleet, and this is Storm." Her hand rested on the girl's blonde curls.

Storm responded by grabbing Leila's hand and pulling to be picked up. Leila obliged her.

Cole dipped his head at the children. "Pleased to meet ya. I think Leila has told you there's a problem."

The boys returned his opener with more silence.

"Okay," Cole said after a long pause, "I'll do the talking for now."

He held up his right index finger. "First off, Leslie—the woman who was here this morning—Leslie believes you kids are in danger."

He put his middle finger up next to his index finger. "Second, she also believes this house is not a good place for you to live."

A third finger joined the first two. "Third, I'm an officer of the law and when she tells me what to do, I have to do it. So it is my job this morning to get you kids out of this house and somewhere..." he scented the air again, wrinkled his nose, "...safe."

Tears slipped down Sleet's face. He looked first to Leila, then to Ray.

"Do—do you want to tell him, Sleet?" Leila asked.

He shook his head and looked down.

Ray put a hand on Sleet's shoulder. "Even after what the house pulled this morning?"

Sleet broke and ran for the stairs, Sophie in hot pursuit.

Leila looked at Cole and shook her head. The force of keeping Rain's secret pushed at her mouth and behind her eyes.

"Give him a minute," she said. "And in the meantime, would you like some coffee?"

"I love coffee," Cole said. Before Leila could move he grabbed the still-full coffee cups on the table and carried them to the sink. When he wrapped his hand around the first one, Leila saw him frown and wondered how much Leslie had said.

She put on fresh coffee and set out clean cups, all the while wondering why the house hadn't reacted to Cole's presence.

Cole smiled at his first sip of coffee and turned with that

expression to Ray.

"So, Ray. Does your brother need help figuring things out?"

Ray shook his head, looking as miserable as Leila had ever seen him. He looked at Storm in Leila's arms and she decided to push a little farther.

"She doesn't deserve to grow up like this, Ray."

Ray pounded the table with one fist, his face flushed. "Don't. Tell me." He ground out the words, struggling to speak at all.

Cole leaned in, one hand still wrapped around the coffee cup. "You need to tell us. You're the man of the house here. Take responsibility for your brother and sister and tell us why you won't leave."

Like Cole's words had thrown a switch, the house changed and threw dread at Leila.

"No!" She said. "Never mind, it's not important!"

Shadows gathered and teemed in the corners of the kitchen, shadows which Leila feared to look at directly because she knew if she did they would have meaning and when she understood she would start screaming and never, ever stop.

She saw Cole's shoulders stiffen and the fact he felt it, too, scared her more than she thought possible.

She looked back to Ray to see if he felt it, too. Ray's face had changed, had hardened into thick, heavy lines like stone. His color gone from red to gray, he drew a breath to speak.

Darkness spewed out of Ray's mouth, a thick, roiling cloud of tumbling shapes and then words grated from the boy's throat.

"You're all bad. You need to be punished."

He walked around the table, his movements stiff and slow, a

predator stalking. Leila wrapped her arms around Storm and pressed back against Cole. The sheriff sat frozen and she could feel the muscles of his torso trembling from rigidity.

"Ray," Leila whispered. Her plea fell into the warm, still air and swirls of darkness ate it.

Ray reached the end of the counter. He turned to look at them as he reached for the drawer with clawed fingers. His eyes glinted amber in the kitchen's dying light. As he pulled the drawer open his face contorted and through locked jaws he said, "Run."

It took Leila a moment to understand. She feared she would scream when she opened her mouth but instead she cried out a warning.

"The knife!"

Ray, his movements now snake-fast, pulled the hooked knife from the drawer and lunged toward Leila and Storm, the blade flicking out with a snick as he closed the distance between them.

Cole still sat frozen at the table. Leila tried to dodge back and turn Storm away and the same moment, tripped over the leg of the bench, and fell. The knife sliced through the air where Storm had been a short second before.

Ray stumbled a little when the blow didn't strike flesh, overbalanced by the force of his movement. Leila saw terror flash over his face, a glimpse of the real Ray, and the mask settled back on his face. IIis lips pulled back to show his clenched teeth and that voice grated from him again.

"Bitch. You can't protect her."

Leila lay on the floor, staring up into the face possessed by fury and hate, knowing there was no escaping the knife a second

215

time.

"I fear no evil," she said. "She is protected and you can't have her."

At the words, Ray staggered a little and Cole whipped around and grabbed Ray's wrist, his knuckles turning white.

The knife dropped to the ground. Leila jerked her foot away to avoid the falling missile. Light pushed through the kitchen window and glinted on the curved blade.

"Ow!" Ray said. "I think you can let go now."

From the doorway to the living room, Sleet spoke, his voice gummy with tears.

"I'll tell you."

Cole looked away from Ray, who was shaking the numbness out of his wrist, and tried to address Sleet.

"You..." His voice scratched over the word like he'd been screaming a long time. He cleared his throat and tried again. "You'll tell me?"

"Yeah."

"Let's go outside and talk."

Cole gave Leila a hand up from the floor and they made a small procession into the brightness outside. Again, Cole knelt in the rocks, this time before Sleet. He took a deep breath and placed one of his big hands on Sleet's shoulder, causing the boy to flinch away a little. Cole left his hand there.

"Sleet, I'll do my best for you. Do you understand?"

"It's not me," Sleet sobbed. "It's him. Rain, my twin brother. It's Rain." His legs gave way and he sat down abruptly.

Cole kept looking at Sleet, kept his hand on his shoulder.

"May I talk to Leila about it?"

Sleet nodded, his gaze fixed on a red rock near his legs.

"Good boy," Cole said, and shook Sleet's shoulder a little. "Good boy."

Leila looked around, feeling like she had just awoken, and saw Leslie watching them from her locked car.

***

Cole gestured Leila away from Ray and Sleet where they sat shoulder to shoulder. Leila saw his hand tremble a little. She looked up to meet his eyes.

"You okay?"

"Nope," he said. "But we gotta see this through. Are you all right?" He asked in return.

"I've been doing this all week," Leila said.

He placed a hand on the small of her back and escorted her around the side of the house.

"I want to talk about what just happened," Cole said. "But I don't want to talk about it, too. Let's just stick to getting the children out for now."

Leila nodded and bit her lip.

"So there's a fourth child?"

"His name is Rain. He's been hiding away in a closet upstairs since Storm was a baby."

"I don't suppose there's any chance Leslie or I could go up there and see him?" Cole asked as if he already knew the answer.

"It was most of a week before I found out about him. No. He would be terrified. And his brothers would probably…"

"…attack me. I know."

217

Leila stood and looked out at the southern view until Cole spoke again.

"So," Cole said. "A boy in the closet who won't come out. And the others won't leave him."

"Yeah," Leila said.

"Do you know when Bill is coming back?"

Leila hated herself for an idiot. She hated even more admitting her idiocy to Cole. It took her time to say it.

"I have no idea."

"And you don't know where he was going. Or what he was doing. Or…anything."

Cole made the statements in such a neutral tone that she felt able to answer him.

"No. Nothing."

"Well. Let's go tell Leslie." He stood.

"What? What are you going to tell her?"

"The truth," he said.

Leslie sat in her car, engine running as if ready for a quick getaway. Leila and Cole walked right up to the window before she rolled it down and when she did a gust of cold air smoothed its way out against Leila's arm.

"Are we ready to go?" Leslie asked.

"No," Cole said. "The children can't leave the house just yet."

She frowned, managing to look disappointed, angry, and frightened all at the same time.

"I don't understand. That house is horrible. They've got to go now. Do your job, Sheriff."

"Leslie, there are four children in the house. Four. One of

them is hiding in a closet. Has been hiding in a closet for…a long time. They won't leave him."

Her jaw dropped. Color washed out of her face.

Cole and Leslie waited in silence.

"I've heard of this," Leslie said. "I've never seen it before." She popped the car door open. "Let's go talk to the boy."

Cole placed his hand on the door. "I don't think so."

"Why not?" Leslie asked.

"Have you ever seen a rabbit die of fright? They sit there all stiff and wide-eyed and you can see their little hearts beating faster and faster and then…they just die." Cole said.

"It's that bad?"

"I think so."

"We'll need to bring someone in," Leslie said. "Someone who deals with this kind of thing. When is the father returning?"

"Let me deal with that," Cole said. "That's my department. How soon do you think you can get someone in?"

"Dunno. I've got to call people who know people and then call those people…" Her eyes got wide. "I've got to go. The East Coast doesn't stay open forever."

"Go," Cole said.

They stepped away from the car and Leslie backed out of the drive and swung around, again with unseemly haste.

Cole stared at the rocky ground as if it offended him. The dust from Leslie's departure settled and around them the whirring of grasshoppers and occasional birdsong were the only sounds.

Eventually Cole looked up and reached to his shoulder to key his mike. He turned his head to speak into it and then frowned and keyed it several more times.

Leila waited for the word "weird" to come out of his mouth.

"That's weird," Cole said. "My mike is dead."

He started fiddling with it.

"Don't bother," Leila said. "It's the house. It drains batteries."

Cole pulled a cell phone from his pocket and confirmed Leila's words.

"All batteries?" He asked.

"Even the watch you gave me is dead," Leila said.

"Okay, then," Cole said.

Leila appreciated his effort to keep his tone light.

"Here's how I see it. Bill could come back in two days. Or a week. Or this afternoon. Or he might never come home. We have no way of knowing. But until we can get that boy—what's his name?"

"Rain."

"Rain. Until we can get Rain out of the house, you are all in danger. Therefore, I believe I'm going on vacation."

Leila stood and processed his statement. Her first mental picture, of Cole sitting in a boat fishing, was followed by the realization he must be talking about staying with them. Then self-doubt set in.

"You don't mean..." she said, and waved her hand at the offensive house.

"I do," he said.

She thought of the house in all its meanness, the kids with their quirks and difficulties, her own weak efforts at behaving like a "real" person.

"What did you do for your last vacation?" She asked.

"Well…" He kicked the ground and then looked up with a grin. "I stayed home and trained difficult horses."

"I've heard real vacations are about getting away from it all?"

"If you mean that kind…well, I don't think I've ever taken a vacation."

"Me neither," Leila said. "Not since I was a kid, at least." And then, because his easy conversation relaxed her, she asked him the real question in her mind.

"Is this really the way you want to spend a vacation?"

"I don't have enough deputies to post someone around the clock out here," he said.

Leila fought a disappointment she felt unreasonable at his evasion but he continued before she could turn away.

"And I would hate myself for the rest of my life if anything happened to you or the kids. So…yeah. This is how I am going to spend my vacation time."

He met Leila's eyes, which made her uncomfortable, but she chose to fight it and return the gaze. After a minute of waiting for her heart to settle, she thought of something to say.

"Vacations are supposed to be—I've heard—about having adventures in exotic locations. We'll do our best to provide."

"In this case," he said, and grinned, "I would prefer boredom."

She nodded solemnly. "Boredom. Check. Two servings up."

Without transition, Cole got down to business. He looked at his watch, said "shit" and glanced at the sun.

"After lunchtime, I'd say. Here's the bad news. I have to go back to town, wrap some things up, make some assignments…you know. It's going to take all afternoon. And I'm going to have to round someone up to look after the horses while I'm on…vacation. Which means I'll have to show them the ropes tonight when I feed. I won't be back until tomorrow sometime."

Leila fought a bitter taste which must be disappointment back down her throat.

"We'll be all right," she told Cole. "We've been all right so far."

"Yeah, well, that's not a completely rational evaluation of the situation," he said. "That's a bit like saying you haven't been hit by a tornado yet so you're going to stop paying attention to the warnings."

"Oh."

He looked around and focused on the high ridge behind the house.

"What's on the other side of that ridge?"

"I don't know," said Leila. "Never looked."

"Come on, then," he said, and started off to see.

She didn't ask why they were hiking around when they both had things to do. The rapid transition threw her off. By the time she decided she really wanted to know what the heck they were doing, her breathing had turned to panting.

Cole reached the crest and extended a hand down to Leila, who picked her way, slipping and scrambling, up the last bit. He hauled her up the steepest three feet and they stood on top of the world. All of Wyoming spread out below them. For the first time Leila saw the view which lay to the north of the house.

She understood, while she turned to look in all directions and the wind tugged at her hair, the smallness of the house and its obstinate evil. And how large loomed the beauty of the world around her.

They plunged down the slightly gentler hill which formed the other side of the ridge. Three-quarters of the way into the valley, Cole stopped and looked around.

"Here," he said, and started picking up medium-sized rocks. "Rocks about this size. Larger will do."

Mystified but willing to play along, Leila began carrying rocks to the cairn Cole was constructing. When he had a small pyramid built, he stood back and surveyed it, then paced back seven large steps. Leila trailed him. He stopped, turned back to the cairn, and bent. At first Leila thought he was adjusting his low-rise black boot. Then he pulled a gun from a holster around his ankle. Leila backpedaled a step.

"This," Cole said, "is a little Smith and Wesson .380. It has a lot less kick than the .45 I'm carrying here." He gestured to his right hip.

Okaaaay," Leila said, hoping the conversation wasn't going where she thought it might be.

"I want you to carry this while I'm gone. Heck, I want you to carry it when I'm around, too. Every minute until this is all over."

"But I don't know how to use a gun," Leila said.

"I figured. That's why we're here. I'm going to teach you how to shoot. Right now."

"But I don't want to," Leila said, trying to keep her voice even and reasonable.

"You need to," Cole said. "You need to be able to defend

yourself."

She considered saying she didn't want to again, but that hadn't worked the first time so she tried a different tack.

"You'll be back in the morning, though."

"Yes. And what if he comes tonight?"

She shivered.

"Can't you just tell all the cops in the state to stop him if they see him?"

"Put out an APB? Yes. And I'm going to."

She nodded, satisfied.

"But, Leila," Cole said, and she could hear him struggling to stay even-tempered. "How many 'cops' have you seen on the highway since you got here?"

She thought. In California she saw them everywhere. She assumed...

"Two?" She offered. "On I-80 when I drove up through. And one on I-25 somewhere."

"And so..." Cole prompted.

"And so he probably isn't going to be stopped."

"We just don't have the coverage," Cole said. "Leila, this is the fifth largest state. With the smallest population in the country. Be reasonable, here."

"But I'm afraid!"

"That's okay," he said. "As long as you do it anyway."

"Okay." She lifted her chin. "I'll try."

"Good girl."

He didn't hand her the gun. Instead, he laid it flat on his massive hand, left side up, and began pointing things out to her.

He started with the safety, showing her the lever which controlled whether the gun could be fired.

"When this orange dot is showing, the gun is live. That means if you pull the trigger, it's going to shoot."

She nodded and shivered, already anticipating the bang.

"Always keep the safety on unless you are going to shoot someone."

"Orange dot," she repeated. "Gun will shoot."

"Good."

"Next. This little button here releases the magazine. Don't touch it. I'm not going to even show you how to change magazines. We don't have time. This gun holds seven rounds if there's one in the chamber."

She frowned. "What does that mean?"

"A round is a bullet. Seven rounds means seven shots. The chamber is what holds the bullet so it is ready to shoot. Magazine holds six bullets. With one left in the chamber, seven rounds."

"Seven rounds. If I shoot the one in the chamber, how do I get another one in so I can shoot again?"

He raised his eyebrows and grinned. "This is the slide," he said, putting his hand on the top of the gun. "When you shoot, the slide will be shoved back and scoop up another bullet into the chamber."

"That's great! I don't have to do anything, then."

"If you are in immediate danger," Cole said. "Immediate danger, click the safety off, point the gun, and pull the trigger. Then do it again."

"Again?"

"Yes. There are two possibilities when you pull the trigger. Either you hit your target or you don't. If you hit your target, you want to hit it again to make sure it stays down. If you miss..."

"I have to try again."

"What else do I need to know?" She asked.

"Just two more things: how to use it safely, and how to shoot it. Safety is first and there are only two rules."

"Two rules. I can handle that."

"The first rule is to never point this gun at anyone you don't intend to shoot. The second rule is to keep the safety on unless you are going to shoot."

Next, he demonstrated a two-handed grip and the way he wanted her to put her feet. She practiced the stance while holding her hands up even with her face. Then, after showing her the safety was still on, he handed her the gun.

"Always check the..." he began, then dropped to the ground as she swung the gun through his position on the way to pointing at the cairn.

She looked down in consternation. The barrel of the gun drifted down in the direction she was looking.

"No! Quit pointing it at me."

She looked down and jerked the gun to the side, pointing it at the ground instead of Cole. He got up, looking disturbed, and stepped close to her.

"Never. Point it. At something you don't intend to shoot."

"But the safety is on!"

"Doesn't matter. Never point it at something you don't intend to shoot."

She blinked back the tears which made it difficult to see.

"I'm sorry," she said. "I won't do that again."

Cole continued his instruction as though he had not just been lying on the ground and she were not struggling with the urge to cry.

With the gun pointed at the ground at all times, he adjusted her grip, then instructed her to turn raise the weapon, and find the middle of the pile of rocks in her sights.

"Now. Take the safety off with your left thumb."

She did. The click of the safety as it slid off felt final, and very unsafe.

"Put your finger on the trigger. Good. Now start squeezing the trigger back toward yourself. Don't jerk on it. Just squeeze it back. And whatever you do, don't drop the gun."

She tried. The trigger took more force to squeeze back than she imagined it would. Then, as it started to move back, she anticipated the bang. Her arms started to shake. Grimly, she kept the gun pointed at the rocks but she couldn't make herself squeeze on the trigger.

"That's all right," he said. "We'll do it together. I'm going to stand behind you and help."

He stepped behind her, extended his arms around her shoulders, and put his hands on hers, steadying her aim.

To her astonishment, having Cole so close to her back that she could feel his body heat and the brush of his uniform against her blouse gave her a pleasant feeling of security. While she reveled in the sensation, Cole lay his right forefinger over hers and pulled the trigger.

Simultaneous with a sound that made her jump, the gun kicked back in her hands and the rocks emitted a spit of white dust, right in the middle of the pile.

"You tricked me," Leila said. "You didn't tell me when!"

Cole chuckled and she could feel the deep thrum in his chest. She decided leaning back against that broad chest would be taking advantage and just stood there, enjoying the sensation of being held without being restrained.

She gritted her teeth against the thrumming in her wrists. "I can do this myself if you just stand there," she said.

He dropped his arms and she steadied the gun and focused through the sights at the rocks beyond. She still had to fight her fears in order to draw the trigger smoothly back, but she did it. Again, the loud clap of sound and the kick. This time the rock dust puffed up lower on the pile of rocks, and to the right.

"That's great," he said, and sounded like he meant it.

"Now the next time, I want you to point the muzzle at the ground, and when I tell you 'Go' you need to raise it up, find the sight picture, and pull the trigger. Got it?"

She nodded, concentrating too hard to verbalize a reply, and lowered the gun.

"Take a few deep breaths," he said.

In the middle of the third breath he told her to go.

She whipped the gun up and pulled the trigger. No puff of rock dust answered the report of the round.

"Why'd I miss?"

"You hurried," he said. "Never hurry with a gun. This next time, I want you to pretend you're doing everything in slow motion. Point the muzzle back at the ground. And take a few deep breaths."

"Go," he said.

She concentrated on relaxing, on moving as slowly and smoothly as possible. The muzzle floated up. There was plenty of time to consider the sight picture, to decide when to squeeze the trigger.

"Excellent," Cole said. "Still low and to the right, but very acceptable."

"But it was so slow," Leila said.

"But it wasn't," Cole replied. "If I had a working watch right now I could show you. That was only about a half second difference. But the other difference is that you hit it. Now, I want you to do that three more times and then we'll head back."

"Why three?"

He remained silent. After a minute she figured it out.

"There are three rounds left," she said.

She hit the rock pile two out of three more times and Cole declared himself satisfied.

Leila's arms ached, her hands buzzed, and her ears rang, but she, too, was satisfied.

CHAPTER FIFTEEN

The dead silent house warned Leila first. With Cole gone in a hurry, Leila felt the weight of the gun at her hip pulling her over to the right. The hush in the house stripped the pleasurable glow of learning, leaving her cold and fearful. The past days' experience kicked in at the thought. She acknowledged the house was talking to her and refused to listen.

She narrowed her eyes and glared at the thick air, then marched through the living room and tackled the stairs.

Guilt and worry over leaving the kids alone so long propelled her up the stairs with no heed given to the gust of cold which wanted to force her back. As she made the top of the second flight, an emphatic thump and a high-pitched cry of distress made her wince.

She burst into the room without knocking and took in the chaos at a glance. Before her, two boys lay in a tangle on the ground. Rain had Ray by the hair. Ray struggled, one hand on Rain's, trying to ease the pressure on his hair, the other hand snaking around Rain's throat. Sleet stood above them, kicking indiscriminately into the fight. Leila looked around for Storm and saw her huddled miserably against the west wall, the stain on that wall seeming to drip down onto the girl's fair hair.

"Quit it!" Leila yelled at the boys.

Sleet glanced over his shoulder at her.

"Yeah, break it up," he said, and resumed kicking his brothers where they lay.

Leila strode across the room, filled with purpose, and bent down to sort the boys out. She grabbed Rain's hand and tried to pry it loose from Ray's hair. The shock of impact and a sharp pain in her calf informed her Sleet had kicked her, too.

"Stop it, Sleet," she said. "Stop kicking."

"I'm sorry, I missed." He said.

Leila made no progress with releasing Rain's grip. She looked for his face and saw it, contorted, purplish, and determined. A glance at his neck showed Ray's arm twisted around it in a choke hold.

"Ray! Quit choking him. Rain! Let go of his hair."

Her shouted commands made no difference.

With strength Leila would have sworn could not have come from such a slight boy, Rain bucked and pushed with his legs until Ray flipped over—right into Leila. She fell, all 150 pounds of her, right on top of the boys.

"Uh," Ray grunted as her weight expelled all the air from his lungs. Rain went limp at the same time.

Leila started scrabbling to get off the dog pile, trying hard not to gag at the smell of Rain's body at close quarters. Sleet grabbed her forearm and leaned his weight backward. The added force allowed Leila to roll off the boys and regain her feet.

Ray pushed his brother's limp body off of him onto the floor where Rain's head hit the plywood floor with a hollow thump. Leila cried out a protest at the sound.

231

"S'allright," Ray said, scrubbing at the place on his scalp where the hair had been pulled. "We hit each other harder than that all the time."

Leila rushed to Rain's side, swallowing hard to calm her gag reflex.

"Why did he pass out? Is he all right?" She asked.

"Well, I was choking him out and then you jumped on top of him. He didn't have any air," Ray replied as she checked Rain's breathing.

Rain lay still and limp, but his breaths came strong and even.

"He'll be all right," Ray said. "Just needs a minute to come to."

"Oh damn," Leila said. "What a mess."

She looked at Storm, still huddled against the wall.

"Come here, darling. It's all right," she said, and opened her arms.

Storm considered her. As usual, the girl's blank face told no stories. Then she uncurled and trotted over to Leila, who wrapped her arms around Storm and rocked her.

As she rocked, Leila thought a breath of air moved through the room, like a monumental sigh. Rain began to stir, moving his head from side to side.

"So," she said after a minute. "What happened?"

"I wasn't trying to hurt him," Ray said.

"I think I asked that question wrong," Leila said, and turned to Sleet. "Sleet, what happened?"

"We wanted to be with Rain," Sleet said. "'Cause we were worried."

She waited for him to continue, but he acted as though that

explanation of events should be perfectly clear. Leila frowned and tried again.

"So you came upstairs…then what happened?"

"Rain came out? He knew you were talking—you and Cole—but we didn't know what was going on."

"I'm sorry," Leila said. "I'm sorry I didn't come up here and tell you kids what was happening."

"Yeah," Ray said. "That makes it all right. Just say you're sorry."

"What?" Leila asked. "That's the longest you can go, Ray, without making an ass of yourself?"

"Who's the ass?" Ray asked.

"Yeah," Leila said. "I screwed up! Now who was the one choking his little brother?"

"You have no idea…" Ray began, when Sleet walked over to where Ray sat and kicked him, hard, in the thigh.

"Hey! Knock it off," Ray said.

You knock it off," Sleet said. His little-boy voice broke with the force of his ferocious tone.

"I don't have to knock it off," Ray said, his deeper voice cracking as he began to yell. "I'm sick of this! I'm the oldest. I should be able to make the rules stick."

"Hey!" Leila yelled. She felt the situation sliding out of control. Ray and Sleet turned to look at her. "Hey," she said again. "What rule did Rain break?"

A hoarse, weak voice replied from beside her. "I hit Storm."

At the pronouncement, Storm's arms tightened around Leila's neck. She turned against the pressure, feeling half-choked herself, and met Rain's gaze. Like the first time she saw him lying on the floor under Ray, something about his steady eye contact made him seem ageless.

"Why did you hit her, Rain?"

"Because she was hugging the wall."

Ray drew in a sharp breath like he'd been hit.

Leila's brain started parsing this statement when a series of short, sharp barks announced Sophie wanted to be let in.

"I'll let her in," Sleet said quickly, and headed out. "Don't say anything while I'm gone," he called over his shoulder.

Leila turned back to Rain. She noticed the sweet curve of his little boy cheekbone and how it contrasted with the depth of understanding in his eyes.

"I don't understand, Rain. Hugging the wall is a little bizarre. But why hit her?"

"We don't hug the wall. We want to, but it's a stupid way to…"

Two things happened at once. Ray exploded into action, driving himself forward toward Leila, Storm, and Rain. Simultaneously, Sleet came pounding back up the stairs with Sophie on his heels.

"What'd I miss?" Sleet demanded, just as Ray tackled the supine Rain, pinning him to the floor. Ray immediately slapped a hand across Rain's mouth.

Rain winced and squirmed, but his eyes never left Leila's. Instead of pain or panic, Leila thought he just looked tired.

Sleet charged into the room and cannonballed into Ray. "Get off! Get off my brother," he yelled, and bowled Ray over.

Sophie jumped into the fray, her paws landing on the floor once, then shoulder muscles bulging and flexing as she took off again to land between Rain and Ray. She growled at Ray and his enraged expression changed. His face, caught in that awkward stage between childhood and adulthood, sagged into an expression of defeat.

Leila couldn't stand sitting there another moment. She got up, Storm still wrapped around her, and began to pace in the only space clear of boys and dog—against the west wall. As if her actions called it, the house started to act up.

The floor undulated under Leila's feet. The walls pressed in on her, pressed in on her as if they wanted to crush her to death. She shook her head and kept pacing. As she walked past the middle of the wall she heard a distant woman's voice screaming, screaming. Storm's arms and legs tightened where they were wrapped around Leila's neck and body.

The voice faded and in two more paces Leila reached the corner and spun, staggering a little with vertigo. But the urgent need to dispel some of the physical tension of the conflict kept her pacing. Moving toward the far wall took effort, as if a giant hand pressed on her.

With each step the pressure grew and with it a sense of doom. In two steps she dimly heard the woman screaming again, screaming as though her heart were breaking along with her body. Then Leila reached the center of the room and the floor tilted down as if trying to pour her toward the far wall. The sudden shift of perspective staggered Leila. She put a hand out to steady herself on the wall and touched the stain which marred it.

235

Without transition she could hear the woman screaming inside her head so loudly she couldn't think. Terror and despair and pain flooded into Leila. She snatched her hand from the wall and instead tried to loosen Storm's death grip on her neck.

Storm's little arm was wet and slippery where Leila grabbed it. She reached up to her face and felt a stream of tears running down her cheeks. And the screaming went on.

"Make it stop," Leila gasped through her sobs.

Hearing her distress, Sophie came over and nuzzled Leila's left hand.

A thought occurred to Leila just as Sophie clawed once at the wall and whined.

She listened, listened to the screaming and to her own thoughts.

She walked away from the wall. The woman screamed once more and then was silent.

Leila stood in the middle of the room, put both arms around Storm, and rocked her. She began humming the only song she could remember from her visits to temple as a child, wishing she knew what the Hebrew words meant. Storm began to relax and Leila looked up at the boys. They watched her as she imagined they might watch a knot of snakes on the floor—all wide-eyed and frozen with some hidden emotion.

"I'm going to put you down, Storm," she said. "Can I put you down?"

Storm released her grip and Leila lowered her to the floor.

She resumed humming. She might not know what the words meant, but the tune sounded mournful, peaceful, and worshipful.

Slowly, still humming, Leila walked back to the stain on the west wall. The screaming sounded more distant this time. She hummed the melody like it was a lullaby for the screaming woman, and kicked the wall hard.

Rotten sheetrock crumbled at the impact and all hell broke loose.

The woman's screaming filled the room with desperation, despair, agony. Leila clapped her hands to her ears and looked around at the children. Hands over their ears, all four of them moved toward Leila in slow motion, their faces reflecting the misery of the screaming. The slow motion nature of the children's charge warned Leila the house was pissed.

A concussive noise, loud as a gunshot, filled the room. Leila jumped and screamed but then couldn't hear her own scream over the continuous wail of the other woman.

She looked to the door and saw the source of the noise. The door had slammed shut. A crack now ran vertically through the cheap wood.

The children still slogged their slow, frantic way toward Leila. She wondered if she, too, were moving in slow motion, and what the children would do when they got to her, but her speculation ended when a cold wind kicked up.

At first her mind tried to discount the sensation of air moving on her face. But the force of hot moving air increased moment by moment, picking up the debris of neglect on the floor and throwing it into the air. With no outlet, the gale swirled around and around the room, colored brown with dirt. The particles stung Leila's face and got in her eyes. She didn't realize her mouth hung open until she could feel dust coating her tongue. She closed her mouth, wanting to spit but too tired to try.

She looked up at the tormented children. Ray, always first, was reaching out to grab at her. She remembered the gun for the first time and a sense of rightness settled into a single idea—if she shot the children she could lie down and rest.

She reached for the gun at her hip and as her hand traveled down, down, she saw Ray's eyes open wide in fearful realization. His fear shook her certainty. Just as this small crack of doubt about her plan crept in, something made her left foot go out from underneath her. She fell heavily to one knee, caught herself from falling further, and looked around. Behind her, Sophie crouched on the floor, paws braced, teeth latched onto Leila's pant leg. The sight of the dog, eyes slitted and teeth showing in a soundless growl, snapped Leila out of herself.

She thought of throwing the gun away from her and decided against it, seeing how easily it could be picked up by one of the boys. Instead, she checked that the leather strap over the top was firmly snapped and abandoned herself to the children's fury.

As they crossed the last little distance to her, she observed their fury and grief and threw away her fear. She opened her arms wide, as if to embrace all four of them, and waited for the onslaught.

Ray hit her and she wrapped an arm around him with all the tenderness she possessed. She held him as he pounded her ribs with both fists. She kept her left arm flung wide despite her urge to curl up and protect herself. Sleet and Rain dove into her, knocking her head back into the wall.

She wrapped her left arm as far as she could around the twins and held them, too, as they tore at her blouse and butted her with their heads. Storm landed on the dog pile last, worming her way through the furious tangle of her brothers to also get at Leila.

As they attacked her, she held them with her arms and held them in her mind, held them with a ferocious love that swelled inside of her until she heard herself screaming.

"I love you! I love you all! I love you!"

The unnatural wind stopped as suddenly as it began. The woman stopped screaming. The sound of all the suspended particles in the air hitting the floor at once made her want to laugh.

With the death of the superheated wind, the fight went out of the children. They relaxed in her arms. Ray stopped fighting last but even he went limp after a few more seconds. She could barely breathe under their combined weight. It felt like the best thing in the world.

"I love you," she chanted. "I love you, I love you, I love you all."

Ray began to cry. He rested his forehead on her shoulder and cried like a much younger child. Rain and Sleet each wrapped an arm around her and another around each other and began to sob as well. Leila held them as they grieved, stroking their backs, then froze when another sound joined in. Storm began to wail, screaming in short, sharp bursts, like a baby might cry when hurt.

Leila joined them. She cried for their pain and loss. She cried for their mother's agony. She cried for herself, for all the years of her abuse, for the young woman locked away inside herself.

Finally, she found she was crying with relief at being able to feel something other than fear.

At some point, as the tears began to ease, she realized her left leg was folded back at the knee underneath her. All she could feel was a painful tingling. Sophie began to lick them indiscriminately, as if to say, "Okay, you can get up and be all right now."

She squeezed the children tightly, regretting the need to untangle from their embraces.

"I can't feel my leg," she said.

Rain, on her left side, looked down.

"Oh my God," he said, and jumped up. "Hey, guys, get off her." He reached down as punctuation to his words and yanked at his twin's shirt, producing a ripping sound which made Leila wince.

The boys untangled themselves and eased off Leila. Storm's shrieks eased off into sniffling and shuddering so hard it shook Leila's torso. She wouldn't let go. Each boy exclaimed when they saw the awkward position of Leila's left leg. Ray swore.

"I don't think it's broken," Leila told the boys. "But it's definitely asleep. I can't get up with Storm on me."

"Okay, okay, we can fix this," Ray said. "Wrap your arms around Storm. We're gonna have to roll you over so we can straighten out your leg."

She wrapped her arms around Storm and bent her head to bury her nose in the girl's hair and kiss her head. All three boys gathered on her left side and began to push her over.

"Ow!" Leila said when they pushed.

The gun, still firmly strapped to her right side, bruised her when they tried to roll her.

"Quit!" Sleet said, "We're hurting her!"

Rain crawled over Leila's leg to see what was holding up the operation.

"She's wearing a gun," he reported.

"A gun?" Sleet asked, and hopped over Leila's leg to see for himself. "Where'd you get it?"

Ray let out an impatient sigh. "We can talk about the gun later. Let's just get it off so we can roll her."

Rain reached for the gun and Leila hissed at him and waved his hand away.

"Don't touch it," she said. "Don't you know that?"

She reached down to remove it from the holster and froze at the memory of how close they had all come…but the pain in her leg kept increasing and she forced herself to touch the damned thing, remove it from the holster, and slide it away from her body.

They rolled her over easily then, and Ray lifted her left thigh while Sleet and Rain unbent her left leg. Despite their care, she still cried out as her knee joint protested the change in position. After that, the real pain came. She lay there and tried to breathe evenly and not cry as warmth and sensation rushed back into the leg.

As a distraction, she thought about what they should do next. Everything she thought of required talking to the children about their horrible trauma. She turned over questions in her head, checking each one for soundness and then abandoning it. Rain saved her.

"I was here," he said. "When he killed her."

"Shut up," Ray said reflexively. "You don't have to talk about it."

Rain looked at Ray but it was Sleet, who didn't even look up from where he was massaging Leila's calf, who answered.

"Yeah, he does have to talk about it. He can talk if he wants to."

Ray dipped his head at Rain and answered him as if Sleet had not spoken. "Okay, then."

Leila turned her head to look Rain full in the face. Tears of pain spilled from her eyes and ran down to make salty mud on the plywood floor.

"Is that what you wanted to tell me, Rain? That you saw what happened?"

"Yeah," he said. "I saw what happened."

"Do you want to talk about it?"

He shivered. "No. That's all."

"Rain?" She almost whispered his name but he looked back up at her as though she had shouted. "Is that why you've lived in the closet all this time?"

"I couldn't just leave her," Rain said.

"You're such a good boy," Leila told him, and reached out and touched his knee. "You're such a sweet boy."

He grabbed her hand and held it, his head hanging. She felt a tear hit the back of her hand.

Leila turned to Ray. "I need your help here. There are so many things I don't know."

"Okay," he said, looking stiff and frightened.

"What is…was your mother's name?"

"Maria," he said. "Her name was Maria."

"What a beautiful name," she said. "And unique, like you kids'."

"My name is actually Sun Ray," he replied. "I just always hated it. It's so…dorky."

"It's a beautiful name," Leila said. "Sun Ray. Maria must have had great hope and love, to name you something so beautiful."

"I never asked her," Ray said. "I was always so mad at her." He began to cry again. "I hated her," he said through his tears.

"I know," Leila said, feeling tired. "I understand."

She thought of all the years she despised herself, despised herself for living with Stu, despised herself because she believed he was right to abuse her, despised herself for her despise.

"What should we do next?" Leila asked the ceiling.

"We need to set her free," Sleet said, looking pale and determined.

"That sounds right to me," Leila said. "But everyone has to agree. Rain?"

"Yeah," Rain said.

"Ray?" Leila asked.

"Yes."

"Well, then…" Leila began.

She stopped as Storm lifted her head from where it nestled on Leila's chest and looked Leila full in the eyes.

"Mama,"   Storm   said.

CHAPTER SIXTEEN

⬜ An agonizing half hour later, Leila thought her leg might hold her weight. Long since bored by snuggling, Storm now sat with her brothers and amused herself by drawing in the dirt with a forefinger.

"You need some Crayons, kid," Leila said.

The boys helped her get to her feet—a graceless process which left her sweating from exertion and pain. Ray insisted on helping her with her first steps, a measure she thought unnecessary until she put her full weight on her left foot and almost fell.

"My knee's all wobbly," she told the boys.

"Does it still hurt?" Sleet wanted to know.

"Yeah. But mostly when I try to walk on it."

She couldn't bend down to pick up the gun. Not without falling on her face.

"Ray? Do you know how to pick that up right?"

"Yeah," Ray said, and scooped the weapon up by the handle, keeping the barrel pointed away from people at all times.

"Great," she said, taking the gun and holstering it.

She dreaded the next step, but kept her voice steady.

"Now what we need is a nice sheet, or a blanket or something like that."

"Why?" Ray wanted to know.

"Because…" she gulped and tried again. "Because Maria needs something nice to lie on."

"Are you kids sure you don't want someone else to free her for us? There are…official people who would love to help."

"Are you chickening out on us?" Asked Ray. "You think we don't know? You think we've been staring at that wall all this time and—" He broke off, unable or unwilling to continue.

"I'm sorry, Ray," Leila said. "I should have thought. So." She looked around. "Who's bringing me the blanket?"

Sleet looked at Rain. "Do you think we should…"

"Yeah," Rain said. "I think it's perfect."

Sleet ran out of the room. Everyone stood and contemplated the wall, the stain, the hole opening onto darkness where Leila had kicked it. In a minute Sleet returned, head tipped up to see over the enormous patchwork quilt which filled his arms.

"Mom never let us use this," Sleet said.

"She said it was her grandmother's," Rain said.

Leila took the quilt from Sleet and stroked the faded colors, felt the individuality of each hand-stitched seam.

"This is perfect," she told the boys.

With a mental apology to the quilt, she spread it out face down on the dusty floor. Storm astonished Leila by trotting up and helping straighten the far edges.

"Okay, now the wall," she told the children. "And no fighting. She doesn't need the squabbling right now. In fact—I think I'll sing to her." Leila began to hum the same tune she used earlier, and reached down, her knee barely supporting the effort, put her hand into the dark hole, and pulled. The texture of the interior made her skin crawl.

A big chunk of sheetrock came free and light shone in on a pair of shin bones draped in scraps of skin. Leila's humming faltered and then she resumed. She stepped back and nodded at the children.

Ray reached in next and tenderly removed a chunk of the wall. Sleet and Rain stepped up and broke more away and then Storm was shouldering her brothers aside and pulling at the wall with more enthusiasm than technique.

Maria's skeletal form began to be revealed. The dry Wyoming air had acted as a preservative, keeping some bits of flesh and skin intact so the skeleton was not completely naked.

The kids worked higher, exposing the upper leg bones. Now Leila saw Bill had built more space into the wall than walls usually have. The separating boards must have been a foot deep and they framed Maria's body, holding her upright. The children's hands tore at the wall and Leila saw the pelvis that had cradled four children in pregnancy. A deep crack ran through one side of it. Around her waist, a rope held her in place.

Leila stopped humming and began whispering.

"I'm sorry. I'm so sorry. We love you. I'm sorry."

"Mama," Storm said again.

The boys joined in, murmuring their love and regret and sorrow as they reached higher and higher.

Another rope bound her neck, the skull sagging to one side. Rain became agitated.

"Cut the ropes. Please cut the ropes off."

"Some one run to the kitchen and get a knife," Leila said.

246

"S'allright," Ray said, and pulled the curved knife out of his pocket.

They sawed at the rope around her neck first as it offended them most. As the rope parted, Maria's upper body fell forward. Leila stepped into the crowd of children without thinking of the macabre nature of the situation, and caught her as she buckled. The upper body came free at the waist and Leila lowered it to the quilt.

"I suppose there was no other way," Leila said.

"No," Ray replied. "It's all right."

Rain put a hand on her wrist and squeezed.

They got the second rope off. The rest of their task went silently. They collected as much of her as they could and laid it all out on the blanket.

The ugliness Leila anticipated from removing Maria from the wall never materialized.

They stood back and looked at the remains. The boys cried without wiping their tears. A tiny vertical line appeared between Storm's eyebrows as she gazed down. Leila tried to kneel at Maria's side but her knee still wouldn't work right. The children all sat down, though. Sophie, who remained well out of the way, whined until Ray reached back and laid a hand on her neck.

Leila leaned against the south wall to take the weight off her knee and waited while the kids communed with their mother. A period of restful quiet ended with a subtle change of the emotional temperature of the room—like light from a window changing without fanfare from late afternoon light to early evening light.

247

"Say goodbye," she told the children, "and we'll wrap her up so she can rest."

"Goodbye," Ray said. "I didn't really hate you. I love you."

Sleet and Rain spoke the single word in unison, and reached out to touch their mother for the last time.

"Mama," Storm said a final time.

"Tuck her in. Wrap her up good," Leila whispered.

They each took a corner and covered Maria's body into a snug cocoon. Rain began to wail.

"Do you know what she needs now?" Leila asked. They looked up at her, faces begging for direction through their grief.

"She needs flowers."

In silent agreement, the children filed from the room. Rain hesitated at the door, then walked out, head held high. Leila looked back one more time as she waited for a subdued Sophie to trail through the door.

"I'm sorry."

She closed the door gently and followed the children downstairs, wishing for a bannister as she leaned against the wall to get down the stairs.

The open front door challenged Rain. She saw tension and longing in his pale face.

"How long since you've been outside?" Leila asked.

"Since...since before," he said.

"Can you do this?"

"I'm afraid," Rain said.

"I'm having trouble walking. Could I lean on you?"

Leila leaned on Rain as they walked through the door, and

Rain clung to Leila.

Outside, Rain blinked and shaded his eyes.

"You can't stay outside long," Leila told him. "You'll burn."

He nodded and went in search of wildflowers. Leila stood and breathed the fresh air, her face turned up to the sky.

A weight she had not known lay on her lifted. She opened her eyes and watched as all the children wandered through the field, walking slowly, stopping, bending. Each child returned in their own time, hands full of flowers. Rain came back first, sagging with exhaustion. Leila reassured him.

"You haven't gotten any exercise in a long time," she said. "You'll get stronger."

Leila sent the children upstairs to cover their mother with flowers. By the time they got downstairs, she had hot chocolate ready. They sat around the table and sipped and talked about what they remembered of their mother.

Exhausted from his outing, Rain went upstairs to rest in the only place he felt safe. Leila sat with the kids in the living room and read to them out of the first book she found—"My Friend Flicka."

In the evening, Leila talked Rain into a shower, to her utter relief, and later, all four kids slept on the floor of the master bedroom with her. Sophie chose a place between the children and the door, curled in circles, then flopped down with a sigh.

The ghost of bad dreams crept up on Leila periodically through the night. Each time she woke she cuddled Storm closer to her chest, felt Sleet's warmth against her back, and fell back into dreamless sleep.

At breakfast the four children made noise, laughed, and even threw little pieces of bread at each other.

The crunch of car tires in the drive ended all hilarity. Leila looked toward the door and looked back at the children. Rain's empty spot at the table glared back at her. Ray got up, dumped the food off Rain's plate, and rinsed the plate. Sleet scooted over on the bench to sit in the middle. Their simple actions revealed to Leila how they had hidden Rain's presence from her for so many days. Ray's discipline, Sleet's commitment, Storm's silence.

Leila wished again for a window looking out on the driveway. She missed Sophie's barking but the dog was out doing whatever dogs do in the morning. The children shrunk in on themselves and Leila wanted to follow suit.

Footsteps crunched toward the door.

"Ray," Leila breathed. "Go open the door and stand behind it."

She reached down to the gun she had slept with and belted back on first thing in the morning.

She backed halfway through the kitchen until the distance to the door felt right, and unsnapped the strap holding the gun in the holster. Ray swung the door open and Sophie trotted in, grinning. Behind her, Cole paused at the threshold, just where the shadow of the house allowed him to see inside.

"Good," he said. "But don't shoot me."

He looked to see who opened the door, spotted Ray half hidden behind it, and greeted the boy cheerfully.

"How is everyone?" Cole asked into an awkward silence.

Leila began to smile at Cole, had a thought, turned white, and sat down, almost missing the end of the bench.

"I think you're going to be very, very angry with me," she said.

The thought of a large man directing anger at her made her quiver.

"What's the matter?" Cole asked.

"Something really wonderful happened yesterday. Some things, really. But you're going to hate me."

"Okay." Cole drew out the word. "Why don't you just tell me, and I'll be the judge?"

"I think I have to show you." Leila turned to the silent children. "Is it okay with you guys?"

Ray understood first and gave her a curt nod. At Ray's look Sleet gave Leila his one-shouldered shrug. Storm's wide-eyed gaze revealed nothing.

"Okay," Leila said. "Come on."

She walked toward the stairs with Cole on her heels. Sophie started to follow.

"No, Sophie," Leila said. "Stay with the kids." She motioned at the kitchen and the dog gave her a look but turned back.

Leila tried the first step up the stairs and found she couldn't do it.

"What happened to your leg?" Cole asked.

"Long story. I think I hurt it bad, though."

He took her arm and passed it around his waist. "Can you make it like this?"

She nodded and braced herself for the psychic difficulty of climbing the stairs. There was no sensation of resistance, however, as they climbed. She turned to Cole at the top of the stairs. He stopped and she saw his nostrils flare as they had when he first entered the house. After a minute of scenting the house, his upper lip curled a little and his face went still.

"I know that smell," he said. "Please don't tell me that..."

Leila turned and walked to Rain's room. The soft, colorful quilt glowed in the illumination of the north-facing window, contrasting the ugly darkness of the ragged hole in the wall. Wilted wildflowers covered the top of the quilt and surrounded Maria's body.

Cole stopped and inhaled sharply.

"Is that what I think it is?"

"Maria." Leila said.

"Oh God." Cole grabbed the door jamb, the same one Leila slid gracelessly down earlier in the week.

"Oh God," he repeated. "She was walled up?"

Leila nodded.

"And you figured it out. And then you fucking tore the wall down and took her out?" His voice rose.

"You..." His voice contained venom.

Leila shrank back. She couldn't help it.

With a visible effort, Cole gathered himself. He began talking, his voice hard as his face.

"It is a crime to disturb a murder scene. I could arrest you right here. But never mind that. Never mind. Because what concerns me. What really concerns me, is how we're going to prosecute Bill now. Do you know how hard it is to nail someone in trial when the crime scene has been this badly disturbed? Do you? No? If he gets away with this...if he gets away..." Cole trailed off, the expression on his face halfway between tears and rage. He spun on one heel, and stalked down the stairs. Leila drew in a shuddering breath and waited to follow until her legs steadied, then limped down the stairs, left knee throbbing at each step.

The kids sat at the table, scooping up food, not looking at each other.

"Where is he?" Leila asked.

Ray avoided her eyes.

"He left," Sleet said with his mouth full.

Leila cried out in frustration.

"Are you gonna finish that?" Sleet gestured at her half-eaten plate.

"No."

"Good. 'Cause I think Rain's still hungry."

"Whatever," she said, and leaned back against the counter. "Whatever."

Rain reemerged to eat Leila's breakfast while she leaned against the counter and fretted over all the things she had not said to Cole. The confines of the house pressed around her mind.

"I've gotta get out of here for a while," she said to no one in particular.

"That's cool," Sleet replied. "Let's go for a walk..."

"...to the barn," Rain whispered.

"Are you sure..." Ray began, but Sleet and Rain ignored him and began clearing dishes off the table.

Storm's expression changed, where she knelt on the bench at the table. The little furrow which grew between her brows and the narrowing of her eyes shouted to Leila that change was coming.

"Barn," Storm said.

Her sour mood forgotten, Leila cheered and swept the girl into the air.

"Good! Yes! Barn is right. We're going to the barn."

The slightest wisp of a smile appeared and disappeared on Storm's face.

Fifty feet away from the house, her left knee began to shoot pain up her leg with each step. She looked up from the ground, realizing she was planning every step to spare her knee.

Sleet and Rain walked hand in hand ahead of her. Rain kept pointing at things and exclaiming, as if his sight had just returned. Off to the south, Storm bent over and peered at something on the ground Sophie was investigating. Ray stood over them both. His pose recalled that of a soldier on guard.

She gritted her teeth, stiffened her left leg, and kept limping along.

Three quarters of the way to the barn, worry over the distracting pain and weakness in her knee found a new worry to join up with. Rain began to stumble in exhaustion.

"Maybe this is far enough for today," she said. "I think Rain's getting tired."

"No!" Rain said. "I can make it."

"It's not a contest," she replied, just as Ray spoke.

"You're too weak," Ray said. "She's right. We should go back."

Rain stopped walking and straightened up. "I need. To go. I've got to check on him."

254

Ray looked at Sleet for support. At the look, Sleet stepped closer to his brother and Rain put an arm around Sleet's shoulder. They both stared at Ray with defiance.

"Okay," Ray said. "It's your funeral."

Leila shivered at his choice of words.

They kept trudging. She grew tired just watching Rain struggle forward with his brother's help. Her knee now hurt whether her weight was on it or not.

She began to sweat from the pain and she could no longer hide the limp from the kids, but the halfway point lay far behind them. Ray came up on her weak side when she paused.

"Lean on me," he said. She looked up at him and saw he understood how hard walking had become.

"Thanks, Ray." She put an arm over his shoulders and he walked with her.

Again she looked around for Storm, who kept getting sidetracked by interesting things on the ground. The girl had her arm slung over Sophie's back as they trailed along. Sophie looked thrilled with the arrangement and stepped carefully forward to accommodate the girl's short stride.

"Ever ridden a horse?" Ray asked Leila.

"No. I always wanted to…"

"You're going to get to today," he said.

Leila thought of their last trip to the barn, of the dark, darting head of the horse that bit Sleet, and shook her head.

"I think I can make it back if I rest at the barn," she said.

"Riiiiight," Ray said.

When she looked, she saw his face broken out in sweat with

255

the effort of holding her up.

They reached the barn. Leila and Rain both leaned up against the warmth of the eastern wall, ignoring the long splinters of the weathered wood. Sleet's pale face showed the strain of the walk. Her blue jeans now tight with the swelling in her knee, Leila leaned on the barn, breathing heavily, and wishing they hadn't come.

Ray looked at her knee and frowned.

"There should be leg wrap in the barn," he said, and then, at Leila's questioning glance, he elaborated. "It's like ace bandages for horses."

"Thanks, Ray. All right," she said, "let's go see some horses. Just not the one in the first stall."

Ray pulled the door open and they slipped in one by one. As Rain passed, Ray grabbed his shoulder and whispered in his ear. Rain shot him a disdainful look and shrugged off his brother's hand. Ray saw Leila looking. He gave her an apologetic-looking shrug.

The hushed interior of the barn combined with the dim lighting and warm, horsey smell to calm Leila. She stood and soaked up the atmosphere, letting her shoulders relax. Some of the pain seeped out of her knee into the soft footing of dust and chaff on the floor.

Sleet grabbed Leila's hand, and turned to hold Storm's hand as well.

"Come on," he said, "I'll show you a good horse you can pet."

He pulled them down the aisle. Toward the other end of the barn a horse poked its head over the half door and turned to gaze at them. The window behind the animal backlit the delicate hair on its head, making its outlines glow a deep red.

"Oh, how beautiful," Leila said.

As they neared, Leila began to pick out more detail. A small white star on the horse's red forehead. The long whiskers on its wrinkled muzzle...

"Why is its nose so wrinkly?"

He's old," Sleet replied, voice hushed. "His name is Fire. But we call him Steady."

Steady's nostrils flared as he stretched his neck toward Leila, and a great puff of warm, sweet-smelling air flattened her shirt and warmed her neck. Behind them, she heard a hoof strike wood, a dull thud which barely registered as she reached out and stroked the horse's face. His eyes half-closed and he lowered his head into her hand.

Caught in the moment, Leila's heart slowed. Then an enraged squeal followed by a thud which shook dust from the rafters startled Leila into jumping. She almost fell when she came down on her left leg, and she did cry out, half in pain, half in fear.

Rain stood up against the half door of Demon's stall, gripping the top of the door with both hands. Leila shook with anxiety, considered her options, and realized she could do nothing.

She anticipated the attacking rush and it came, the sound of a thousand pounds of flesh driving forward on small hooves. Demon's head darted forward into the light, ears pinned back, nostrils flared.

Rain stood his ground. The script playing out in her head changed. The horse checked its attack. For a split second, boy and horse stood frozen. Then Demon's ears appeared out of his mane. They flicked straight forward. A low nicker filled the barn and Demon pressed up against the half door and lowered his head against Rain's side. Rain laughed, the first time she heard him do so.

Ray pursed his lips and blew out the breath he had been holding. Leila realized she should also begin breathing again.

"See?" Sleet said. "Demon is Rain's horse. He was always real mean. Except to Rain."

Ray walked away from the reunion scene.

"Why's he so mean?" Leila asked.

"When dad got mad at Rain he used to make him watch when he beat Demon," Ray said.

Leila's gut clenched and acid heat burned her stomach.

"They'll be all right, now," Sleet said. "Is that why you're wearing a gun now? So you can kill him?"

His hope sounded pitiful, and posed a question Leila was not ready to face.

She pictured Maria's body. She imagined Bill torturing Rain by beating his horse. She saw again the black bruise on the side of Sleet's face.

Ray and Sleet waited on her answer.

"I...I will do whatever I have to. To protect us."

The boys nodded as though her answer satisfied them.

Rain slipped into the stall with Demon, murmuring to the horse all the while. A few moments later he called out.

"Everybody look out!"

Ray swore and pulled Leila back against Steady's stall just as

Demon came trotting out of the stall with little Rain on his bare back.

"You don't even have a bridle, you idiot," Ray called out.

"Don't need one," Sleet called back. "I'm just going to ride him in here for a few minutes."

"Does anyone else think this is a bad idea?" Leila asked.

"Of course it is," Ray said.

"He's fine," Sleet said.

"We should do something," she said.

"Sure!" Ray replied. "Why don't you just walk over there and take him off Demon."

Leila didn't like his sarcasm but saw his point.

Demon stood foursquare in the middle of the aisle, head high, ears pricked, and surveyed the barn. From her safe distance, Leila drank in the sight of Rain, looking taller and more relaxed than she had ever seen him. Rain saw her looking and laughed again. He nudged the horse forward and Demon lowered his head and walked toward them. Sleet squeezed Leila's hand and smiled up at her.

"He's back," Sleet said. "Thank you."

Leila pondered her reply. Her thanks to the children ran just as deep as the gratitude Sleet just expressed. She opened her mouth to say so and closed it again, jaw tight, as she heard the rumble of a truck approaching the barn.

Demon broke into a trot at the sound, tail high, ears flicking, and somehow Rain made him turn in place when he reached the end of the barn. They stood in a group, Leila, Storm, Sleet, and Ray, with Demon and Rain flanking them, and stared down the length of the barn. No one spoke, but Leila knew from the trembling in Sleet's hand and the tension in Ray's shoulders that they all dreaded Bill's return as much as she.

After the truck engine shut off, after they heard boots hit the ground and begin moving toward the barn door. Only as the big sliding door began to be pulled open with a glare of light did Leila remember the gun. She put her right hand on it and popped the snap open.

The dark figure, silhouetted by the sun, put a shoulder to the sliding door and pushed it all the way open. Leila blinked rapidly, willing her eyes to adjust to the flood of light. Beside her and above her, she heard Rain's rapid breathing catch as if he were about to start sobbing.

"No. I can't," Rain whispered.

The sliding door clanged to a stop, the man turned toward them, and Demon took off at a dead run, Rain bent over the horse's neck with his fingers wrapped in the tossing sea of mane. Sophie took off after the charging horse, barking.

"Oh shit," yelled the man at the far end.

Leila recognized the voice. Jimmy.

"Rain! Stop!" She yelled. "It's Jimmy!"

She realized he didn't know Jimmy. The hand had only worked for Bill for six months.

"Stop! It's okay, Rain!"

"I can't," Rain called back. "He's running away."

Jimmy dived out of the way of the charging horse. Demon whipped through the open door, Rain looking small on his back. Sophie followed, spine reaching and bunching with each bound forward. The sound of rapid hoof beats assured Leila the horse would not stop any time soon.

Jimmy ran down the aisle.

"Tack room," he called.

Ray broke from his frozen stance and dove toward a door across from them, pulling it open for Jimmy just in time to keep him from plowing into it. Jimmy disappeared inside and reappeared seconds later with a bridle. Without a word he ran out the back door of the barn, into the corrals. She heard a whistle followed by the sound of hooves trotting toward the barn.

"We have to do something," Leila said.

"We can't," Ray replied, sounding angry. "The only way to catch him is on a horse."

Just then the sound of another set of running hooves alerted Leila that Jimmy was doing just that. Sophie's barking sounded ever more faintly across the open prairie.

"Oh God," Leila said.

"You can put the gun away now," Sleet offered.

She did, wondering when, exactly, she had drawn it from the holster. Her knee gave one warning twinge of pain and gave out, leaving her leaning against the stall door again and trying to hide her pain.

"We should get some ice on that," Ray said.

"There's ice out here?" Leila asked.

"No, back at the house."

She wanted to stay in the barn and wait for Rain and Demon to come back. But Ray's observation about ice drew her attention to her knee. She could feel the seam of her blue jeans pressing into the swollen flesh there.

"I don't think I can make it back," she said.

"That's why you're riding," Ray told her. "Take one step forward."

She obeyed, leaning against the barn for support. As she stepped clear, Ray lifted a halter from where it hung next to Steady's stall and swung open the stall door. Steady nickered and lowered his head. Ray slung the halter around his nose, drew a strap up behind his ears, and buckled it at the horse's jaw. Leila watched with fascination, remembering how horse crazy she had been at thirteen, how she had craved riding a horse like craving water on a hot day.

"I wish things were different," she said.

Sleet looked up at her from where he still held Storm's hand.

"I always wanted to ride a horse but this isn't a great way to start."

"It'll still be fun," Sleet said, and patted her back. "And it's okay. Rain'll be fine. Don't worry."

Ray led Steady to a block of wood in the center of the aisle.

"Can you make it this far?" He asked Leila.

She gritted her teeth and limped over, hating how helpless she must look to the children. Ray helped her up on the block of wood. Steady stood, unmoving, on the other side, his back even with where Leila now stood above him. Ray directed her to lie belly down on Steady's back, across him.

The pain attacked her thoughts, fuzzing them out around the edges. Her knee throbbed with each heartbeat. Her need for ice erased any initial hesitation she might have experienced in riding a horse for the first time. She bit her lip and lowered herself onto the horse.

"Now grab his mane and swing your leg over onto the other side," Ray instructed.

A series of comical struggles followed. Ray went around Steady to help her get her leg over and sit up. In the meantime, the horse stood true to his name. Finally astride, Leila sat hunched forward clutching at Steady's mane. Ray frowned up at her.

"Sit up straight!" He commanded.

Leila complied and found she felt less like she would fall off the minute the horse moved.

"Okay, let's go. Sleet, please don't let Storm wander off," Ray said.

"I got 'er," Sleet said.

They exited the barn at a slow walk which Leila found terrifying. The horse moved in odd ways under her. She could feel every step in the back muscles she sat on and she kept slipping off to one side. Ray glanced back at her.

"Relax," he said, "and quit looking at the ground."

Between Ray's barked commands and the adventure of going over uneven ground, Leila did not begin to enjoy herself until halfway back to the house. When she did, the day turned beautiful despite her worry over Rain.

At the house, she asked Ray how to get off the horse.

"Lean forward against his neck, swing a leg over, and slide down."

He made it sound easy. She barely managed and she grunted with the pain when her left leg hit the ground. Ray dropped the lead rope on the ground and helped her inside.

"What about Steady?" Leila asked, trying to distract herself from the pain.

"He's trained to ground tie," Ray said.

The children positioned Leila on the love seat in the living room, put her leg up, and applied ice. Sleet showed Storm how to hold the ice on Leila's knee and Storm stood there, frowning slightly as she concentrated on the task.

"Gotta run Steady back," Ray said.

"You're not really going to run him, are you?" Sleet wanted to know.

Ray cuffed his brother on the ear, but more gently than usual.

"Not our old boy," he said. "We'll just walk."

"Is there any Tylenol or Advil or something in the house?" Leila asked.

Sleet went off in search of some. She leaned back against the couch, closed her eyes, and prayed for Rain's safety, still not convinced prayer had a point but willing to try it in this situation.

Storm, meanwhile, got bored with holding the ice. She balanced the bag on Leila's knee and climbed into her lap, her baby hands cold when they touched Leila's neck. After achieving her perch, Storm went still, looking at Leila until she opened her eyes.

"Rain?" Storm asked.

Leila didn't know whether to smile or cry.

"He'll be okay," Leila said. "Jimmy will bring him back."

Storm relaxed against Leila's chest and they rested like that until Sleet returned with Advil.

Between the ice and the Advil, the pain in her knee began to subside. She felt Storm's limbs jerk two or three times as the girl fell asleep against her.

Then Leila fell asleep, too. She dreamed of Rain riding free over the prairie on Demon's back. He laughed, and in her dream, she laughed, too. She heard the front door open and close and chose to ignore it for the lovely images in her dream.

CHAPTER SEVENTEEN

 "What a beautiful picture," a male voice said.

Leila awakened with a gasp, turned her head, and saw Bill standing in the doorway between kitchen and living room. He leaned on the frame and stared at her, waiting for his presence to sink in.

"Bill," Leila said. The word thrummed in her chest and she felt Storm awaken, stiffen, then go limp.

"Where is everyone?" Bill asked. "Upstairs?"

His question dashed the last of sleep from Leila's brain.

"Well," Leila looked around for Sleet. "Ray was down in the barn helping Jimmy. And Sleet was here when I fell asleep. I'll bet he got bored and went down there, too."

"I see." Bill frowned, as if he did not see.

Immediately, Leila needed to placate him, to explain.

"I do usually keep a better eye on them. They're usually with me all the time. But," she waved a hand at the ice on her knee, "I sprained my knee and…"

"Are you okay? What happened?" Bill asked.

The full mental picture of how she sprained her knee came back to her. Finding Maria's body. The children's attack, the way she held them all… Panic and anger welled up with equal force.

"It was just a little accident," Leila said. "I stepped wrong when I was walking down to the barn."

Bill looked thoughtful. "Maybe we should get you into town to see Dr. Paddock. You must think this is a terribly small, hick town, but Dr. Paddock is the best, and right here in Elk Crossing."

"I think I'll be all right," Leila said. "If it's not better by tomorrow I'll go."

Her thoughts ran a thousand miles an hour, trying to sort out what she had done in his absence, trying to figure out ways to hide what she knew while making polite conversation.

Bill still stood in the doorway. He eyed her in a way that gave her an unpleasant shiver.

"You're probably in a hurry to get out of here," Bill said, "but why don't we have some coffee first? I would love to hear all about how it went while I was away."

Leila started to obey despite herself, moving to push Storm off her and sit the rest of the way up. As she shifted her weight, though, she pressed her right hip toward the couch and felt the gun pinched between her hip and the couch. She covered a surge of gratitude for the reminder with a wince.

"I'd love some coffee but between Storm and how badly my knee hurts, I think I'll stay right here," she said.

"Yeah, of course. How 'bout I make the coffee and we'll sit here and drink it?"

Leila smiled at him. Her lips felt wooden and she could only pray her smile didn't look as fake as it felt.

"That sounds great," she said.

He left for the kitchen and Leila thought furiously about what to do about Maria's body, Rain galloping over the

267

prairie...everything. Her thoughts chased around and around with no resolution.

He returned with two cups and gave one to Leila, who balanced it over Storm's head and sipped.

"So how are the children doing?" Bill asked.

"Oh, they're fine. We had a good time while you were vacationing."

Bill declared he was glad to hear it and then asked a question which made Leila's heart stop.

"So how would you feel about staying on here? The children could really use a woman around. They haven't been well since their mother ran off."

"I'd...I'd have to think about it?"

"Fair enough."

The kitchen door scraped open and slammed shut. Storm, eye still squeezed shut, flinched at the sound. Bill turned, his solid, bulky appearance when still transformed into the grace of a predator in motion.

"Ray! My boy!"

"Hi, Dad. How was your trip?"

Ray's eyes flicked to Leila's face and he shook his head very slightly, once.

Bill's eyes narrowed at the brief exchange of eye contact.

"Ray. Go get Sleet. I don't understand why he hasn't come downstairs."

As Ray moved past his father for the stairs, Bill clapped him on the back.

"Good boy," Bill said.

Leila saw Ray stagger forward half a step from the force of the blow and wince, then continue as though nothing had happened.

"They don't come very well when they're called," Bill said. "Independent little shits."

He drained the last of his coffee, set the cup on the trestle table, and walked toward Leila.

"Now," Bill's booming voice notched up, "how's daddy's little girl? Still pretending to be asleep?"

As he neared Leila he reached out his arms to pluck Storm off her chest. Leila panicked.

"She's just tired," Leila said, wrapping her free arm around Storm's trembling body. "I took the kids to the barn this morning to visit the horses and she walked the whole way."

Bill stopped at her protest, hovering over the pair on the couch. She lay there and stared up at his heavy, regular features and tried to not tremble like Storm was trembling.

"Well. What a fine little momma you are," Bill said. "You're right, she can rest."

He sounded as though he felt quite generous, granting permission for Storm to stay with Leila. She bit back the words "thank you." and imagined them all somewhere else—anywhere else.

Careful footfalls on the stairs warned her Ray had found Sleet. Bill turned and broke into a wolfish smile when the boys rounded the corner.

"There's my other boy! Sleet! Come and give your daddy a hug."

Sleet hesitated then continued toward his father, moving in

269

little marionette jerks into the room. Leila could see the sheer effort it required to force himself forward. Bill closed the distance in two quick steps and grabbed Sleet up in a bear hug.

"I missed my little Sleety Wussy," he said, and reached up and scrubbed the boys scalp with the knuckles of his closed fist.

She and Sleet looked at each other helplessly, she from her recumbent position, pinned by Storm and hobbled by her knee, and Sleet from over his father's shoulder, pinned against the man's barrel chest. Sleet gritted his teeth against the pain but the glisten in his eyes warned Leila he wouldn't hold out forever.

Anger bloomed in her chest. She waited to see if the feeling could be attributed to the interference of the house but decided a moment later the burning in her chest was all hers.

"Ray," she snapped. He turned to look at her. "Are there any ace wraps in this house?"

"I'll go get them," Ray said, and moved off.

"That's a great idea," Bill said. "Ray really seems to jump when you say 'boo.' I love a woman who can get some obedience out of these children." Bill finally let Sleet down—too hard—and Sleet staggered over to stand near Leila. Too angry to reply, Leila ignored Bill's jab at the kids and shifted Storm toward the couch, concealing the gun more completely.

She imagined shooting him right now and even in her imagination she couldn't point the gun at another human being and pull the trigger. She heard Cole's voice giving her instructions yesterday. "Don't pull it unless you or the children are in immediate danger."

And afterward he said she must shoot immediately once she

270

pulled it out. A plan occurred to her, but it depended on being able to get up the stairs at a normal pace.

Ray came back with two large ace wraps and knelt on the floor next to Leila's knee, putting his back to his father. Leila's skin crawled in sympathy with the feeling he must have, turning his back on danger like that. She knew the feeling too well.

"Wrap it tight, Ray. I'm tired of not being able to walk well."

Ray looked up at her words and she saw hope on his face. He looked at Storm—through Storm—and raised an eyebrow. She gave him a tremulous smile which she hoped Bill would attribute to the pain of having the knee wrapped.

"That's good, boy. You're real good at that," Bill complimented Ray as he worked.

Her plan almost came unraveled a moment later. Bill cocked his head and stiffened.

"We're missing someone," he said. "How could I have forgotten?"

They all froze in place. Leila thought of Rain. Then she heard it, faintly, barking.

"Oh, you mean Sophie?" She asked.

Bill turned on her. "Who else would I mean?"

"I'm just—I'm just not used to anyone referring to their dog like a person," she stammered.

Ray's hands had stopped at Bill's statement. Leila nodded at him to continue, widening her eyes a little to make the point he should hurry. He finished, pulled the end tight, and fastened it.

Bill walked to the front door. "Now what's she barking at?"

The barking became louder as if someone had turned a giant

volume button. Just as Bill opened the door, however, the sound faded, then cut out. Leila heard Bill step just outside and start calling the dog.

She shoved Storm off her and onto the couch, and hurriedly unbuckled her belt. At her glance, the boys sprang into action. Ray went out to stand with his dad. Sleet positioned himself at the door to the kitchen. Leila's numb fingers fumbled with the holster, trying to pull it off the belt, leather dragging against leather. Bill called again, then she heard Ray's voice, too quiet to make out words, but the sound was of reasonable conversation.

"I don't get why she's not coming," Bill said.

Ray replied. Again, his voice too quiet to make out words.

The holster came free. Leila jerked the gun out, threw the holster behind the couch, and jammed the gun—barrel first—into the waistline of her jeans at her back. She buckled her belt again with a silent shout of joy. She looked at Sleet and jerked her chin back toward the stairs.

Sleet said what was obviously the first thing that came to mind. "All right! She's standing up!"

The sound of Ray conversing with his father out front went quiet but they didn't come inside. Leila walked to Sleet. The knee sent a stab of pain through her leg with each step but held her fine.

"Hey!" Leila called toward the kitchen door. "I almost forgot. We made a surprise for you."

The strong, happy tone in her voice surprised her, then she thought of all the time she spent with Stu, acting one way, feeling another, just putting on a show.

The sound of his heavy footsteps coming closer sped her heart rate even further. When he entered the living room, he rewarded her with a big, easy grin.

"Glad you could stand up!" Bill said, "What's the surprise?"

"We thought you should have something special to come home to," Leila said. "We left it upstairs."

She wondered if she imagined the hitch in his stride when she said the last word. Behind Bill, Leila saw Ray's eyes widen in fear at her words. He shook his head, stumbled on the tile. Leila couldn't do anything to reassure him with Bill looking straight at her.

He stopped well within her personal space and looked at her. "Let's go, then. I love surprises."

Leila couldn't think of a good way to get him up the stairs ahead of her. If he went behind her the first thing he would see is the gun. Timid little Sleet saved the day. He reached, grabbed his father's hand, and started walking him toward the stairs.

"Come on, Dad, I'll show you."

Bill and Sleet headed for the stairs with Leila in hot pursuit.

She saw Ray catch on as Sleet and Bill stepped on to the first riser. Ray came alongside her left. She threw an arm over his shoulders and they walked after Bill and Sleet. Leila stumped up the stairs with more determination than style. She and Ray turned for the second flight just as the pair ahead made it to the hallway. Sleet paused there, looking down to judge their progress.

"Hang on, Dad, she's a little slow on the stairs."

Sleet dragged his father down the hall when Leila and Ray made it plain they would get up the final flight in seconds. For the

273

first time Leila realized she was letting the boys help her set up their father. When the thought occurred to her, she wanted to vomit.

The horror and sickness of the situation threatened to overwhelm her but the trap was already beginning to close. She had no choice but to go forward.

Bill and Sleet were almost at the door to the room. Leila let go of Ray and limped down the hallway toward them, feeling the gun chafe her back with each step.

She realized too late that Sleet's hand in his father's made him a hostage. The sickness inside her grew, and with it her forward momentum. Only three feet separated them when Sleet pulled his father into the room. She kept moving, terrified to enter the room but even more frightened for Sleet.

Three more steps. It's too quiet in there.

She took another step, then heard Sleet cry out.

"Ow! Put me down! You're hurting me!"

She took the last step and turned into the room. What she saw confirmed her worst fears. Bill held Sleet pinned against his chest with one arm. Leila could see Sleet struggling to draw deep enough breaths against the force of his father's arm. Sleet's legs dangled two feet off the ground. Bill smiled at Leila, showing his teeth.

"Well," he said. "I'm delighted."

"You are?" Leila asked.

"The greatest tragedy," Bill said, "is that no one was ever able to admire my little project."

Leila shivered. The darkening color in Sleet's face warned her

Bill's vice-like grasp across the boy's chest was hurting him. Searching for inspiration, for some way to distract Bill, Leila found she knew something else.

"Bill. Why don't you put Sleet down and tell me about your vacation?"

"I think the boy's fine here," Bill said. "But I've been dying," and he let out a gruff laugh, "to tell someone about what I did."

To Leila's relief, Bill shifted his grasp on Sleet, as though the boy were simply an orator's tool, used to emphasize points in his speech. Sleet drew in a great gasp of air and the color of his face lightened toward normal.

"See, Maria here," Bill gestured at the body on the floor, "was my first. And it always disappointed me that I lost my temper. In Mexico—well, that was different. I took my time."

Ray moved restlessly behind her. She dropped her hand to her side, palm flat out, and hoped he got the message.

A clear picture rose in her mind of how she could make him put Sleet down. The revelation almost dropped her to the ground. Visions of all the times Stu had charged at her, fists raised, attacked her at once.

"So," Leila said, and lifted her chin, "you're one of those cowards who only kills the defenseless."

Anger passed over Bill's face, then astonishment. He smiled.

"I misjudged you," he said. "When I met you, I thought you were just another of those poor, beaten-down women who would do anything. I really thought I could keep you here to watch the kids."

The wonder in his voice combined with his keen assessment

275

sent a sharp stab of self-hatred through Leila. She chose thought rather than folding in on herself.

"Yeah, well," Leila put as much mockery in her voice as she could, "you obviously weren't too bright about it."

Bill's biceps flexed and the bar of his arm across Sleet clamped down. Sleet wheezed, his eyes wide, and fixed on Leila.

"You know," Bill said, "I haven't seen Rain…" He stepped to the closet door and flung it open, releasing the caged smell which still hung there. Despite the smell, he actually poked his head into the closet to check the corners, as if he couldn't believe his eyes, before he whirled on Leila.

"What did you do with him?"

"Me? Nothing. He's out riding Demon right now," Leila said.

The soft sound of Storm coming up the stairs whispered against her ears, then, like a shout.

"Well," Leila said, needing to pressure him, "If you're just going to stand there and yammer, I believe I'll just go call the cops."

Bill laughed, an animal noise like the call of a hyena.

"How're you planning to do that?"

Ray spoke up. "I imagine I'll just beat your puny ass and sit on you while she drives to town," he said.

Bill took one big step toward them, but didn't let Sleet down.

"You little fucker," he said. "I'll deal with you next."

Leila laughed in his face. "Ray's right," she said. "You don't have the balls. In fact, I'll bet you're lying about everything. Maria must have died of disappointment in her ball-less man."

Bill's face went dark, fury drawing blood to the surface.

Storm's feet pattered up the hallway. Sleet heard the footfalls, leaned down, and bit his father's forearm, latching, champing down, and twisting his head from side to side. Bill roared and flung the boy away from him. Sleet hit the wall and slid limply down as Leila reached for the gun. Instead of the gun, Storm's little hand found hers and latched on.

"Oh, look," Bill said. "It's a three-for-one deal. I'll kick all your asses down the stairs."

In desperation, Leila dropped to her right knee as the left protested at the sudden movement. She reached across with her left arm and scooped Storm up, away from her gun arm, then reached back and grabbed the gun. It snagged on her waistband.

Bill, old rancher that he was, recognized her posture and flung himself at her. Just as she began to give in to fear and despair, Ray tugged at her waistband and the gun came free. She swept it up, shouted congratulations to herself for remembering to flip off the safety, and pulled the trigger.

The first shot stopped his forward momentum. The second dropped him to the ground.

One thought pushed Leila forward, rising with Storm clutched to her—the need to make sure he was dead.

The left knee almost buckled but with the help of the adrenaline she didn't feel the pain. She rushed forward, gun still pointed, and looked down at Bill.

Blood poured out of the open wounds on his chest. She made herself look at his face and found him looking back at her. She stifled a scream. When he opened his mouth to speak, frothy pink blood oozed out. He mouthed two words at her.

"Finish it."

For the first time Leila's agenda matched Bill's. She wanted him dead. Now. She looked down at the gun in her hand and thought about shooting him one more time. Where would she point it? At his heart? At his head? The reality of the situation rose up on her like an ocean wave, curled over her, and dragged her under.

She staggered away from him, bent and vomited, staggered a few steps farther, and slid down the wall to sit huddled on the floor. Her vision went foggy and for some reason the gun kept clattering on the floor. She looked down to see what would make it do that and saw her hand still gripped it although all the strength had gone out of her arm and her hand was shaking.

Storm wiggled in her arm. Leila released her automatically. The girl wandered over to Bill, looked at him without expression, and went to join Ray where he knelt over Sleet. Through her fog she saw Sleet stir.

"Back with us?" Ray asked his brother.

Sleet groaned.

"Yeah," Ray said. "You're gonna have one hell of a headache. Can you move your arms and legs?"

Despite herself, she looked over at Bill and saw the end. His hand relaxed and his head rolled to one side. The eyes were still open, but he would never see another thing.

The wave of shock still had her, rolling her over and over, deep beneath the surface.

Sleet sat up, wincing, and took a long look at his father's body.

"Good," Sleet said. "That's good."

Downstairs, someone pounded on the front door. A deep yell followed the pounding.

"Sherriff! Open up!"

Ray stood up. "I guess I should let them in."

At his last word, the sound of wood breaking was followed by the crash of the door as it was improperly opened.

"Never mind," Ray said. "I think I'll stay."

Cole took his time getting upstairs. Silence filled the room where the children's parents lay, punctuated by the occasional call, either from Cole or from a woman.

"Clear!"

Finally, Cole poked his head around the door. Leila sat against the wall the door was on, so he didn't see her at first.

"Everybody okay?" he asked, ignoring the fact that Bill was clearly not okay.

"I think everyone's fine," Ray said. "But she needs help." He looked at Leila.

Cole popped around the door and saw Leila.

"Oh God. I'm sorry, darlin'," he said, then turned and yelled out the door. "Williams! Get in here!"

The brawny female sheriff's deputy from the station walked in and surveyed the room.

"Leila's in shock," Cole said to her. "Do your thing, Williams. Let's get them all outside."

Williams knelt down beside Leila and explained the course of events to follow.

"You're going to put the gun down now. Put it down. That's right, open your fingers."

After Williams got her to release the gun, Leila found she could not stand up. The knee would not hold her weight.

"Okay, then, we'll do it together," Williams said.

She got Leila's right leg under her and then heaved her to her feet. Cole watched from across the room where he stood with the huddle of children.

"What happened to her knee?" Cole asked Ray.

"She got it bent funny and then lay on it for a while," Ray said.

"Everybody go downstairs," Cole told the children. "Stay together. I'll be right behind you."

The children moved as a group to leave the room. Ray didn't even look at the body as he walked past. Sleet paused, kicked him once in the ribs, and then trailed after the others.

At the top of the stairs, Leila found she could go no further. Cole scooped her into his arms and trooped down the stairs.

"You're shivering," he said as they descended. "That's okay. It's normal. Shooting someone really takes it out of you. Especially the first time."

Leila began to cry.

"Good," Cole soothed her. "That's good. Much better than shivering and staring off into space."

"I don't understand," Leila said between sobs, "why feeling safe is making me cry."

"Me either," Cole said. "But it seems to work that way."

Cole got them all outside to where the coroner stood, smoking and staring at the house. He put Leila in a patrol car and told Williams to take her and the kids to town, then frowned.

"Isn't there a fourth one?"

The shock of realizing she forgot to worry about Rain pushed the shock of shooting Bill out of her mind. She explained what happened to Cole.

"Drive them down to the barn," Cole told Williams. "Find that last kid and get them to town. Get Leila a doctor, round Pat up to sit with them, and take statements. And send reinforcements."

"Where do you want to house them?" Williams asked.

"See if they can crash at Pat and Jim's."

Leila couldn't wait to go. She twisted around in the car's seat to look at the kids when Williams opened the back door.

"Hurry. Get in."

They parked at the barn, next to Jimmy's truck. Williams came out a minute later followed by Jimmy carrying Rain. The boy's arm hung down and swayed back and forth with Jimmy's steps.

"Rain!" Sleet shouted.

"It's all right," Williams told them. "He's just really tired."

Jimmy crammed him into the patrol car and Williams moved a limp hand out of the way to shut the door. With every mile Williams drove away from the house, Leila felt a little stronger.

***

Doctor Paddock frowned at the condition of Leila's knee. "We need an MRI. I'm guessing you stretched the ligaments too far and there's a nice surgery in your future."

"She can't go to Casper right now," Williams told the doctor.

The doctor engaged in a brief staring contest with Williams and lost. Instead of going to Casper, Leila ended up with her leg strapped into an immobilizer. Doctor Paddock handed her a set of crutches. "No bearing weight on that leg. And ice fifteen minutes out of every hour."

Leila dreaded giving a statement. But after Pat flung open the door to her home, fussed equally over her and the children, and made them all something to drink, she felt equal to the job.

For her part, Williams made the chore into something approaching therapy. She chose Pat's homey kitchen as her interview room, served Leila coffee, and then listened hard. She asked questions which knitted Leila's fragmented mind together. She listened some more. At the close, Leila thought she understood the value of the Catholic practice of confession. Clean of secrets, emptied of the stresses of the last week, she knew she could move on to whatever lay ahead.

Williams spoke to each of the children alone, as well. Ray volunteered to go first, walking into the kitchen with head high and shoulders straight. Sleet went next, shuffling his feet forward, head lowered. Rain sat shoulder-to-shoulder with Leila and trembled while his twin was away. They had needed to shake him awake to walk from the patrol car into the house, and Leila figured only his exhaustion kept him from collapsing in terror at being out among people after spending so long living in that closet.

"Do you think you can talk to her?" Leila asked him. "Alone?"

Rain nodded. "I gotta," he said, and when Sleet emerged, Rain pushed himself up and walked willingly into the kitchen.

Finally, Williams came out and considered Storm. "I've never heard the child say anything. Does she speak?"

Leila shook her head but felt Storm draw a deep breath.

"Daddy." Storm said. "Bad."

Williams' eyes opened wider. And she got down on one knee before the little girl. "Anything else you want to say?"

Storm just stared at her.

They spent three days with Pat and Jim before Leila thought to ask the question what came next.

Pat found her standing in the kitchen staring dully out the window and pried the questions out of her.

"It's not hard to become a foster parent," Pat told her. "I've already talked to Leslie about it and she's all in favor. We'll work out the details."

"I need to get a job," Leila said. "I've never had a job before."

"Unemployment in Wyoming is four percent right now," Pat reassured her. "You'll find something."

A week after the shooting the story broke in the Casper newspaper. On the front page. Pat showed her. "You might as well see this. You'll be the talk of the town now."

Leila groaned and read the story, which wrote of allegations and questions and seemed lurid in nature while still quite missing the reality of what actually happened.

"Oh well," Leila said, and let it drop.

A knock on the door sounded the following morning as Leila and Pat sipped coffee in the kitchen. Pat sighed and looked lovingly at her coffee.

"I'll get it," Leila said.

She opened the door to Stu. Shock froze her muscles and her smile of welcome turned into a rictus of fear.

"I found you," Stu said, sounding like a little boy who just won hide-and-seek.

Leila shook herself free of fear and chose thought.

"You found me," she said. "Now turn around, get back in your car, and leave. Me. Alone."

She watched as his face worked its way from surprise to ferocious anger. He stood on the step below her and she wondered if he really was as small as he looked just then.

Stu's jaw clenched. He hurled himself toward her. She knew what he would do before he did it. Observation of the acute type only captives and the abused are capable of had sharpened her understanding of his every move.

When his foot left the second step and he lowered his head to bull through her into the house, she reached out with a flat hand and shoved his chest hard. He stumbled backward, missed a step, and landed on his tailbone, his legs splayed out in front of him.

She waited for him to get up. He did.

"I'm going to make you regret that," he hissed.

She felt Pat walk up behind her. His expression changed to one of a polite visitor immediately.

Leila hobbled out of the house and walked right up to him. She didn't want Pat overhearing her next words.

"No," she said. "You're not going to do anything to me ever again."

She took another step, as if to occupy the space in which he stood. He backed up a step.

"You are going to leave now."

She took another step and allowed some of the rage she

284

remembered from her days in the house to surface.

"You are going to go home and wait for divorce papers."

He backed up again, and she kept walking.

"You are going to never contact me again."

She wanted to walk over his body like a steamroller. She felt she could if he would just fall down again.

"If I ever see you again, I'll make you regret the day you were born."

He backed his sore tailbone right into the door of his car and winced.

She stood, still closer than comfort allowed, and studied his face with its wide eyes and slack jaw. She smiled and realized the situation lacked one thing, a question he had always asked her before leaving for work in the morning.

"Do you understand my instructions? Because there'll be hell to pay if you don't follow them."

"Yes! I understand. Just—just let me get in the car, okay?"

She backed up then, enough for him to swing the door open, and stood and watched as he gunned the engine and sped off.

"Who was that?" Pat asked.

"My soon to be ex-husband."

After coffee, Leila couldn't control her exuberant energy any more.

"I gotta get out of here," she said. "Do you mind watching the kids for a little?"

Pat didn't mind at all. "In fact, they're almost too easy to watch. Like they're walking on eggshells."

Leila sobered for a minute. "They have been their entire life.

285

No one's told them it's okay to change."

She walked to the hardware store because she had a question. Wizened old Randy welcomed her like a war hero returned but asked only one question.

"Can I help you find something?"

Leila laughed. "Once again I have a non-hardware related need. Is there any place I could buy some Crayons?"

"But, Leila," he said. "We sell Crayons. We have a toy aisle."

Back with the children, Leila asked for printer paper and sat down with Storm to teach her to color. The boys, who hadn't seen a Crayon in years, wanted to play too.

Half an hour later, bent over Storm, who sat in her lap and scribbled furiously, Leila paused to listen to the sound of happy children.

"Do you have a light green?"

"Hey! That's cool."

She looked up, a true smile on her face, and saw Cole peering in the open door, smiling just as broadly as she.

"I was going to knock," he said.

"That's all right. Just come in."

ACKNOWLEDGMENTS

To my husband Kelly McLoud who provided a weird but effective combination of encouragement, support, and butt kicking. David Paulson's enthusiasm makes him the best friend a writer could ever ask for. My at-home children Hawk, Ya'el, and Logan, who extended respect by (usually) leaving me be when writing. Shannon McLoud whose many long conversations about books and writing inspired me over and over. Erin McLoud's sheer grit gave me hope for the next generation—a necessary component of producing art. Mary and Gary Paddock—friends extraordinaire who read and believed. Christina Caldwell and Adelaide Myers for ploughing through the first draft and saying things like, "When's the movie coming out?" Stacey Roberts for his generosity in providing wisdom despite never having met me. Florin Petre, a most talented Romanian photographer, graciously gave me permission to use his photograph for the cover. Sandy Ackerman volunteered, despite knowing nothing about my writing, to design the cover. She is now a valued friend. Kind and willing pre-readers agreed to peruse the final draft. You know who you are and I am grateful indeed. Finally, this book would not have been possible without the direction, strength, and wisdom added to my life by Judaism and Buddhism. Gratitude nourishes.

ABOUT THE AUTHOR

Heather McLoud wakes up most mornings with two thoughts. "I'm sure happy to be alive," and, "Coffee!" These spontaneous urges are followed by a determination to write while the coffee is consumed. She works as a Registered Nurse—a profession she loves for its intrinsic meaning. At home in the foothills of the Colorado Rockies, she is kept company by two teenagers, two dogs, two cats, two goats, and a jumping spider. Heather can be reached at heathermcloudwriter@gmail.com.

Made in the USA
Charleston, SC
25 August 2016